REBELLION ROAD

It took a year after Joe Johnston surrendered for Duncan Wade to work his way back to his father's plantation in western Alabama. There was no sign of life about the place. But back of the house, on his mother's seat under the magnolia tree, his father sat, hunched over. His untrimmed hair and beard were gray, his shirt was yellowed like his hands—he looked so old!

There wasn't a decent change of clothes for Duncan to wear when he had scrubbed himself and thrown aside his tattered, verminous gray uniform. Guerrillas had looted the house, breaking and burning what they couldn't carry away. Forty field hands had worked the plantation, but with freedom all but three had wandered off.

That first day Duncan went to see his mother's unmarked grave. And presently he heard horse's hoofs, and a pretty girl on a handsome bay horse was standing by him. It was Marian Villerand, daughter of a rich neighbor. He recalled her as a tomboy brat whom his mother had loved. She was to warn him to be careful, to control his high temper and give offense to none—not the white Union soldiers, and especially not the freedmen. The laws were oppressive, the courts were packed, and she didn't want anything to happen to him. "You've got to live," she said, "and get rich and marry me!"

Rebellion Road is the story of the violence that ensued on Duncan Wade's return. In less

(*continued on back flap*)

$3.00

asily have been
Reconstruction.
d decidedly un-
the Wades and

e point of view
veholders. The
d girls for that
e. But they hate
t it as the cure
ays.

he picture em-
s and Southern
given everything
and others who
sperous though
were gentlemen
drunken, cruel
loyal to their
ere confused at
nly a different
ho were black-
en with bitter
oung men with
urpose in theirs.

ggle of rebirth
gallant Marian

Other Novels by HELEN TOPPING MILLER

DARK SAILS: *A Tale of Old St. Simons*
SHOD WITH FLAME
THE SOUND OF CHARIOTS
TRUMPET IN THE CITY
BORN STRANGERS: *A Chronicle of Two Families*
WE HAVE GIVEN OUR HEARTS AWAY
CAMEO
WITCH WATER

REBELLION ROAD

by
Helen (*Topping*) *Miller*
and
John Dewey Topping

THE BOBBS-MERRILL COMPANY, INC.

Publishers

Indianapolis   New York

Copyright, 1954, by HELEN TOPPING MILLER
Printed in the United States of America
Library of Congress Catalog Card Number: 54-6497

To Ruth and Web Garner

REBELLION ROAD

PRELUDE

IT WAS, so Emma pointed out, his duty to go to the funeral. However deep-rooted lay his dislike of Hugh Wade, argued Emma, the fact remained that Hugh's wife was dead after lying ill a whole winter, and with so few neighbors left in the river country common decency demanded that the Villerands pay their respects. Marian, the younger Villerand daughter, had been spending half her time at the Wade house lately, Emma said, and definitely Marian would be humiliated if her parents did not appear.

"You know what I think of Hugh Wade," fumed Julian Villerand, his reddish spike of a beard trembling with irritation. "A hide-bound old secessionist Democrat—thinks Jeff Davis was a god, thinks we're going to win this fool war. Poor planter too. Most of his people took off as soon as Lincoln said they were free."

"Alabama is a seceded state and we have a son fighting to win victory for the Confederacy, Mr. Villerand," his wife reminded him. "Even if you have such radical ideas you should be discreet about expressing them."

"Young hothead!" Julian grumbled, keeping his eyes away from his wife's too shrewd gaze. "I could have got him a good job in Montgomery. Safe too. Governor Moore was indebted to me."

"You wouldn't be proud of young Jule if he had been willing to hide out in a safe political job while all the other young men were fighting. Hugh Wade's son was one of the first to go.

9

Marian says his father hasn't heard from him in months; they don't even know if he is still alive. About the funeral— Juliet and I will go in the carriage. You'd best ride. Marian went over early this morning. I couldn't stop her," she put in hastily, answering her husband's annoyed gesture. "You've encouraged both of them to do as they pleased, Mr. Villerand, you know you have. The funeral is at two o'clock. Your clothes are laid out and I told Cassius to get your shaving things ready."

"Going to rain anyway," Julian muttered.

"The sky always looks this way in spring. I hope it won't rain into an open grave—it means another death soon."

"Some more of your old Gullah superstition!" He snorted as he tramped off on his short legs and small, narrow feet. Emma, his wife of more than twenty-six years, was a head taller than he.

Twenty-six years! It seemed incredible to Julian Villerand that so much time had passed since that day he had flung himself on his horse in a fury and galloped off down the Tombigbee road, leaving Florence Duncan watching him from the porch of her father's house with distressed, unhappy eyes.

That was the day she had told him that she was going to marry Hugh Wade, ten years older than she, a childless widower since the fever epidemic of '31.

"But I'm the man who loves you!" Julian had protested then.

"I'm sorry, Mr. Villerand, but Mr. Wade insists that he loves me too." Tears had quivered on Florence Duncan's lashes; her voice had been choked and uncertain.

"And Wade is the man you love!" Julian could recall yet his incredulous, cheated anger; the pain that had got him by the throat, the aching weakness that made it difficult for him to maintain the rigid dignity that his short stature made imperative. He had stood taller than Florence then, though. He liked to remember that—her hair level with his lips, her slight, sweet body so light and frail beside his own stockiness—even when he was hating Hugh Wade for his six feet of dark, saturnine charm.

"Mr. Wade is the man I love," Florence had said then.

All the way back to the new place Julian had built on the Selma road those words had been beaten into his ears by the thudding hoofs of his horse, by the slam of the gate, by the crashing bang of his door. No man, he had sworn to himself in bitter fury, could love brown-haired Florence as he loved her. Not Hugh Wade, who had had another wife and mourned that wife for five years! Where had those twenty-six odd years gone? Now Florence was dead. Now he must array himself in proper garments and stand by mutely and impersonally while her tiny body was laid in the grave. Emma decreed it, and Emma throughout their married life had had her way. He knew now that he had always given in to Emma as a kind of continuing penance to make up for never having really loved her.

The very next day after Florence Duncan's final rejection of him Julian had left for the east, taking the old Federal road that was still marked by three blazes on the roadside trees and still called the "Three Chop Road." The road followed the old horse path of the Creek Indians, but had been widened so that carriages and wagons of the settlers who were streaming into Alabama from the older states could travel it in safety. The country was counted safe now from the menace of the red man. Alabama was a state.

It was over this same road that he had come to the Tombigbee country in '28, from South Carolina, a young man setting out alone to make his fortune, with an urge for adventure. Charleston and the Low Country where he had been born were already old, set grimly in a pattern of custom and tradition. His Grandmother Villerand, a pious Huguenot and the only mother he had ever known, was dead. He had sold his inheritance of land and slaves and with gold in his belt taken the western trails, fired as hundreds of others were by the tales of the rich black land to be had cheaply in the Alabama and Mississippi country. At a land sale in the little village of Selma, he had bought a huge tract not too far from the rivers, bordering on a trace that was now a highroad, as Selma was rapidly becoming a city.

Then he had met Florence Duncan and fallen abysmally in love with her liquid brown eyes, her low caressing voice, her quick white hands. So he had built a long house on his land with wide verandas and a kitchen set off to the rear. He bought slaves to wait on Florence and a horse for her to ride—only to learn in stunned misery that she wanted none of them. So over the same road he had come, full of fire and purpose, he traveled east again, sullen torment raging within him at every mile. In Charleston, where he lingered most of a winter, he had married Emma.

Emma was older than he. She was neither fragile nor lovely like Florence, but she was rich, practical and fairly good-looking. With Emma he had brought five wagonloads of handsome furniture and ten slaves. He admitted now that he had a very good life with Emma. She was capable, a bit domineering, but a good wife for a man who had early determined to be both rich and important, and for more than a quarter of a century that determination had been Julian Villerand's life.

His wife had given him three children, two handsome daughters and a son. By Florence Hugh Wade had only one son, a lad who offended Julian by being tall and jaunty while his own boy, young Jule, had unfortunately inherited his own short body, his reddish hair and freckled skin. Now both boys were lost somewhere in this idiotic chaos of a war—and now Florence was dead. He lay back in his chair while Cassius stropped the razor, and tried to win some release from the knowledge that he would never see Florence again, never again hear the voice that had always been able to make his heart quiver, never know again the torment of lying awake of nights burning with wretchedness as he thought of the woman he had loved in Hugh Wade's arms.

Had ever any other man been such a devoted fool? Did other men let their frustrated dreams live on endlessly to cloud every other hope and desire?

Julian asked abruptly, "Cassius, did you ever love a woman?"

Cassius stood, looking blank, his coffee-colored face inscrutable, the shaving brush in air. His mouth twisted, pursed, pondering. A thin mouth with no thick liver-colored lips. Cassius had white blood and gloated in it.

"No, suh," he said thoughtfully, "cy'ant say ever I did. Not real love no woman. Married up with th'ee of 'em, but when Lily got sold off it didn't make no never-mind to me. Ada, she died. Rosie—I ain't know where she went, come freedom. Now I ain't got no woman and I better off."

"Much better off," agreed his master.

"Po' Mis' Wade, she dead." With the uncanny prescience of his race Cassius appeared to interpret Julian's thoughts. Always the Negroes read white people like that, as though what they felt and thought emanated in some fashion from their paler skins.

"I know. I've got to go to the funeral. Did you polish my boots?"

"Shine 'em good and make Tuby soap you' saddle and rub down that hoss."

"You'll drive the carriage for Mrs. Villerand, Cassius."

"Yessuh. You goin' wear that ole blue coat any more, boss?"

"No blue coats, Cassius. Not a popular color now in Alabama. When the war's over I'll give you that blue coat, brass buttons and all."

"Why ain't the war over now, boss? Mr. Linkum say come

las' New Year's all the nigger free. They goin' fight till they unfree us, boss?"

"I reckon you'll stay free. This war can't last much longer. Lee is losing too many men."

"Ain't been any fightin' down this-a-way, Boss. Reckon they'll be fightin' down this-a-way?"

"God help us, I hope not! Get me a black cravat, Cassius."

Now she was dead and forever gone, he told himself as he rode the narrow black-soiled road to the Wade plantation. Gnats swarmed up from a marshy stretch, his horse danced and threshed his head and tail and in the carriage ahead Julian saw Emma flapping her handkerchief and his older daughter, Juliet, pulling down her veil. Juliet had been married since last summer to Felix Destrade of New Orleans. Destrade was older, wealthy, with a fortune made in the wine and distilling business, an enigma of a short dark man whom Villerand had never been able to know very well or like very much.

That match had been Emma's doing. She it was who had sent Juliet off to Louisiana to learn arts and manners from the Sisters in New Orleans, and Julian suspected that young Duncan Wade, Florence's son, had been a reason. If Emma had ever suspected his own unrequited love she had never spoken of it, but all the years of their marriage her attitude toward the Wade family had been one of reserve, gracious it is true, but still somehow on guard.

Destrade traveled widely, making voyages through the blockade to France and Spain, even to California. During his long absences Juliet came home, afraid, now that the Yankees held New Orleans and there were Union gunboats on the Mississippi. Both his daughters were tall and had dark hair like their mother; Julian was glad of that. Too bad young Jule had had to be born a runt like himself. Julian Villerand knew a moment of tenderness, wondering where that rascal was now. Not yet nineteen, he had gone off to fight with General Maury, flinging hot words behind him because he had been opposed.

The road ran alongside his own fields and Julian observed them with pride. Only a few of his black people had slipped away when the news of Emancipation came south. Most of them were contented, being well fed and comfortably housed. War was far away from the river valleys of Alabama on that spring day of '63. Cotton was high and the young crop looked promising, the green rows free from grass, three plows moving deliberately down the middles. Julian sat straight in his saddle, feeling adequate and prosperous again. His spirit was already rising a little because never again on the earth would he glimpse the slow, judging look of the woman who had rejected him.

The Wade place looked fairly neat, a somehow desperate and haphazard neatness, the look of a house and grounds from which the woman's cherishing hand had been removed. There were daffodils in bloom—"Easter flowers" the women called them—but grass was creeping into the beds, and the trees and shrubbery all needed pruning. There were no other carriages along the drive and Julian knew the reason for that. When Nathan Bedford Forrest had needed horses to oppose the threat of the Union Colonel Streight's attacks in North Alabama, every planter in the river valleys had given up his carriage and saddle horses to the cavalry. All but Julian Villerand. He had told himself obstinately that no gentleman could afford to ride a mule, and that his wife and daughters could not be without a respectable vehicle.

Alabama was divided in mind about the war anyway. The governor distrusted Jefferson Davis, fought for State rights. Men in the northern counties were deserting the Confederate forces by the hundreds, and some had even enlisted with Federal troops. Generals Joe Wheeler, Forrest and Roddey were desperately trying to keep the Yankees out of Alabama, but Julian knew that so long as Alabama fed Lee's army, their chances for success were not too sanguine. A time might come when it would be expedient to escape from the brutal kind of war the Federals were inflicting on the Tennessee Valley, and if that time came Julian Villerand had no intention of being caught without proper means of conveyance. So he hitched his handsome mount boldly beside a lop-eared mule equipped with a sidesaddle, waited for the carriage to be backed into the shade and helped his wife and daughter to alight. Together they mounted the wooden steps to the open front door of the Wade house.

Three people stood waiting in the wide, cool hall. One was Hugh Wade looking stooped and dejected in a black coat a bit faded on the seams, broadcloth trousers and a home-ironed shirt. Julian and Emma shook his hand murmuring conventional sympathy. Juliet made a little bow and whispered something inaudible. Beyond Hugh stood a black woman, starched and rigid, with fiercely grieving eyes under a white cap and lips that trembled. And standing by her, holding to her hand was Julian's younger daughter, Marian, seventeen years old, rumpled, obviously tired, her eyelids hot and swollen, her hair escaping in damp curls from the snood that massed it on her slender neck.

Marian regarded her family with a look of relief, tinged with irritation. "I was afraid you weren't coming. They're ready to begin."

Emma led Juliet to two chairs near the front of the big parlor, where close to the coffin a very old minister with white hair and rheumy eyes teetered on his toes, balancing a heavy Bible on his palms. Julian looked about, found a seat at the rear, but even there he could not avoid the sight of Florence's small face upturned, in her varnished wooden coffin, ivory-still and frigid as a cameo. And her hair—good Lord, it was white! Julian ran his hands over his own head anxiously, but knew there was no gray there. No gray either in Emma's dark tresses, though Hugh Wade's thinning locks were gray and lanky.

I'd have taken better care of her. I'd have given her everything. I wouldn't have let her die, Julian was thinking, the old bitterness returning.

Hugh Wade tiptoed in, and people sitting near rose and pressed his hand. A group of Negroes had gathered at the door and they began a low, rhythmic humming, broken now and then by sharp sobs. Marian slipped into a chair beside her father as the preacher cleared his throat. "You'll have to help carry her," she whispered. "There aren't enough men. I told them you would help."

Julian gave a little involuntary moan. He could not be one to carry Florence Wade to that last resting place! Yet a look about the room told him that he must. Women, boys, very old men—not six able-bodied males in the rooms. All off with Forrest, with Maury, with Johnston, even with Lee. And no Negro could be persuaded to carry a corpse, unless it happened to be one of his own family. They had to be bribed and almost coerced into digging a grave—and since last January and Lincoln's proclamation, with the thought of freedom running through the race like a fire, like a heady brew, coercion was no longer expedient or wise.

The minister blew his nose, fluttered the pages of the Book. "I will read from First Corinthians," he announced in a voice that quavered.

Julian smelled honeysuckle. It made him a little sick and sweat stood out on his wrists. As he wiped it away he saw that his hand trembled. Tears had come again into Marian's eyes. She reached for his hand and held it. There was honeysuckle in bloom that night, Julian was remembering. When he had ridden furiously away from the scene of his humiliation, the perfume was strong on the evening air and he had breathed it, hated it. He was grateful for the long prayer that gave him time to compose himself; then he fidgeted through what seemed an endless eulogy. Words registered but faintly on his brain. What were words? She was dead. "This lovely life . . . beautiful example of womanhood . . . devoted wife and mother . . ." Julian Villerand almost snarled aloud. Devoted wife to Hugh Wade, the fumbler, the ineffectual, who had let her die!

Then at last the coffin was closed. The Negroes keened and women sobbed when the nails were driven in. A wormy little man with one arm and a too-long black coat raised his voice: "Will kind friends please assist us in bearing the remains?"

Julian moved forward reluctantly, shoved along by Marian. Then he was lifting that inert burden, that precious freight, stumbling with a few others out of the house, across the yard, through a gate. Abruptly he was aware of Marian there, helping to carry too. In a low mutter he ordered her back, but she shook her head. Beyond her the Negro woman Louisa panted, trudged. A long way across the meadow to that burial plot. Bard Leonard, a one-legged neighbor was waiting there with coiled ropes. The ropes shrieked and rasped on the wood as the coffin went down. Julian turned away, suddenly, strode off down the slope without looking back.

At the avenue where his horse was hitched an old man, tottering on a cane, halted him. "Heard the news, Villerand? Nate Forrest is running hell out of Streight's Yanks up towards Gadsden. Even got gals out with guns up there so they say. By Jupiter, we'll lick 'em yet!"

Julian nodded numbly. He was having a rather humiliating struggle to lift his bulk into the saddle.

It hit him abruptly that he could be getting old. But he wasn't old. Florence had not been an old woman. It was the long illness that had turned her hair white. War and worry had killed her. Hugh Wade had let her die.

He would hate Hugh Wade as long as he lived.

I

THE AVENUE was not changed. He had expected to see the great trees laid low, the fences destroyed; he had even steeled himself to find the house burned to the ground like so many he had seen on his long, weary tramp through Georgia. But he glimpsed the roof between the trees and hurried toward it over a grass-grown track.

Once this carriageway had been wide and sanded, but now weeds grew in it and heavy wagons had rutted it deep after rain. In his mother's day no wagon was ever allowed to travel the avenue. They went out over the field track across a wooden bridge over a creek and to the main river road. Likely that bridge was gone now. No cavalry troop ever left a bridge intact behind them.

The house came into view, a width of sun-blistered clapboards, the glint of glass. At least there were still windows unbroken. The grass grew high where the lawn sloped down toward the marshy pastures. Duncan remembered a night long ago. He had been seventeen then and Juliet a few years older. There had been lanterns strung in these trees and a bower built for the fiddlers, and all this sward had been clipped with shears as smooth as velvet by small colored urchins crawling on their knobby knees, his little mother strolling purposefully behind with her parasol to see that no grass blade escaped the blades.

He stood still for a moment, his legs aching with weariness, the weakness that still lingered in flabby, dried-out muscles. The six-mile ride on the back of that jolting wagon had not rested him. The mule had been lean and old and slow.

"Mighty lucky I got to keep this-here mule," Bard Leonard had drawled. "Had him hid in the swamp so much he forgits is he a mule or a alligator. Et him, I reckon, could they catch him. Everybody got hungry enough to eat mule before crop come in last summer. You been a long time gittin' home, Mister Duncan."

"I had a long way to come, Bard. Afoot most of the way."

"In May it was a year since Dick Taylor surrendered over towards the line. We sure cotch hell in Alabama that last year before the surrender."

"We waited a long time up in North Carolina before we were paroled. They fed us—fed us a little."

"Didn't feed you much by the looks of you" was Bard's laconic comment.

"They didn't have very much themselves. The country up there was bare as an empty meal bin; even the rats were hungry." Duncan almost got out the question then that had lain like a red-hot lump in his throat for months. "The old gentlemen . . . is he . . ."

"Right peart, Mister Duncan. Right peart."

Duncan felt like running when he got down from the wagon at the gate, but now his feet were heavy and aching again, even with the house in sight. The tall cedars beside the front steps had grown gnarly, and one had the top broken off. The boxwoods were up to the window sills, and his mother's climbing yellow rose sprawled over them, rank and untended. He had got the news of her death after Gettysburg and it added despair to the agony of that battle. Tal Leonard, Bard's son, coming up with Sanders' Alabama replacements, had brought the word to Duncan.

"They had a nice burying, Dunc," Tal had said, trying to be comforting. "I'd went home—had to help Pap get the cotton planted." So casually had Tal passed over the dubious business of too many desertions from the Confederate forces. "I helped carry her up the hill. Wasn't enough men—two women helped carry."

Duncan lifted his eyes to the little hill now where an old brick wall crumbled and one tall shaft caught the sun. Great-grandpa Wade. Came west from South Carolina in 1816, when the Creeks were still a ravaging menace in Alabama. There would be no stone above his mother's grave. That was one of the things he had planned to look after when he got home.

Strength came back into his legs again and he hurried a little, cutting across what had been a posy bed. Somebody had been cutting pokeweed there. That would be Louisa, always ranging around after greens.

There was no sign of life around the house and the front door was closed. Duncan had never seen it closed before in summer, and a touch of returning unease, of the haunting panic that had pressed upon him so long, came back again. Now he almost ran around the house, over the trampled, grassless space at the back, where there was a mounting block, and a brick kitchen set off from the house by a covered walkway, and the great magnolia tree with a wooden seat built around it.

On that seat his mother had sat of mornings, waving a palm-leaf fan while she directed the bleaching of linen, the shelling of peas or the dipping of hanks of spun yarn into a steaming dye pot. Now Duncan's father sat there, hunkered forward, his elbows on his knees.

Hugh Wade wore a yellowed shirt, and gray hair, too long, hung over his collar beneath a frayed straw hat, pushed back on his head. His beard, grown gray too, was untrimmed and stained. His hands were thin and yellow. Duncan's heart gave a sick jerk. His father looked so old! Old and thin and dejected and alone.

"Pa!" It was a yell, choked with emotion. "Pa—I'm home!"

Hugh Wade staggered up, steadying himself with one hand against the tree. He stood staring for a minute, then stumbled toward his son, trembling hands outstretched. "Well, sir! Well, sir!" he cried, grasping Duncan by both shoulders. "Well, sir, I gave you up. I gave you up months ago."

They shook hands, pawing at each other affectionately, babbling incoherencies, tears streaming down their faces.

Duncan tried to laugh. "Wades never give up—didn't you know that, sir?" He held his father erect, maneuvered him back to the seat. "Sit down, sir. You're shaking all over."

"I'm all right," gasped the older man. "Just excited. Sit here now, sir. I want to know where you've been all this time. Looked for you last summer—watched for you all the fall. Came winter, and no word and I sort of gave up."

"I was a long way from here when I got paroled, finally— July that was. I'd lost my horse, away in the spring, and I didn't have any money and there was nothing much to eat. So I wandered up into Virginia from Durham, North Carolina, to work awhile for my room and board on a repair job on the railroad bridges. All the Negroes were drunk on freedom up there, and none of 'em would work, so some of us out of the army got jobs on the roadbed and the bridges. That's where I got these—" Duncan held out his callused palms. "Then we moved on down through North Carolina, but what work was to be had there was paid for in scrip, and it was no good after a few weeks. I didn't even have the price of a stamp to send a letter home, Pa."

"You walked? You walked home?"

"Got a ride once in a while, but mostly I walked. Stopped along to help hang some tobacco or pitch hay to get a meal. Slept in barns, under bridges, anywhere there was shelter."

"Damn war to hell!" Hugh Wade prayerfully twisted his hands into fists. "It was bad here—too bad. Bad times in Selma, a year ago. They mighty near laid that town flat. General Wilson came down through this country. Burned the military school up at Tuscaloosa, destroyed everything as he went. River was high—that's all that saved us here, I reckon. We lost her, Duncan—spring of '63."

"I know. Tal Leonard brought me the word. But she'd been gone some time then."

"It was in her breast, all that winter, but she wouldn't give up. Got thinner and paler. Then the swelling began and she couldn't lie down. Couldn't get her breath. She used to sit up all night, scraping lint for the soldiers. The doctor went, with Bed Forrest's cavalry. I did what I could. Nothing much anybody could do. Louisa took care of her. I wrote you—guess you never got the letter?"

"We got mail once—that was before we went south across the Rappahannock. After that I was on detached scout duty most of the time till they shot my horse. Later we got some more horses, but we lost them, one after another. No shoes. They went unshod till they got lame. No fodder when the grass dried up in the hot weather. I carried my saddle for a while, then I had to throw it away."

"Tal Leonard was killed. I reckon you heard?"

"No, I hadn't heard. I figured Tal was at Appomattox when Lee surrendered. Some of the Alabama brigades were over there. Bard never mentioned it."

"Bard thought you knew, likely. Tal was killed at Petersburg when that crater blew up. I reckoned that you'd been killed there too."

"I was there—not ten miles away. But all the commands and divisions were getting scrambled then; men got lost from their regiments and never found them again. I served under seven commanders in one war. Ended up under Johnston. He would be fighting yet, I guess, if he hadn't got peremptory orders from Marse Robert. Nobody wanted to own that we were licked. I saw a captain who'd gone through Gettysburg and the Virginia campaign sit down beside the road and blubber like a whipped young one."

"Come into the kitchen, son." His father struggled to his feet. "You must be hungry. Ought to be a pone of bread left in the oven. No coffee though. No coffee for a long time. No whisky either. A little while after Dick Taylor surrendered to Canby, down yonder, a renegade Yankee named Applegate came here with a gang of ruffians, illiterate scoundrels like himself. They hung around a week, waving pistols at everybody, stripped the house of everything they fancied, destroyed a lot that they couldn't carry away."

"I heard about that fellow Applegate. I met some Mississippi boys up toward the Tennessee River. They said he'd been over in Mississippi, stole a lot of valuable papers from some woman over there, a prominent woman."

"Wife of the Treasurer of the Confederacy. Offered to sell 'em back to her for ten thousand dollars. Mrs. Thompson hired some lawyers and they tracked him up to Huntsville and got the papers back for three hundred dollars. He's still around—stranded down here, they say. Fooling around in Yankee politics."

"Louisa—the people, are they all gone?" Duncan asked after a little silence.

"Louisa stayed." His father held open the kitchen door. "So did Josuff and Parmy. They're chopping cotton today."

"Louisa chopping cotton? She was always a mighty proud house servant."

"They share the crop now. Freedmen's Bureau sets the wage and they've got a garrison of troops up in town to enforce their rule. It's work or go naked and hungry for the people now, but Louisa still cooks what little we have to eat and Josuff putters round the place. Here's bread, son, but no butter any more. Wilson's troops took our last cow—but some other outfit would have got her anyway."

The kitchen still smelled like home. Duncan sank on a backless stool, polished to a sheen by the warm buttocks of generations of house slaves. He ate the cold corn pones and drank the cool water his father brought from the cistern.

"Over a year now since the war ended," he said presently. "What has that year done to Alabama?"

Hugh Wade let himself down into a sagging, splint-bottomed chair. His dejection, his feebleness, Duncan discerned, had been more of a mood than a reality. There was still an alert steeliness about him, a glint of fire in the dark eyes under prominent brows, strength in the quick movements of his long, yellowed fingers.

"We had almost sixty days of no law or authority whatever in this state. Most people stayed at home, kept as quiet as they could, were careful what they said where it could be overheard by any ears, white or black—and prayed. Everybody was hungry. All the stores had been looted or destroyed, meat carried off, corn stolen or burned. Most of us were in rags too—like me." He held out his arms in frayed sleeves. His dry grin was rueful, but Duncan could see no self-pity in it.

"The horses?"

"They went early. When Forrest needed mounts for his troops. Josuff hid out the mules, but old Derry went lame from being staked out in marshy land, and he's no good any more. We were told we'd get our horses back when the regiments were dismounted, but we never did."

Duncan remembered the horses he had seen, disemboweled, stiff legs in air. "They tried to get the horses first, always. They hamstrung and shot them. Both armies." Some horses had been eaten later, he knew, but he would not speak of that. "They let you alone, at least," he said.

"I let them alone. A lot of houses were destroyed, but they left this one stand. Josuff hid out a sow, so we had a little meat for a while. The sweet-potato crop was pretty good last fall too.

But I wouldn't take their ironclad oath, so of course they took all the cotton."

"Who took it? Our people?"

"No, our people just drifted away a few at a time. They had heard all the fabulous promises made by the Federals and the Freedmen's Bureau. They thought they were going to get forty acres and a mule, that all the big plantations were going to be confiscated and divided up among the blacks. I don't know what happened to most of our black people. They found that cross-eyed boy we called Henry last spring, when the freshets went down. He'd tried to cross the river in a little leaky boat and drowned. Louisa says she knows where some of ours are. They were good people, Duncan—simple, honest and deluded. God knows what will become of them now!"

"You still haven't told me who took the cotton."

"I wouldn't take their oath, so I was a Confederate sympathizer and therefore the cotton was contraband. They had taxed the crop so high anyway that nobody could make much off of it except the hands—they got forty per cent and the Yankees got part of that, you may be sure. Josuff got some money, and Louisa and Parmy. Josuff's too feeble to do much beside putter around the place, but the Freedmen's Bureau says I've got to pay him wages and maintain him. Thaddeus Stevens—he's our arch enemy! Bring the arrogant South to her knees, strip her bare and then flog her till she repents—that's his idea, but not Johnson's, I think. Johnson's a Southerner. He may see justice done."

"A renegade Southerner!" said Duncan bitterly. "Elected on a Black Republican ticket. Our army hated Lincoln, but they respected him. Johnson, they despised. We planned if we took Washington Lincoln would be a hostage, but Johnson we'd hang."

"The young," said Hugh Wade thoughtfully, "are vengeful."

"How about the old?" demanded Duncan, picking up the last crumbs of bread with a moistened forefinger. "Are you satisfied to let them rob you, spit on you, humiliate you?"

"The old have learned to wait. They have seen the day of the despoiler pass. They know that all they have to do is wait."

"And starve while you're waiting!"

"Nobody has starved, but some poor people have had to eat 'Congress bread.' The generosity of the victors. Feed the benighted, obstinate creatures so they can live to pay more taxes. By the way, you don't have a gun, do you?"

"Where would I get a gun? They even took our canteens and pocketknives away when the regiment was paroled. A few officers were allowed to keep their horses, but the beasts were half dead anyway. These shoes—" he thrust out his feet, thin-soled, shapeless—"came off a dead lieutenant from Georgia. When our colors went he shot himself, and the burial detail divided his clothes. We left him a coat, buttoned up to his chin. A waste to bury good clothes with any wear left in them. There were men on both sides who were buried naked."

"You're tired." His father rose and picked up a bucket. "I'll get some water. You'd better have a bath and get some rest."

"Yesterday I stripped off and washed in the Black Warrior River. Do we have any soap? That was what we missed most. We lay around, foul and stinking, and talked about big steaming kettles of soap. One corporal from Arkansas stole a pot of it, red-hot out of a yard, but it didn't last an hour. By that time we'd got lousy too. Are any of my clothes left upstairs?"

"I don't know. Your mother gave out some things—there was no Osnaburg or linsey any more to make clothes for the people. They were getting destitute for wearing apparel. Then those guerrillas came—Applegate and his gang——"

"I'll look." Duncan got up, the weary pain making his legs tremble again. "Leave the water here. I'll come back and scrub

myself. These things—" he scowled at the tattered uniform—
"ought to be burned. Even Parmy wouldn't be seen in them."

"Parmy wouldn't scorn any garment that would hold together." Hugh Wade started for the cistern, turned back. "The
reason I asked about a gun—they took every weapon we had
on the place. Even my grandfather's old 1812 musket. I could
shoot a little game now and then if there was anything to shoot
it with."

Duncan cursed angrily, as he took the covered way back to
the house. The wide hall that divided the main house was bare
now, dusty, echoing. The carpet was gone and the mahogany
tables and yellowed portraits of dead and gone Wades and
Duncans. Only one was left, a dim, crudely painted likeness of
a young girl holding an impossible flower—some great-grand-
mother of his father, Duncan remembered. The picture hung
askew and was defaced. A sooty beard had been daubed on the
faded, prim young face and the small virginal breasts had round
holes burned in the canvas where the nipples would have been.

Angrily he jerked the portrait down, shattered plaster and
dust raining with it, and turned the tarnished frame to the wall.

Applegate had been there, and Applegate was now stranded
in Alabama, his father had said. Duncan licked his lips with
vengeful intent. It was true that the young were vengeful. His
father had spoken the truth there.

II

THERE WAS little left in the big, dark wardrobes in the upper rooms. In the southeast chamber, the room where Duncan had been born, the bed was carelessly made and a soiled cotton nightshirt dangled from a bedpost. Obviously Hugh Wade still slept here. The room had a musty, masculine smell now; nothing of his mother was left in it except two lanky cotton dresses and a bent and rusted pair of hoops hanging in a wardrobe and a faded straw bonnet with dried-out ribbons impaled on a hook.

He remembered the billowing silks his mother had worn, with the skirts tilting jauntily as she came down the stairs, but remembered too that most of the silk dresses in the South had gone into making those futile balloons that had been sent aloft to spy out the movements of the Federal troops. Duncan had seen one shot down on the upper James, lolloping in the water, and he had wondered then if some of the piebald breadths of that slammock had ever been worn by his own mother.

In his own room cobwebs draped every corner and their thick lacework was over the chest and the rungs of two remaining chairs. The bed was stripped, the feather bed turned over the footboard, and thin drifts of feathers revealed that this tick had been slashed, and then sewed up roughly with cotton string. Applegate again, no doubt, looking for hidden money or silver. He pulled out the drawers in the chest, found one worn undershirt, one dress shirt with yellowed, stiff bosom, a few rusted collar buttons, one white glove and nothing else.

There were two faded pairs of cotton pants, the pockets all
turned outward; and the broadcloth coat he had had made for
some wedding, already turning green at the seams. The waist-
coat and trousers that had companioned this bygone elegance
were both missing. He wondered if Parmy or Josuff had
been protected by his wedding garments from the sudden chills
of a black-belt winter.

No shirt at all, unless Louisa had some things hidden somewhere from pillagers. From his window he could see the old
loom house where in his boyhood vast lengths of cotton and
linen fabric had been woven by the dark-fingered girls, then
cut and sewed into shirts and chemises and billowing petticoats
under his mother's direction. The shingles on the loom house
were mossy and curling now, the door hanging on one hinge.

He put on the undershirt and a pair of the lanky trousers.
They smelled of mildew and were shrunken and tight but they
were clean. In the kitchen he barred the door and scrubbed himself in the wooden tub his father had made ready, using lye
soap from a ferkin, lathering his body and his hair, scrubbing
his body afterward with a coarse tow towel of the sort he had
seen often hung on the fig tree for the field hands to use.

Hugh Wade was still sitting under the magnolia tree. Overhead great white blooms were opening and bees made the air
vibrant with their murmurings. Duncan dropped down beside
him and laid a hand on the older man's wrist, feeling dryness
there under the brown skin, and a wiry tautness that had nothing of weakness in it.

"What do we do now, sir?" he began. "Life has to go on.
What can we do now?"

Hugh Wade studied him, frowning. "Those the only
clothes you could find? Gad, what a pair of scarecrows! Two
gentlemen of Alabama, you and me. Now that you're home
again—and thank God for that—what do you intend to do?

You must have had time this past year to consider your future. Do you plan to stay here?"

Duncan looked perplexed. "But where else would I go? At least we've still got the place. Or can they take that away from us too?"

"Yes, we've still got the place. And one mule able to work. The Wellborns lost their land last summer. Sold for loans and taxes. Four hundred acres of black bottom land, worth thousands, and a colonel from Wisconsin bid it in for six hundred dollars. The Willborns gathered together what they could, joined a wagon train and left for Texas. Settled somewhere on the Brazos River, I heard, and the old lady, Tom's mother, died out there."

"Can they sell us out too?"

"Nobody knows what they can do. This is a conquered province and that rag-tail Congress in Washington makes the rules. June last year they appointed Lewis Parsons from Talladega provisional governor. Then in the fall they ordered an election. Bob Patton in Lauderdale County was elected governor. We sent Lewis Parsons and George Houston to the United States Senate, but they've never been allowed inside the door as yet. Neither have any of the men we sent to Congress been seated, although we did everything they asked—framed a new constitution, revoked the Ordinance of Secession, asked to be readmitted to the Union. At least Andrew Johnson recognized Alabama as a state, one of the states necessary to ratify the constitutional amendment against slavery, but there will be opposition in that rump Congress and bitter opposition here if they try to dictate the political status of the Negro in Alabama."

"So much for Alabama. What about the Wades?"

"The Wades could not be poorer than we are now. Like everybody else down here I bought Confederate bonds. There's a trunk full of them upstairs. Not even very good paper, though the seals and signatures are imposing. One of them might last half a day to stop a hole in your shoes, but no longer. There are fifty thousand people in this section, people like us who always lived bountifully before the war, who are in dire circumstances now. Brave people. They formed the Nineteenth Alabama, they produced leaders like Joe Wheeler and John Pelham."

"Pelham was killed on the Rappahannock," Duncan said. "I was transferred to his command in '62." He would forego his wish to assay the present, indulging his father in his desire to review the past.

"Hundreds of boys from north of here, from counties where there were few slaves, or none at all, died at Shiloh in their butternut breeches, fighting under Joe Wheeler," Hugh Wade rambled on. "A year ago, when it looked like there was no hope for the South, about two days before the surrender, I think it was, they started burning the cotton. Thousand of bales were burned in Selma, in Montgomery—even out on the plantations they poured turpentine over the bales and burned it, to keep the Yankees from getting it. Then the crop was poor—everything worn out, the tools, the mules, the people hungry and weak, the seed inferior—and what little we did raise was more than half of it confiscated. Just what future can you see ahead for us, son?"

"I was asking you, sir. I've been away five years. But the land is still good and strong, if they don't rob us of it. I saw plenty of big places burned out and devastated, between Petersburg and Tuscaloosa. At least we've got one mule and three people left. I'm young—in a little bit I'll get my legs in shape to go. I figure they've carried me about seven thousand miles in the last five years, but they held out to Demopolis." He tried to laugh, to put a bright face on the outlook, but he knew it for a desperate effort and he felt dubiously that it fell more than a little flat.

"You were born a gentleman," Hugh Wade said. "So was I.

The country is filled with free Negroes now, decent people most of them. They can be contracted through the Bureau, but a man's no good in the field without stock and tools. If Andrew Johnson wants to persuade Alabama back into the Union without rancor or antagonism he could send us a few carloads of mules."

"The artillery had them, but they wore them out. There must be mules, but I suppose there's no money to buy them. Are all the banks out of business?"

"One or two in the state are trying to resume again. Even the state is bankrupt—had to borrow thirty-five thousand dollars to pay the expense this year—borrowed it in New York, I heard."

"When the war ended we heard big tales from the Yanks about the gold that was buried down south. Some fellow who'd been discharged from a New Jersey outfit organized a party to come south and dig around the ruined plantations for the gold they thought was buried there. Who buried any gold around here?"

"If anybody did," said his father, "it was Villerand."

"Juliet's father?"

"She got married. I reckon you heard?"

"Yes, I heard." Sixty-two, that exultant year when the South was still strong, still determined and the tide ran high. He had had a horse then, been sent east to Stonewall Jackson's command. Somehow, the letter had got through.

I'm blotting this with my tears, Duncan. But after all I am older than you. It was jolly for a while, wasn't it? Now I'm marrying Felix Destrade. He's older—from New Orleans. The family are pleased. Don't forget me——

No, he had not forgotten. But a year later he had torn the frayed letter up and thrown it into the Shenandoah River.

"She married a Frenchman—distiller, rich. She comes home and stays around most of the time, though. Villerand appears pretty well off, which is unique in a country where the fashion is elegant destitution." A touch of acerbity was in Hugh Wade's voice. "Villerand made a speech 'while back, just before county election, reminded people that Alabama had been wealthy before secession, implied that we'd been foolish to listen to hotheads and impractical patriots. The speech—" he grinned dryly—"was not too well received, I heard. I wasn't there. Prudent people stay home and hold their tongues, and I count myself a prudent man."

So she was at home and still married to the whisky distiller whose name was Felix. Duncan felt a dry hardness tightening in his chest. For weeks, while that letter had lain folded inside his coat, he had caught himself clenching his teeth till they ached.

"If Villerand has money, what's he doing with it?" he asked.

"You hear rumors. One is that he's projecting around on some railroad idea." Hugh Wade's face stiffened scornfully. His son knew that his father had despised Julian Villerand for years, that it went far back and had something to do with his mother. "That bowlegged Carolina sharper," Hugh had called Villerand at first, and then when the other man grew corpulent, he had scorned him with "Frogbelly."

"Well, the country needs railroads," Duncan agreed. "I saw what we had all torn up, bridges burned, and river barges sunk or leaking." He got to his feet. "I'll walk around a little. My legs have quit aching now. I'll get stiff if I sit still too long."

"Want to wander down with me and see how the people are getting on with the chopping?" His father raised his thin body, all bones now but still alert and quick with purpose.

"Later I'll wander down. I thought I'd walk up the hill yonder."

"Yes—yes, do that. You'll find everything badly overgrown, though, I'm afraid. Nobody to tend it now. Porter wandered off too. He's on one of those vagrant jobs now, Josuff says.

They gather the Negroes up, contract them out to the planters, but I couldn't manage that because they have to be fed. Hard enough to keep Parmy filled up." Wade put on his stained old hat, moved off toward the lower gate.

Ranger should be there at that gate, Duncan was thinking, with his white nose and chestnut head over the bars. That colt had been his father's pride, followed the old man everywhere. Where was he now—a few bones and a rotting hide in some stinking Tennessee gully? Duncan had seen so many of them, those lost proud horses.

He crossed the yard, went through the pecan alley, where the trees were grown so tall and dense now that their branches met overhead to make a sea of pale-green dimness below. They had carried his mother up this way. Two women had had to help carry, Tal Leonard had said. Now Tal was gone too, buried in that trench, no doubt, with the other shattered bodies at Petersburg. Duncan resolved to walk over to Bard's place some evening and talk to Bard about Tal. Bard had always been a respectable white farmer. He had lost a leg in the Mexican War.

Duncan had a little trouble finding his mother's grave. All the brick-walled enclosure swarmed with periwinkle and myrtle, dewberry vines snatched at his naked ankle, a rosebush run wild slapped him in the face. A little width of raw, washed earth revealed where the new mound lay. A handleless blue pitcher was half sunk in the soil, with an inch of stained water in it and the dried stems of some flowers.

He stood there, very still, wondering how she had looked in death. Thin and pale, his father had said. Had they buried her in a blue dress? She had always liked to wear blue. It set off the wheaty sparkle of her brown hair, the clear amber of her eyes. She had been such a small person to contain so much pride and determination. Like so much that had been proud and beautiful, like all the trappings of the proud people, she was lost now. She would have hated this country now, Duncan was thinking, been revolted by this scarecrow creature who stood here reverently mourning the ending of what had been spirited beauty. She would have been revolted by this penniless ragamuffin, her only son!

"When I get some elegant clothes and a good pair of boots I'll dress up and come back to see you, Mother," he said aloud, "and you shall have a monument, the tallest, whitest monument in Alabama."

Fatuous boasting, he told himself. Then he stiffened suspiciously and strode over the broken wall, listening, hearing the clink of a shod horse approaching along the lane.

A girl was riding on a bright bay, a girl with dark hair under a scrap of black hat tied with blue ribbons beneath her chin. Her long blue skirt was tucked up, but she shook it down quickly and frowned, flushing, seeing him standing there. She pulled the horse to a quick stop. "Get away!" she ordered sharply.

Duncan stared. That hair—those storm-colored gray eyes . . . "Juliet!" he exclaimed, moving near her.

She pulled the horse aside, held her crop at the ready. "I'm not Juliet. You keep away. Don't you come near me!"

"Your pardon, Miss," Duncan said coldly, "but it happens that you are trespassing on private property. I mistook you for an old friend, Miss Juliet Villerand. She has another name now—but I've forgotten what it is."

"My Heaven!" she exclaimed. "Do I look as old as Juliet? I know this is private property. I ride here nearly every day. Nobody minds if I ride here. Who are you, anyway?"

"Once I was Lieutenant Duncan Wade. Now I'm what is left of that noble character. These rags, young woman, cover a proud heart still."

"Duncan? But you were killed—you were killed at Petersburg!"

"I didn't like being buried in a trench at Petersburg—so I

came home. I was choosing a better place here, beside my mother. And who," he inquired with a tinge of acidity, "is rich enough now in Alabama to own a horse like that?"

"I own him. Duncan Wade, don't you know me, really?"

"I've been off to the wars for five years. Wait a minute—that hair! You're the little one."

"I'm Marian. And I'm not flattered a bit that you forgot me. I was madly in love with you, Duncan Wade, when I was fourteen, but you never gave me a glance. Now I'm grown up. I'm practically an old lady. I'm glad you weren't killed at Petersburg. So many boys didn't come back, but some came home last summer. You were a long time coming back. Were you in prison?"

"No, I was just walking. It was a mighty long walk from where the war ended for me. And I had to work along the way to get something to eat. Young Jule—" he remembered the arrogant, redheaded young Villerand son—"is he——"

"Fort Morgan. He's buried down there somewhere. Father has never been able to find his grave," she answered quietly.

"I'm sorry. Jule was a merry rascal. You shouldn't ride alone, Miss Villerand. This country is full of riffraff and strangers and that's a very good horse."

"I ride only in the fields. I ride over to see Uncle Hugh Wade. He talks to me about you. Now he won't talk about you any more. I must bring some more flowers to Aunt Florence. Those I brought the other day are all dead."

"You brought those? You knew my mother?"

"Of course. I loved her. I was with her when she died. I even helped carry her coffin up here. I helped Louisa dress her and comb her hair."

"Did you put a blue dress on her? I've been wondering."

"Yes, it was blue. It was a little bit faded, but Louisa dipped it in indigo. It looked pretty nice. I put a flower in her hand —a Cape jasmine flower."

"Thank you," he said gravely. "She would have liked a Cape jasmine flower. I thank you, Miss Villerand."

"A long time ago you used to call me Maggie. When you looked at me, which wasn't very often. You were always looking at Juliet."

"She was very lovely to look at. Is she still beautiful?"

"Well," said the girl slowly, "she's going on thirty and she's married. To Felix. He's getting fat. He doesn't come up here very often—on account of traveling so much and getting his export trade started again, so she says. For a long time the Yankee army took all the grain, Juliet says, but now he can get grain for his distilleries. Yes, I reckon Juliet is still beautiful." She breathed a little sigh, gathered up the reins. "I'd better start along home."

"You'd better give up riding alone, Miss Maggie Villerand. What if I had been a deserter or a guerrilla or one of these scalawags left behind by both armies?"

"Well, you weren't. You were Duncan Wade—raised from the dead. And you scold just like my father."

"At least your father talks sense." Duncan was on the point of adding, "for once," but he remembered that the old hostility between his own father and Julian Villerand had never been allowed to affect the members of the younger generation. For some odd reason he was glad of that.

III

MARIAN RODE home slowly, deep in thought and remembering. The ending of the war had obscured for her both its beginning and the long anxiety of its duration. With the blithe eagerness of youth she had accepted what was now, today. She was not happy that seeing Duncan Wade again brought it all back—that old, rich, carefree time. True, there had been rumblings then of trouble, hot political arguments whenever men came to call or to dinner, a few friendships broken. She was remembering now how the eyes of the house servants had troubled her in those times when the unrest began, how they had looked withdrawn and judging, dark enigmas who whispered among themselves in the kitchen or the yard. The white people's day was waning, and with the mystic prescience of their race the Negroes had known it then. But it was bitter remembering.

Naïvely arrogant, the young people of her set had danced and picnicked, or ridden off at dusk on possum hunts with troops of colored boys leading dogs and carrying lanterns. Sometimes the young fellows she knew had argued about current affairs, but usually the girls ordered them to hush. Who cared about stupid old Stephen A. Douglas? What if the Black Republicans did elect that rail splitter from Illinois? Who wanted to hear about him?

As for South Carolina, that firebrand state, everybody knew that it was a mildewed and bigoted place, drenched in futile pride, pathetic in its conceit. Even Emma and Julian Villerand, who had been born there, declared that they would not want to live again in South Carolina. What, demanded the young and the brash, could you expect of a place where the people lived on crabs and grits and made a public holiday out of hanging pirates? Where old ladies, fusty and rigid with outmoded traditions, sat arrogantly in ancestral pews and young people languished in aloof, moldering houses?

Of them all, young Jule had been in those days the only one who defended South Carolina, exulted when Sumter loosed the delirium of war on the South. Marian remembered her father's arguments about the poverty of industry, the lack of steel, the insanity of believing that any war could be won with sabers by yelling boys on horseback with plumes in their hats.

Her mother had been very quiet that first spring. Marian had had no time to worry about Manassas or the threat of blockade, because Duncan Wade had been the first to rush off to fight, and she had long adored Duncan Wade from the agonized, frustrated distance of adolescence, knowing that he was fatuously in love with Juliet, four years older than he and insolent then in her fresh beauty.

To Juliet, Duncan had been only one of a train of bedazzled young men. But her young sister had always been convinced that secretly Juliet nursed a passion for Duncan, though she called him that "silly Wade boy" when she was teased about him. A match with a younger man, their mother had argued, would be most unsuitable. A woman's life was difficult enough when everything was properly in balance. Duncan was impetuous, of the hotheaded, high-tempered metal of the plantation gentleman, a temper that could be broken but would never bend. The first of the county to go, now Duncan was the last to return.

As she turned in at the Villerand lane Marian felt a little cloud of sorrow for Duncan. Things were going to be rough for him at home. A ragamuffin, he had scorned himself, and a ragamuffin he had appeared. Hugh Wade had been so terribly unlucky. She had heard it talked at home. Stubborn, said her father, imperious, full of old notions of honor, slave to a bygone code. No act of legislation, no ruling of the Church would ever move the gentlemen of Hugh Wade's generation from their standard of unyielding ethics.

"He could have taken the oath," argued Julian. "He could have saved himself from persecutions. He could have saved his cotton."

Marian had flared up at that. "He'd never take that oath, any more than I would!"

"At least, my dear," her father warned, "be discreet about making statements like that where other people can hear you."

"Jule would never have taken their foul oath either. You know he wouldn't."

"Your brother would not have been able to take the oath. He was ineligible. He fought for the Confederacy."

"Then Uncle Hugh Wade wouldn't be eligible either. He gave all he had to the Confederacy," Marian persisted.

"You're acting very ugly, Sister." That was Juliet, being reproachful and sisterly. "I'm sorry too to see Mr. Wade so reduced, but Papa says he could have managed better. Just as Papa did."

Marian tightened her lips at that, held her tongue. Juliet did not know that Duncan was back. I won't tell her, I'll never tell her, Marian was saying to herself as she neared the house. It was a silly vow, of course, for inevitably the black grapevine would bring the news. The mystic speed with which servants knew all the white people's doings over the countryside was a marvel accepted but unexplained.

"They smell things," Marian had declared once. "Lelia goes out the kitchen door and sniffs, and in ten minutes she knows everything that goes on: who's getting married, who's having a new dress made, who's bought a horse. When the Lawsons had that fight and Henrietta went back to Talladega to her mother, Cassius knew about it before the carriage got across the bridge."

"You will learn, as you mature, that you must not listen to servants," her mother had lectured. "Above all you must not question them. No lady displays curiosity or listens to gossip, and her name must never be spoken idly or maliciously. Duels have been fought over that matter."

A lady might eschew gossip, but in that case Juliet fell short of ladyship, for undoubtedly Marian would be shortly hemmed in a corner and pumped dry of everything she knew about Duncan Wade. Of course she knew practically nothing except that he was here, handsomer than ever, in a grave, sun-darkened saturnine fashion, that he was a trifle bitter and still domineering, as of old when he had stirred her to aching fury by ordering her around as though she were a child.

Thank goodness, Juliet was safely and rigidly married to Felix, and would be married forever, Felix being a Catholic and divorce an unthinkable disgrace, relegating any lady to social limbo.

She turned the horse over to Tuby, mounted the front steps and waited for Cassius to open the door. The jalousied summer doors were kept bolted now, the times being so unsettled, and Cassius gave her an elderly, disgusted look out of his flat maroon eyes. Cassius had white blood and a tendency to get above himself, as Emma mourned.

"Your Mama ain't be pleased," declared Cassius, drawing his thin lips down. "She ain't like you runnin' round by your lone."

"Nobody likes it except me. I like it a lot, Cassius."

"Ain't safe." He carefully made the bolt fast. "Just last week now——"

"I know. They stopped that silly girl of Debow's, and like an imbecile she jumped off her horse and ran away screaming, which was exactly what the scalawags wanted—the horse. If I poke Diablo in the right spot he kicks out and bites. You

needn't worry about me. I suppose you've heard—" she made
a try at it— "that young Mr. Wade has come home."

Cassius looked baffled and slightly indignant, as though he
had been defrauded. "No 'm, I ain't, Miss Maggie. Must have
come lately. Las' I heard he was killed somewhere up in Vir-
ginny."

"Well, now you know, so enjoy it." She gathered up her
skirt and headed for the stairs. There was dust on the polished
treads, cobwebs on the beautifully turned spindles. She ran a
finger along the frame of her Charleston grandmother's portrait and it came away smudged. "This house is filthy!" she
flung back at the servingman, but his dry mouth and aloof eyes
held no distress or apology.

"Yes 'm," he agreed. "Cy'ant keep no big house clean widout
nobody to do it. Got to hire and pay now, Miss Maggie—hire
and pay."

Marian went to her room and kicked out of her habit, tossed
it in a heap onto a chair. Then seeing her morning dress lying
where she had discarded it, she picked both garments up with
an angry fling and hung them on pegs in the press. That no-
good, miserable Rhoda! She hoped she was hungry and miserable in Mobile or wherever she had taken herself off to.

She heard movements in Juliet's room and it occurred to
her that Juliet had a lonely life. A married woman was so re-
stricted—she could not go out often without her husband. But
why didn't Juliet go back to New Orleans where she belonged?
It was true that Felix was gone a lot, and Juliet did not greatly
care for her mother-in-law, who was old and wheezy and soft
and spoke only French, nor for her sisters-in-law who were
all old maids, acid and critical. Marian wrapped herself in a
peignoir and went to Juliet's door and knocked.

Her mother's voice answered, "Come in—quietly, please."

Juliet lay on her bed with a folded white cloth over her eyes,
and the odor of camphor was strong. Emma was shaking some-

thing out of a bottle and dabbing Juliet's wrists with it. She said, "Oh, it's you. Go along, Marian; your sister has one of her sick headaches."

"Sillabub," remarked Marian. "She *will* eat it and she knows it makes her bilious."

"Oh, be still!" snapped Juliet. "You've been riding around again. I smell horse. Papa will raise Cain."

"Not unless you tattle—which very likely you will. I was going to tell you something exciting, but now I won't do it." Marian reached for the doorknob.

"Come back here!"Juliet pulled off the bandage and sat up with a jerk. "Mama, can't you do something with her? She's always annoying me deliberately—when I feel so utterly wretched."

"I'm not annoying you. I'm leaving. Give her some blue mass and salts, Mama—you know she needs it. Why she isn't fat as Lelia is a mystery to me."

"That will do, Marian," Emma said sternly. "Go away now and try to behave yourself."

"Don't let her go. She's heard some news and now she'll keep it to herself, the nasty little thing!" Juliet wailed.

"Ladies," said Marian primly, "should not gossip."

She went back to her own room and fell back on her high bed, rolling over happily, letting her hair fall out of the pins and straggle over the pillows. There were no starched pillow shams any more, thanks be! Nobody to starch or flute them now that 'Phrony and Rhoda had gone off with a lot of other free Negroes. She could hear Juliet complaining peevishly, and her mother's murmured comforting. A door slammed below and she heard the bolt snick and heels on the stairs and knew that her father had come in. He puffed as he climbed. He was getting fat too. Duncan Wade had been so thin. Thinned down, tough as leather, and as brown.

She shut her eyes and recalled the dreary day when Duncan

had ridden away to join the army, jaunty in his new grays, his shining boots, wide hat and saber; on a high-stepping black horse with Ceph', a colored boy, riding behind on a bay. She had waited down at the gate near the bridge, half hidden by honeysuckle and cedars, and Duncan had seen her and briefly touched his hat. Hardly aware of her then, she knew. She was a little one, the fledgling, frying-size Villerand brat, who hung around the edges of frolics, always carefully shepherded by a black mammy or her hovering mother.

But now he knew that she was grown, that she was a woman. She had seen amazement in his eyes, and incredulity, and she had seen a kindling of interest there too. She beat the pillow with her fist, tingling all over, thrilled and ecstatic. I saw him first, she gloated. She shan't spoil it. She's not going to dazzle him again, get him all moony-eyed and abstracted as he used to be. Even in those awful clothes he had looked jaunty and exciting, compared with short-legged, black-whiskered Felix Destrade. How Juliet could bear even to be touched by that creature—oil on his hair, perfume on his handkerchief, and his smug, white-toothed smile that had dollar signs glinting in it! Juliet might as well have been bought as the slave girls had been bought—for depth of chest and roundness of hips, for clear eyes and a pleasing voice.

Felix's old mother, outraged because her son had married outside the Church, had refused to come to the wedding. She was very likely mean and nasty, and Marian let herself feel sorry for Juliet, but only briefly. She had too much to think about, mapping her own campaign. She was twenty years old, and most girls were married at fifteen. If they were still single at eighteen their mothers began to worry. Juliet—heavens, Juliet had been almost twenty-three! In a state of desperation, no doubt, when Felix came along with his shining carriage, his money, his offered security. Men much older than Felix had quietly shouldered guns to follow Joe Wheeler or Braxton

Bragg, or saddled their best horses to ride away after Bedford Forrest. But Felix had been content to run the blockade and fetch wines from France and Portugal so that fat cravens could be convivial in Mobile or Montgomery while they plotted how to ship their cotton north up the rivers to sell in Louisville, or even in Pittsburgh.

Marian wondered if Juliet detested Felix; if that was why she seized on any excuse to come home. Certainly there were no longer any Yankee gunboats threatening New Orleans, though Juliet argued that the city was intolerable now, with fear of rioting in the streets and so little left to buy in the shops.

Maybe, Marian speculated, she could persuade her mother to give a party. But no, a certain sensitive caution warned, that wouldn't do. With most of the planters around the river valleys in straitened circumstances any festivity would be misunderstood; it might even have the tinge of treason to the fiercely proud and loyal Southerners. Anybody who was a bit too prosperous these days was suspected of consorting with the enemy. That there had already been whispers against her own father she knew, though all conversation here at home was studiedly casual or else carefully guarded. But she remembered her young brother's furious anger when the family had tried to keep him from enlisting. Jule had said some hasty and dreadful things then. And today Duncan Wade had asked, with a tinge of incredulous bitterness in his voice, "Who is rich enough now in Alabama to own a horse like that?"

No, definitely, a party would not be wise. To flaunt freedom from poverty, when poverty was the patiently accepted lot of people never before accustomed to privation, would be bad taste at least. She would have to study some more subtle approach to the problem of interesting Duncan Wade and of curing him from being too aware still of Juliet.

In books men nursed hopeless passions forever, but Marian had never believed that any man could be so hopelessly stupid in real life as to go on adoring a woman when he knew that she was forever lost to him. It made very moving poetry, but very little sense to her practical mind. At least she was still free to ride over to the Wade place whenever she chose. The family scolded about it, but nothing drastic, like locking up her saddle or forbidding Tuby to bridle her horse, had ever happened yet. And Uncle Hugh Wade was her friend; he would be on her side.

It might be wise to make her own position clear immediately: let Juliet know once and for all that she wanted no interference with her plans. She got up from the bed, marched to Juliet's door and opened it abruptly. Juliet was lying back again with her eyes closed. Their mother sat by the window with the blinds drawn, half dozing, some sewing ignored lying on her lap.

"What I was going to tell you, when you were so rude to me," Marian began loudly, "is that Duncan Wade has come home."

Both women opened their eyes, but there was no dawning interest or excitement in their looks.

Juliet sighed. "He certainly was in no hurry to return," she said. "There must have been some pretty girls up there in Virginia. Did he bring a new wife home with him?"

Panic exploded in Marian's mind. "I—I don't know," she faltered.

"I only hope, if he did, that he didn't pick an impossible creature like that Maryland girl the Gaines boy married," Emma said. "His mother is brokenhearted. She hasn't left her room in weeks." Emma looked sharply at her younger daughter. "My dear, how many times must I tell you not to parade around the halls in deshabille? Go and dress yourself properly, or remain in your room. Papa has come home, and Cassius might come up any minute. Though he has a dark skin, Cassius is a man, too."

Marian went out limply, feeling chastened and laid low.

Nothing to do now but learn the truth. It was ill-bred of a lady to question servants, but she had to know. Before morning Lelia would know if Duncan Wade had brought home a wife. Cassius would know. They prowled the night like cats; they absorbed rumor and scandal out of the air. There were ways to get things out of them without asking questions, and Marian knew all the ways. By sundown next day she had the answer. Duncan had not brought home a wife. If he had rashly married a wife, he had left her behind, where he found her.

Juliet was full of questions next day, and Marian answered them grudgingly. How did Duncan look? Was he staying in Alabama? Had he been wounded or captured? To them all Marian gave the same short, irritable replies.

"I don't know. He didn't tell me." Then at last she flared, and flung her challenge. "If you're in love with Duncan still, kindly remember that you're a married woman!"

"Don't be an idiot," said Juliet scornfully. "I was never in love with Duncan Wade. Even if I were, what business is it of yours?"

"Because," said Marian desperately, "it happens to be my business! And you keep your hands off, do you hear?"

"Don't tell me that you have any idea that Duncan might fall in love with you," her sister drawled.

"Why shouldn't he?" Marian demanded.

"Oh, no reason, really," Juliet admitted. But it fired the younger girl to burning fury that Juliet laughed as she said it.

IV

PRIVATE JOHN RANKIN had been born and reared in Wisconsin and what he remembered most about his youth was the cold of the Green Bay country.

There had been the winter when he was nine years old. The summer before, his father had built the new three-room house of up-and-down sawmill planks which he meant to cover with siding another year if the flax and hay crops were good and the trapping business profitable through the winter. Private John Rankin recalled the two big front rooms of that house, each with two beds and a trunk and a few splint-bottomed chairs.

In the beds the elder Rankins and their seven sons slept, and in the middle of the largest room stood the loom where his mother clacked bobbins and sley, weaving the rag carpets that covered the floors of the new plank house and the floors at some of their neighbors'.

"Sleep in your pants, boys" was their father's favorite jest, "else you won't have no pants in the morning. She'll have 'em cut up in the hit-and-miss."

Vividly Private Rankin remembered the sleet storm of that winter when he was nine. It came through the cracks of the house driven on a north wind that blew for two days. The beds had to be shoved hastily into the middle of the rooms, and the bright rag carpets, laid over straw, were soaked. Then the temperature took a wild slide downward and everything in the house froze solid. The carpet billowed in icy waves and all the younger Rankins were kept on the beds by their anxious mother, who had a fear of lung fever.

They played and wrestled and fought. Goose feathers from the ticks and tufts of fuzz from the wool comforts floated on the frigid air. Wrapped in fur scarves and heavy coats, with felt boots pulled on over their socks, they found the dash to the outhouse a thrilling adventure. Frost lay in furry buttons on every nail of the kitchen wall, though the stove roared, red-hot on top.

Private Rankin thought about the pots full of snow that sat on that stove often in winter, to be melted into wash water; and about the icicles that hung to the ground from the barn eaves, the sting of a frosty pump handle on a damp palm. He was remembering all these while he soaked up the Alabama sun, feeling it burn through the shoulders of his blue coat, feeling the sweat run down between his shoulder blades, exulting in being warm. Other men of the garrison detail cursed the early heat, but Private Rankin loved it. It seemed that his bones had been cold most of his life. Now he was really warm for once. After the cold rains of the Tennessee hills while he was with Thomas, after the marching in frigid mud and icy rain on the way from Louisville to Chattanooga, he welcomed the sun. Now he was warm at last and he meant to stay warm. He shifted his chair around the corner of the building to a sunny spot where the bricks glowed, and tilted it back against the wall, his long legs stretched out halfway across the plank sidewalk. There he dozed till a shabby young man in a decayed Confederate uniform, who was followed by an old Negro, stepped awkwardly over his sprawling feet.

Private Rankin sprang up with an irate bellow. "You, Reb, you look where you're a-walkin'!"

Duncan Wade, wearing the gray coat Louisa had sponged and steamed and pressed as best she could, gave the bluecoat a deadly look. "Keep your legs off the public walkway then, Yank."

Private Rankin glared about for his weapon, remembered that he had left it inside against orders, shook his fists. "Got an idee to run you in, Reb. Insultin' the military."

"You won't run me in," Duncan drawled scornfully. "Since when did the Fed army do their sleeping on duty? Come along, Uncle Josuff."

"That ain't allowed neither. Ain't no niggers gits called 'uncle' down here no more. That old colored man, he's your ekall. You treat him ekall or you rot in jail, Reb, you hear me?"

"I could hear you if I was over in Mississippi. You've got two buttons unbuttoned down there, Yank. Against regulations."

Private Rankin made a wild grab at his nether apparel. Uncle Josuff gave him a slow look of pity out of his seamed and rheumy eyes. "Whole county full up wid white trash, Mist' Duncan," he muttered as they passed.

"Don't you call me white trash, nigger!" Rankin shouted.

Two other soldiers came out of the building. "What's the trouble out here?" a burly one demanded.

"That Reb and his nigger give me lip," Rankin growled.

"Ain't no Reb owns no nigger any more. Whyn't you arrest the Reb? What you let him git away for? Ain't no Rebs allowed to insult the military forces of the United States."

"He's gone now." Private Rankin knew a flicker of relief. These damn' uppity Rebs, licked and beat down into the ground, but the pride in them as defiant as ever! Every one of 'em ought to be run out of the country and their property confiscated. Not that Rankin had much sympathy with the doggone free niggers either. With the feral instincts of the white primitive he hated and feared the black men, never having seen one till he came south with the regiment. Some of the officers had been drilling black boys in the woods at night, but Private Rankin didn't relish that too much—not in those swampy dark woods where snakes and varmints might lurk, not out in the blackness with those unpredictable Africans.

"Teach 'em to shoot and white men all look alike to them," he protested. "Same as all of 'em look alike to me. Enough of 'em down here to take over the whole country, did they know it. Dunno why they ain't done it—save us all this mess of a war."

"They loves Old Massa," sneered a trooper, "but they ain't love him so much but what they're ready to cut Old Massa's throat, now we turned 'em loose."

Duncan Wade walked on into the mercantile establishment of Horning and Hale. The store had a stripped and desolate look now. Old Horace Horning came shuffling out of a dark region at the rear. He blinked at Duncan with no recognition in his wary eyes.

"Ain't very smart to wear those clothes on the street, boy," he remarked. "This garrison we've got here can get plumb ugly. Who are you and what can I do for you?"

"I'm Duncan Wade, Mr. Horning. I'm wearing these clothes because I haven't got anything else to wear."

"Old Hugh's boy? Well, sir! Everybody here thought you'd been killed up there in Virginia. So you got back finally, did you? Have you stuck in one of their stinking prisons?"

"No, sir, I was never captured, but I had to walk back and work along to eat."

"Guess your pappy was mighty glad to see you coming. How is the old gentleman?"

"I left him chopping cotton. He sent me to town to get some clothes. The Yanks went through our place like a plague of locusts."

"Plague ain't over, either. We need us a Moses down this-a-way," Horning grumped. "Things ain't good, Wade. Hell and molasses, no! I'm uneasy for fear they're going to get worse. Take Andy Johnson now—he's got good intentions; but Stevens and his gang, they want to see this whole country trampled into dust, and they've got Johnson hamstrung and hog-tied. You want some clothes and you ain't got any money. That's it, ain't it? I can guess 'em right every time."

"We've got cotton planted. Forty acres. And some corn."

"Took Hugh's cotton last fall, I recollect—every bale. Price was high too. Hugh couldn't settle his account with us then— no fault of his. Always kept paid up when he could. Trouble is, we've had tight times too. Credit ruined, north, east, every-where. State of Alabama flat busted too. Could I find you a piece of goods, how'd you get pants and coat made out of it?"

"Josuff's still around. He's old, but he says he can still cut out a pair of pants and a coat, and Louisa can sew. Josuff cut all the clothes for our people when we had fifty or more of 'em on the place. I thought maybe I could get enough rough goods for Josuff to have some pants too. Poor old fellow's mighty near naked."

"So are all the rest of us. When the blockade closed in, all the woolen stuff we had sold out in one winter. Then the army took everything the mills turned out. All I can get now is some stuff that's half shoddy—and not much of that. I'm wearing it myself—you can see——" He held up a leg, seams wearing green and shiny, knees getting threadbare.

"I'm destitute for clothes, Mr. Horning. So is Josuff. This old uniform is so rotten it won't hold patches any more. I've lain out more nights than I've slept under a roof these last few years."

The old man's eyes misted. "We owe everything to you boys. More—because we sent you into this war knowing that we couldn't provide what you needed to win it."

"We sent ourselves in, sir. Nobody could have kept us out after Sumter."

"Murder for politics—that's war. Murder for a whole country. Wade, I know if it's possible for you to pay me, you'll do
it."

"If they take our cotton again or the crop fails, I'll work.
There'll be public works or something. A ruined country has
got to be built back again. I'll pay you, one way or another."

"You'll have to pay your old colored man too. Orders from
the Freedmen's Bureau. You have to pay, feed and maintain
any free man of color you employ, even to cut out a pair of
pants." Horning reminded him.

"He's getting a share of the crop—forty per cent, Pa says,
for the people who stay on the place."

"And keep. Feed and maintain, whether you've got anything to do it with or not. I've got a couple of bolts back here
. . . have to keep my goods hid . . . can't leave anything
out in plain sight any more. Lost a barrel of sugar last week,
first sugar I've had shipped up the river since the surrender.
They come in with a paper and bayonets. Supplies needed for
the needy—sign this paper, it will get sent to Congress. Congress! A congregation of buzzards up there waiting for the
corpse to stop breathing." He led Duncan back through a dark
hall, smelling of rats and molasses. "This stuff is brown. Looks
like butternut, but it will cover your backside. Keep you respectable for a little while, maybe."

In the back room Horning carefully closed and barred a
heavy door. There was little light, save what sifted through
a barred, dirty window. Sitting very close to this was a little
gnomelike man, round-bellied, round-headed, with a fringe of
reddish-gray hair and a scanty drizzle of beard. He looked
up from the newspaper he had held close to his nose.

Duncan said, "Howdy, Mr. Hale. Glad to see you survived
the war."

Hale let the legs of his chair fall with a thud, pulled his

glasses down and blinked over them. "My Lord, it's young Wade!" he exclaimed. "Did they dig you up along with the rest of the corpses, last election?"

They shook hands gravely and Duncan had to relate again the story of his long return.

Mr. Horning lighted a hanging lamp, picked the charred wick even with his fingers. "Emanuel and me survived the war," he remarked. "Now we're wondering if we can survive the peace."

"We lived through the sixty days," Hale said. "That was an evil time, young feller. All these Northern troops moved in on us and most of 'em were bounty men. Some couldn't even speak English. They even put uniforms on some Negroes and armed them. Most of us, black and white, stayed quiet and said nothing. Drunken soldiers liable to knock your door down, 'most any time day or night."

"My father thinks Johnson would like to treat the South with justice, but the army certainly hated his renegade guts— our army," Duncan said.

"That gang in control up there in Washington would like to give Johnson the boot, if they could get the votes in that piece of a Congress. My opinion, Grant's the man we've got to worry about. He talks fair. Just reading a piece about him in the paper here. Jim Stanley's paper—maybe you remember Jim? He prints this *Greenville Advocate*. Just a young feller— little past twenty. I knew his folks, good people over in Lowndes County. He fought with the Seventeenth. Started his paper without a dime. Took up a collection around to buy type and paper to print on. Jim says Military Government is ahead for Alabama and Grant is the big military eagle. Drunken old 'Useless Grant'—lived on a farm once up here in Missouri, lived on pone and pot liquor same as the rest of us. What you reckon to do with that no-good bale of shoddy, Horace?"

"Young Wade here needs a new pair of pants."

"Set the seat in a week out of any breeches you'd make from that goods. Shoot a straw through it."

"I don't plan to do much sitting down, Mr. Hale. So it holds together till crop time it will do me."

"Just measuring." Horning walloped the brown bolt over and over on the counter. "Figure you can get two pairs of pants and one jacket out of this, does your colored boy know how to cut to save. Let you have it for twenty dollars. Take your note. Make out a note, Emanuel."

"Ink's all dried up. Got to boil some bark and indigo and make some fresh."

"Put a little water in it. Just so it will make a mark, we'll recognize it."

"The last time I tried to write a letter home I used a charred stick," Duncan said. "Then the writing all rubbed off, so I gave up and threw it away."

"Wouldn't have got through anyway, likely. Never did hear from my boy. I heard he was killed up at Stone's River, but never did know how or just when," said Hale. "His mammy won't believe he's gone. Keeps sunning his bed every week, waiting for him to come back. How's he going to get that bolt of stuff home, Hod? Carries it wrapped up he might meet some gang of scalawags and lose it."

"Why couldn't your boy cut it here, Wade?" Horning inquired. "Tote it home a little at a time in a tow sack? We could pack it in some rags to hide it, but they don't bother the Negroes much. Encourage 'em to rob the white people any way they can. Negro steals your hog he gets acquitted. You take a shot at him and you get ten years."

"If you had anything to shoot him with," Wade remarked.

"Who says I haven't?" Horning said slyly. "My grandfather built my house—built places to hide in it. Indians it was, in those days."

"Well, keep quiet about it," advised his partner. "My pistol's down my well, in the bottom of a bucket of tallow. Never know who's listening." The round little man looked about cautiously. "Billy Maupin told somebody he had a barrel of sorghum—figured to let it work and run some liquor off of it. Had it hid in his smokehouse. Next morning the smokehouse was burned down and the sorghum was gone when they got the fire put out. So was all their meat."

"How long is this going to last?" Duncan demanded. "We own we're beat—why can't they leave us alone to put Alabama back together?"

"We ran out on 'em," Horning said. "We turned up our arrogant Southern noses at their Union. Now they've dragged us back into it they're going to rub our noses in humility till we stink of it. Ever chase a runaway hog back into the lot? Spend an hour getting him penned up again and the planks nailed on —what do you do, if you're human? Wipe the sweat off your face and give the dumb hog a kick in the rump. They've got us penned—now we're getting our rumps booted. And they don't forget it took four years to get us in. Be a long time, I'd say. Ten years maybe."

Ten years? A decade of tragedy, of retaliation, reconstruction! His father, Duncan was thinking, would be a broken old man. He himself would be thirty-six—middle-aged, practically. "We'll fight again, if it lasts ten years," he said.

"With what? Pitchforks and staves? Anyway, I'll be dead and gone, what with the grub we get now and carpetbaggers more worrisome than a mess of chiggers." Mr. Hale seemed content with that idea.

"When you going to bring old Josuff in to cut out this stuff?" Horning asked.

"He's here now. I left him outside. He's probably asleep. He brought along his shears. Sharpened 'em this morning."

"Thought of everything, didn't you? All but the ink. In a

mighty hurry to get dressed up. Got a girl in mind, I reckon. Plenty of 'em left behind, poor pretties, who won't ever see their own sweethearts again."

"In those pants he'll never dare get down on his knees— that's gospel," Hale drawled. "You'd better pick a good-looker, Wade. Your mother was the handsomest woman in this county. Had every single man round these parts addled in the head. Even old Villerand, though he was an ugly, short-legged redheaded little runt then. You can't go back on the breed and pick an ugly one."

"What would I do with a girl? It takes money to court a nice woman."

"Good horse too. Couple of horses is better. Who's got a good horse any more?"

"Villerand." Hale let the name fall again, and the two old men's faces seemed to tighten. There was a sharp, pregnant silence. Duncan pondered that withdrawal, that silence, as he went toward home. Villerand had been one of his mother's suitors. He had heard that before. But then Villerand had been someone to smile about. His father and Julian Villerand had never been friends, but Hugh Wade had never displayed resentment—or had it been suspicion he had seen in the eyes of Horace Horning and Emanuel Hale?

Once, Duncan was thinking, he had loved a girl. Her face had gone to war with him, on long weary marches, over winter-hostile hills and through icy rivers.

It was jolly for a while, wasn't it?—but now I'm marrying Felix. . . .

To hell with women, anyway! Then another inner voice spoke harshly to his spirit. Why be an utter fool? He was on his way to a ruined plantation to eat corn bread and greens with no seasoning but salt. He was on foot, wearing the rotting habiliments of a defeated army, and in the seams vermin still crawled in spite of Louisa's scalding. He had had not a penny in his pocket in two years. He might not have a penny for a long time to come. A fine prize for a woman!

Old Josuff roused him from his bitter musings. "Git through them woods and we's all right, Young Boss. Git's dark mighty sudden in them woods."

V

THE VILLERAND PLACE had suffered but little from the war. True, half the whitewashed slave cabins were empty, gates were left open that had penned fat Villerand horses, mares and foals. The stable roof had a mossy look, but pigeons still did their awkward courting dance on it, talking to one another in liquid syllables.

Cassius still wore his white coat, but he insisted on wearing a pair of blue uniform pants with it, and pinning two large brass medals on the front of it. He would have surrendered the wages Julian Villerand paid him every Saturday night rather than surrender those medals.

"But what do they mean, Cassius?" his mistress inquired.

"They's Union soldier medals, Miss Emma. I's a corporal and a patteroller."

"And what is it that you patrol, Cassius?"

"I patteroles Saturday night. Does any white man push a free man of my color out in the street I reports him to the captain."

When he had gone out of the room Marian said, "Leave him alone, poor old silly thing!"

"But the Negroes are being shamefully exploited and deceived. They've been told that all the big plantations are being divided up and each of them will get forty acres and a mule."

"What could Cassius do with forty acres and a mule? He'd be too lazy to work the land or curry the mule, and in no time

61

some trashy Copperhead or carpetbag Yankee would take them away from him."

"He could still go on being a patteroller," said Emma with her dry small laugh. "Your father is having a guest tonight for dinner, Marian, some Union general or other. So watch that quick tongue of yours. We must not offend these people, your father says, as he wants to launch some new business projects that they could block completely."

"I hope this one is not like that General Hubbard. It was disgusting the way people fawned over that man. At Mrs. Athol's party for him, he pinched Mildred Simcoe's arm, on the veranda."

"We have to live with these military characters, my dear. They have tremendous power because they report only to General Grant and the Secretary of War in Washington, and if we can live in peace with them it will be more pleasant for everybody. This is Major General Swayne who is coming here. He outranks even the governor. He is said to be a very fine gentleman, a graduate of Yale. He was wounded last year and had to have his right leg amputated. Whatever he is, he will be our guest and we have the obligation of hospitality."

"I won't say a word, but I won't simper or smile either. Go ahead and fawn over the Yankees if you must, but I am still seceded." Marian marched up the stairs, her silk skirt swishing over her hoops. No Villerand gown had ever been surrendered to be made up into military balloons; Julian Villerand had scoffed at that idea as absurd and futile, and, as so often happened, he was more than a little right.

In a sunny upper room Juliet sat on a low chair, scratching a dimity ruffle into precise folds with a quick-flashing needle. She began almost instantly. "You haven't told me what Duncan Wade looks like now. Is he greatly changed?"

Marian tightened her lips a trifle. "Not as I remember him

—no. I saw him at his mother's grave. Terribly shabby—and as dark almost as Cassius."

"You have no business riding across the pastures, as you know very well. Maggie, Duncan Wade must not come here—not with military people dropping in on us every whipstitch. I remember what a firebrand Duncan used to be."

"He won't come. He knows you're married—and he was always proud and touchy. Please remember that you're much older than Duncan."

"I suppose you made it a point to tell him how old I was?"

"How could he help knowing when we all grew up together?" Marian pulled up the shoulder of her frock, which had slipped down to reveal a dimpled, ivory shoulder. "Jule and Duncan were always fighting when they were boys. Then they joined together to fight any other boy who came around. If anybody enjoyed the war it was Duncan. Maybe he refused to surrender and that's why he was so long coming home."

"He'll be in trouble almost immediately with his temper and that sarcastic tongue of his." Juliet sighed. "He used to make me absolutely furious."

"And absolutely maudlin, as I remember."

"How can you remember? You were practically a child."

"I had my hair up and my dresses down when the war began. Mama was only a year older when she was married. There's a Yankee general coming here, I suppose you know. We're to be very polite to him because he holds the power of life and death over us all."

"Nonsense!" Juliet said. "No Yankee general has that much power. I shall be polite to him because I'm a Villerand and a lady, and he'll likely chew tobacco and wear spurs in the parlor like some of those creatures who were around last winter."

"Or he might be like that Hubbard man. Olivia Clanton said

whenever he looked at her she felt as though she hadn't any clothes on."

"What a disgusting thing to say—or to repeat! I hope somebody will warn Duncan Wade to be careful. Nothing would please these scalawag soldiers better than to put a Confederate officer in jail."

"If I'm not allowed to ride over there, I certainly won't be able to warn him," mused Marian, looking off smugly. "You might go in the carriage in all your genteel married state and sweetly suggest that he refrain from knocking any insolent Yankees down. Why must we have the creatures in the house anyway? Even Mama was complacent about it."

"Papa says somebody has to do something about building Alabama back again, and Felix agrees with him. And they are the conquerors; they can make things much worse for us if we display hostility. Papa has managed very well, Felix thinks. He's very clever about business and there must be business if anyone here is to survive."

"Jule used to say that Papa was a Copperhead."

"I don't believe it." Juliet's face flushed and her eyebrows drew into delicate, angry points. "I don't believe Jule ever said such an infamous thing."

"He said it and I heard it. He was furious because Papa didn't want him to enlist in the Seventeenth."

"Papa thought his only son should be something more than a mere trooper. And he gave that son for the South, and now Mama can't even so much as put a flower on Jule's grave." Juliet dabbed her eyes. "You should be ashamed of repeating a silly thing like that. Jule never meant it when he said it. You had better watch your tongue, too. Women have found themselves in trouble, insulting the Union people."

Marian slid from the edge of the bed and made a mock curtsy. "General Swayne, your humble servant, sir," she piped in a mincing falsetto voice. "Take my all for the glory of the Union and Andy Johnson—take my soul and body——"

"My word, you mean General *Swayne* is coming here?" demanded Juliet. "He's in command of this whole district."

"To wine and dine and consult with Papa about something. Shall I send Tuby out to find a lizard to put in his soup?"

"Heavens, no! Walk on your tiptoes and speak in whispers. Felix says that man would like to do away with all civil authority in Alabama. General Grant is a liberal beside Wager Swayne."

"What shall we wear? Shall we be poor destitute Rebels in four-year-old dresses, or shall we dazzle him in those silks Felix had sent that came from France?"

"We're in mourning, remember."

"Poor Jule! And I know he'd hate me in that old dress. Smells of dye. Absolutely I reek like a chamber pot every time I wear it."

"Sister, if you must be vulgar and low-minded, will you please go and be it in the kitchen? Or the stable would be a better place for such coarse unladylike behavior."

"Well, it does smell like that! Diablo snorted the last time I went near him in it. All right, I'll be frail and pitiful. And you can trail your elegant filaments and be languid and bereft. If you make the right impression maybe they won't steal all our cotton."

"They didn't steal our cotton."

"I know," said Marian soberly, as she turned to the door. "I know."

Juliet got up and closed the door after her, closing her mind with equal firmness. Marian had no judgment, she was a Rebel, she was all emotion and impulses. That was the trouble with the South, as Felix had often pointed out. The people mistook fire and fervor for common sense. They went off half-cocked, like plunging into a war without knowing where they would get guns or powder to fight it with, then refusing to admit their mistake till they were crushed and prostrate. But Felix was no Copperhead, his wife was certain. He merely had clear sight, he saw things in balance, was not dazzled by the glitter of one side of the shield so that he overlooked what was deadly and certain concealed behind it. Papa could see clearly too. Papa argued that Alabama should return in humility and contrition to the Union, deploring her folly, and Papa was usually right, though hotheads like Duncan Wade would never admit it.

Juliet decided to brush her hair straight back and pin up the curls that hung to her shoulders. 'Phrony should be here to fix it. That was the bad thing about this silly war—no 'Phrony to press flounces and twine curls around a dark finger. No Lissa to sweep the pussy willows from under the bed and flute the curtains. They'd taken themselves off—to Mobile, Cassius said, riding a steamboat with a lot of rough colored Union soldiers. Juliet hoped they were good and hungry now, that they had to sleep on the ground with mosquitoes devouring them. And 'Phrony, the thief, had stolen her green tulle scarf.

General Wager Swayne had a young, weather-marked face with a long nose sloping up to a high, sunburned forehead. His hair was already receding in front. He wore a long mustache and a small, jaunty beard. His eyes were very dark but with no softness in them. Brown eyes, Marian was thinking as she watched him covertly, were usually liquid and mild, but his had a hardness almost glassy. He moved them with a thoughtful caution, rested them on whatever he looked at as steadily as he might have sighted a gun.

No one or nothing would ever fool him, she was certain. He had learned a trick of deadly surveillance, of keeping his own thoughts well hidden while he turned the minds of other men inside out. His lower lip was soft but straight, as though it had long been grimly disciplined. His ears had no lobes and lay flat against his head under brushed-back wings of hair. His collar was high and tight and every button of an obviously new blue coat was firmly buttoned. Marian wondered if this Ohioan, who could not be forty yet, had ever kissed a girl, shed a tear or repented a decision.

There was a terrible decisiveness about him. In the parlor with Cassius strutting around with glasses of wine on a tray, General Swayne appeared to choose with deliberation the spot where he would stand, the chair he finally condescended to sit on, the particular glass he would drink from. He used his crutches deftly. He was courteous without warmth, his manner guarded and a little withdrawn. Her father, Marian decided dubiously, was talking too much, and all the time Julian talked General Swayne was appraising him with reserve, if it was not actual contempt that she saw in his eyes.

Emma was the gracious hostess. Whether he was friend or foe, it would have been impossible for Emma to be ungracious to him. She had been a Michaux from Charleston, and the delicate nuances of hospitality were as instinctive with her as breath. She gave Cassius the nod to refill the general's glass, and presided over the silver coffee service with the dainty movements of her white hands that always fascinated her younger daughter. Marian had tried often before the mirror to make her blunt fingers flutter in such delicate motion, but with little success. She was a heavy-handed Villerand, she accepted patiently, "a horse trainer" she told herself scornfully, with little grace to charm a man as her mother was obviously charming General Wager Swayne.

He seemed reluctant to join her father in the library when the dinner was ended, but Emma led her daughters to the little back parlor. "Your father has railroad business to talk over with the general." She quietly closed the door.

"All their eyes are alike," Marian burst out. "They explore. I could just see his mind working, thinking we'd buried the

silver and dug it up again, reckoning how much money Papa
has hidden away—and he's convinced that neither Juliet nor
I is as good-looking as you, Mama."

"You have too much imagination," Juliet said. "He was
very reserved and definitely on guard against being charmed
by any Southerners whatever. And I doubt if Papa gets anything out of him, whatever it is he wants."

"He wasn't on guard against Mama," Marian insisted. "She
could get anything she wanted out of him, I'll bet a horse."

"Ladies do not bet, Maggie," chided Emma. "It is most unladylike."

"If I did bet on that proposition, I'd win," Marian declared.
"Why can't we sit on the veranda? It's stuffy in here."

"The library windows are open. We'd appear to be listening.
Haven't you any needlework, Maggie?"

"I hate needlework. Anyway, I lost my needle—the last one
I had."

"And needles are still scarce and hard to get." Emma
sighed. "They must not have made any all through the war. I
suppose all the steel went into weapons. I can't even buy a
kitchen knife, and Tuby has sharpened ours till they're thin as
straws, not even strong enough to cut up a chicken."

Marian fidgeted. She itched to know what was being talked
about in the library. Whatever her father proposed, General
Swayne was going to oppose, she was confident. She knew
that young Jule, her brother, had left home convinced that his
father was not sincerely in sympathy with the Southern cause
no matter how loudly he protested. The Yankees, Jule had
argued, used these wavering deviators to their own advantage
but despised them in their hearts for their divided loyalties.
Any man who was a man, he spouted with his hot young
fervor, hated a traitor, even when they employed him, knowing
that a tool that turned in the hand can turn both ways. That
was when he had called his father a Copperhead.

By the murky look in her husband's eyes when the men finally emerged, Emma knew that whatever it was that Julian desired of their conquerors he had not succeeded in obtaining.

The general was bowed out gallantly. A waiting orderly brought his horse around, took his crutches and helped him to mount. But it was Tuby who had rubbed the horse's coat to a gleam. Emma repressed a tiny ironic smile at the bland acceptance of servitude from one of the race the Northern armies had declared to be equal to their own.

Julian exploded before the general was out of sight. "It's that damned Congress! Can't they see that they're pulling down the recovery of the whole country by keeping the South under and obstructing our progress? How can we develop our resources without railroads? How can we build railroads without money? No—they want us to crawl and grovel. To hell with them! I'll get the money. I'll lick them yet."

"My dear, the servants may be listening," his wife warned. "I've heard that they are bribed to carry tales, and it's even suggested that they're encouraged to inform on their own masters."

"Poppycock! I'll say what I please in my own house."

"This year," Marian remarked casually, "you could lose all your cotton."

"I'll talk to Patton. Who should be more interested in the future of this state than the governor?" Julian shouted. "If we can get the bonds endorsed, we can build a railroad without a damn cent of Federal money."

"Provincial governor," Juliet suggested, "governor by the kind permission of Congress—and they can throw him out any time they choose."

"Papa," Marian remarked, when they had gone upstairs, leaving him to his brandy and his sulks, "appears finally to have seceded."

VI

PRIVATE JOHN RANKIN did not like the new lieutenant who had been sent up from Montgomery to command the garrison.

This young fellow from Delaware, a state Private Rankin had never heard of, was all full of stupid notions. Every soldier in the garrison was to keep his boots polished, his coat buttoned with the darned sun getting hotter every minute, and have his hair—and his beard, if he owned one—trimmed by the company barber. Furthermore he was to take baths regularly.

As though these orders were not offensive enough, it was also a command that every man be courteous to women, no matter what their station, and that if sneers and insults were offered they were to be ignored in proud silence.

"So we should bow from the waist, I guess, when some little dainty in a faded dress turns up her nose at us," fumed a corporal from Iowa. "If they call us smelly Yankee scum, we should fetch 'em a bouquet or something! Anyway, I pushed one off the sidewalk into the mud before he got here. She dropped her parasol and called me a name. 'Vulgar beast!' says she. 'Rebel bitch!' says I. That shut her up."

"And we ain't to drill no more Negroes or incite 'em to riot or stealin' or disorderly conduct," a lanky sergeant put in. "Just when I got them apes I been workin' on so they know 'port arms' from 'parade rest,' and which is their right foot.

Git me a brigade of 'em and I could take over this whole country."

The lieutenant's name was Eric Wilkins, which was a dandi-
fied name, fit only in the mind of his command for a mother's
boy with lace on his pantalets. That Wilkins had ridden with
Burnside and seen hard service for four years did not outweigh
his heresy for thinking these Rebels were people. He was too
pretty too, with brown hair that had a stubborn wave in it, a
new uniform with all the buttons gleaming, black eyes that
could flash or smolder and then turn abruptly cold and grave,
and a chin as hard and stubborn as a plowpoint.

"Me," announced Private Rankin, "I'm going to push one
more gal into the mud. Next one gives me a dirty look. I won't
even wait for her to say a word. Just let her cut her eyes
around scornful and in the dirt she goes, right on her sweet
little tail, and to hell with Lieutenant Petunia Wilkins!"

With a howl of laughter, the lieutenant from Delaware was
christened. Behind his back thereafter he was "Petunia" Wilkins.

"You'll git you a stretch in the guardhouse," they warned
Private Rankin.

"Huh! I already got four bricks loosent up good on the
back wall of that-there place," Rankin scoffed.

But he went about nursing his grievance, sweltering in his
buttoned-up blue coat. He took details sullenly, worked off his
spleen on innocent shopkeepers and farmers who came to town
on Saturdays, cluttering up the streets with their mules and
their shabby, unpainted wagons. He ordered men roughly to
move on when they stopped to talk in groups on the plank walks,
shouting at them and waving his gun in menacing fashion when
Lieutenant Wilkins was not at hand. He boasted, in the billet
he shared with six others, of his insubordinations; tossed a
bowl of oatmeal at the cook because he said it had a fly in it,

leveled looks of raw contempt at the back of the erect young lieutenant from Delaware.

Then came the day he had been waiting for. Petunia Wilkins was nowhere in sight. The girl had on a blue silk dress and a saucy little bonnet, a silk reticule hung on her arm, and dark hair lay in two curls over her shoulders. Her eyes were gray and stormy as she regarded Private Rankin standing rigidly in her way, his gun on his shoulder, cartridges in a belt shining across his chest. "Let me pass, please," she said coldly.

"You can walk around. Plenty of room," Private Rankin sneered. "The Army of the United States has the right of way in this town."

"The Army of the United States has also abominable manners!" she snapped.

Private Rankin did not move. He was having fun. "Mud out yonder's good enough for you Rebel hussies," he remarked, giving her a shove with his elbow.

Abruptly a mine seemed to go off under his chin and he staggered and fell on his back. He blinked up dazedly into the lightning eyes of Lieutenant Wilkins.

"Report to headquarters, Soldier!" barked Wilkins, who had stepped inopportunely from a near-by doorway. He turned to help Marian Villerand recover her balance and her lost reticule. "I apologize for this ill-bred fellow, Miss," he said, brushing the soil off her silk bag. "The Army of the United States does not condone such conduct toward ladies."

Marian gave him a scornful look. "Indeed?" she asked crisply. "The ladies of Alabama have learned to expect ungentlemanly conduct from your Army. Not quite so brutal as the ladies of Georgia and South Carolina experienced, but certainly there has been nothing to lead us to count on any consideration whatever from your troops."

"I have said I was sorry, Miss. I promise you that there

will be no more of this rudeness—not while I am in command here, at any rate. I am Eric Wilkins. May I escort you wherever you are bound?"

She raked him slowly up and down with her smoke-colored gaze. Anger made her vibrant. Why did these stupid Yankees have to be handsome and engaging? Why didn't they all look like the scoundrels and scalawags they were?

"No, thank you!" She was curt. "If you will restrain your riffraff and ragtag soldiers from insulting me and manhandling me, that is all I ask." She moved away, her head high because people were watching, people she knew, people who formed unfavorable opinions of anyone who consorted with the Union troops.

But the lieutenant fell into step beside her, apparently undismayed. "You have a right to be indignant," he said. "You have also a right to be forgiving. At least you could accept the apology I offered."

She walked a dozen paces, ignoring him stiffly. Then her tongue got the best of her. "Why? Why should I be forgiving? You are the trespassers here, not I. I was born in this county. I have lived here all my life."

"And we are here to maintain peace in your county, to protect you," he said. "We are here as friends."

"We prefer to choose our own friends—and you are the only people from whom we need to be protected. There would be peace here if you would take yourselves off and leave us to restore our own country by our own efforts and in our own way."

"You have people here who are destitute—even hungry." He modified his brisk stride to her angry, pattering pace. "We are trying to take care of them. Supplies are being sent from the north and east continually."

"Nobody was ever hungry in Alabama till the armies swept over this country like locusts." She kept her face stiffly averted, moved faster, but he stayed alongside. "Even our black people were all well fed and contented. You've tried to turn them against us, but you haven't been too successful at it. Most of them would come back now if they weren't ashamed or intimidated by your bureaus and your bayonets."

"That is another matter, Miss. The blacks are restless and resentful. Without our Army you would be helpless against them."

"Pooh!" she sneered. "Your Army is twice as obnoxious and alarming to us as our poor, pitiful servants could ever be."

They had walked a long way on a shaded street, and Marian was so furious that she had scarcely noticed where they were going. She had been vaguely aware of watchers, the curious who were probably wondering at seeing Villerand's daughter walking with a Union officer. She hoped her rigid demeanor and hostile attitude had squelched any gossip. At least they had not taken the direction of the Yankee jail. Now she found herself suddenly at the gate of the town cemetery. That was an old romantic rendezvous. She stopped short and faced about, setting her chin into grimness to match her stony voice.

"May I please proceed now about my business?" she asked. "I appreciate your saving me from that creature of yours. Now may I be released from official custody?"

He smiled, and she held sternly to her defenses, feeling them wavering. "You look like my little sister," he said. "Her name's Margaret and she has spitfire eyes like yours when she gets mad. Naturally you hate us. If the South had won we would have detested your occupying forces, I know. I'm not justifying either side, or complaining. I'm merely saying it's all a great pity. I like this country." He looked across the green burying place where white slabs stood in grass grown tall and silvery with bloom under dark cedars that laid green patches of shadow.

"You fought hard to conquer it," she remarked, "but now

that you have conquered it why do you wish to destroy it? Why must you make laws that frustrate what we could do for ourselves? If we must be part of your union, will you be stronger by keeping us weak and prostrate?"

"I do not make the laws, remember. I only obey orders. Even if I don't particularly approve of the orders, even if I hate what I'm commanded to do, I must obey because I'm a soldier. Were there fighting men in your family?"

"My brother was one. He was killed at Fort Morgan, we heard. He was nineteen years old."

"When I was nineteen I enlisted with Burnside's cavalry. We fought from Cumberland Gap to Petersburg with a dozen other battles and some tough campaigning in between. While we were driving your General Longstreet away from Knoxville my father died. The war was over before I got the news. I should be at home right now, running his flour mill and taking care of my mother and sisters. Instead, I'm standing here while you hate me. And I don't even know your name," he finished ruefully.

"You are not required to stand here. Or am I under arrest? If not, I have no intention of standing here any longer myself."

"Certainly you are not under arrest——"

"Then good afternoon, Lieutenant." She walked away very fast, her blue skirts swinging, spots of carmine burning on either cheek. He followed, very rigid of spine and grim of eye, a few paces behind. Two soldiers in blue who were leaning on a wall hesitated a breath before snapping to salute, and Marian heard his barked reprimand. A one-sided smile softened her militant frown. Showing off like a little boy, she thought.

She walked back to the courthouse and looked about for the carriage. Presently it came bouncing up, out of a rutty side street, with Tuby sitting stiffly up front and flicking the horses with his whip while her mother urged him on from the back seat. Emma looked worried and pale, though she held her haughty great-lady pose. Where she stood waiting Marian could hear two rough men muttering behind her.

"Some folks still rides in carriages. Me, I ain't even got me a mule to bust the middles in my cotton."

"Me, I ain't got no cotton," said the other. "I ain't borrowin' no money to hire free niggers to grow cotton for the Yankees to steal."

"Looky yonder. Got to have a nigger help her into the buggy."

"Villerand's gal. He ain't lost nothin' in this-here war."

Impulsively Marian turned on them. "You're very wrong. Villerand lost a son in this war," she said.

Emma moved over, dragged her up nervously. "My Heavens, Marian, don't notice white trash! Drive on quick, Tuby— drive straight home. What happened, Marian? I saw you with that soldier and I was terrified."

"He was an officer. He's in command here, he said. One of the soldiers insulted me, and that officer knocked him down. Then he apologized!"

"For heaven's sake, I can't believe it! But did you have to walk with him all the way to the cemetery, just to let him apologize? What will people say?" her mother worried.

"No doubt they're already saying that you had General Swayne out to dinner. What do we care what they say? Certainly I wasn't being friendly with that lieutenant. I just couldn't get rid of him, though I was definitely nasty—and he seemed a nice boy, too. His father died, he told me, and he was needed at home, but he has to stay here because he has his orders."

"So many of them were nice boys—our boys, theirs too." Emma sighed. "That is the evil of war—what it does to decent people. What's the matter?"

Marian was tugging at Tuby's sleeve. "I left all my parcels

in Mr. Horning's shop. Turn around, Tuby, we'll have to go back. Turn around this minute."

"Ain't no place to turn till the crossroads, Miss Maggie. Us be dark gittin' through that swamp, does we have to go back."

"But I left the sugar the cook wanted for the peaches and the thread and Cassius' tobacco. And the goods for Juliet's petticoats."

"Pulled a white lady out of her carriage 'while back, goin' through that swamp. Bad colored boys done it. Took all her money and her earbobs and tore her clothes, stole the hoss and cut the harness and lef' her there afoot, just one ole colored man wid her," insisted Tuby. "Beat the ole man too."

"Who was that? Odd I hadn't heard about it."

"It was that white lady lives across the river up where the boats come in, Mistis. All the colored knows about it. Cassius, he know."

"Eugenia Freer? I'll drive over there tomorrow and see her," Emma said. "Drive on, Tuby. You can go fetch the parcels in the morning. You'd expire with fright, I suppose, if we were molested, even if we didn't."

"Them bad colored boys don't like white folks' niggers," explained Tuby. "Says why'nt we be free like all our color got free."

"But you are free. Doesn't Mr. Villerand pay you every Saturday? And feed you beside?"

"Yes'm. Pay me six bits. Find me ole clothes too, but it ain't no use tellin' them rough people that. Git loose, they says. Git you a piece of some white man's land and a mule."

"Nobody has got any white man's land—or a mule! That's all Yankee talk, Tuby. They want you to hate us, the best friends you have in the world. Who'd doctor you when you get the ptisic every winter, if you got loose, as you call it? Who'd feed you? I'll wager 'Phrony and Lissa are plenty hungry by this time."

"Maybe so, Mistis, maybe so." Tuby, sitting slumped in the seat, clucked at his horses. "Git along, you Rastus! Ain't goin' to git cotched along here." At the edge of the swampy land where the road narrowed over little wooden bridges, he plied the whip vigorously and the wheels clattered over quaking planks.

"If there were any outlaws within twenty miles, they'd certainly hear us, Tuby," reproved Emma.

"Might hear us, but they aint' goin' cotch us."

Marian sat clinging to the arm of the seat while the vehicle bounced and swayed. She was thinking pensively of Lieutenant Wilkins. Not all the Northern men came tramping into Alabama in iron boots, to intimidate and betray. He liked the country, he had said. Even though the sun had been hot as tophet, too hot for May. But of course, whatever happened, the poor man could never be accepted in Alabama, never live happily or find friends. That was another tragedy of this war—that the seething hatred could never be healed, not in her lifetime anyway, nor in the lifetime of Eric Wilkins.

There was Duncan Wade, his life blighted. Uncle Hugh would be all torn up inside if Duncan got into any trouble, and if Duncan had been in town today he might have killed that offensive soldier and probably been promptly and horribly hanged. She had better warn Duncan to walk discreetly and avoid offense. War hadn't softened his legendary fiery temper, she suspected.

She would ride over as soon as she could and warn him. Uncle Hugh shouldn't have any more trouble; he had never got over Duncan's mother's death. She had seen the old man often sitting in the graveyard. They had had many long talks there.

Duncan would never see that Lieutenant Wilkins was a decent young man, forced into a punitive role through no wish of his own. Duncan would see only the detested Union blue, through an angry haze of remembering. Petersburg, the lieutenant had said. He had been with Burnside at Petersburg. But Burnside had made a fiasco of his attack at Petersburg and been relieved. All the South had gloated over the abortive failure of that crater affair.

Perhaps Duncan and Lieutenant Wilkins had lain in opposing trenches, shooting at each other. That was a romantic idea and Marian's young mind dwelt on it, tried to picture what would happen if those enemies should meet and recognize each other.

Impulsively she said, "Since we've taken to entertaining Yankees, we might invite that lieutenant to supper."

"I can think of no reason at all why we should," said Emma coldly. "Your father had business dealings with General Swayne. I hope you're not getting silly ideas about that young man—just because he spoke to you respectfully as any gentleman ought. Any man of decent breeding, that is."

"Oh, no, I'm not getting ideas. There's no use having ideas —not about anybody."

Not about Duncan either. He was still remembering Juliet— the Juliet who had only laughed at his devotion in the long ago. Marian recalled the laughter, and tingled with defensive fury at the thought of it.

Now Juliet had fat Felix. Plenty good enough for a woman as heartless as Juliet.

VII

OLD JOSUFF had done a fairly creditable job on the suit of brownish cloth for Duncan Wade. True, the pockets were not quite straight and the collar of the coat had a tendency to roll, but when Louisa had pressed it with her heavy old iron it had a respectable if not a stylish air.

"Look good enough to wear courtin', Mist' Duncan—" Louisa beamed—"did you have you a nice starched shirt."

Then, her maroon eyes suddenly flaring to a gleam, she dashed to the mahogany sideboard and dragged out a drawer that squeaked in protest.

"This-here tablecloth—" she brought forth a yellowed bolt of linen—"Mist'ess, she ain't never hem this-here since it come from across the water. All the rest been cut up and scraped for lint long ago, make bandages for the soldiers, but this piece she ain't cut. Look—" she unrolled the goods, heavy and glossy, on the big dining table—"cut a power of shirts out of this goods, does the boss say we kin."

Old Hugh fingered the rich linen, misty-eyed. "I got this for her out of Belfast in '58. She said you'd be getting married, Duncan, and there'd be an infare and she'd have to set a big table. I didn't know she'd saved it. She cut up about every piece of cotton after Shiloh. They made bandages at the church and she'd make Lemuel take a mule off the plow and drive her in to town. After Lemuel left between dark and day one night, I drove her myself. She was failing then, but she wouldn't give up. If she had lived I reckon this piece would have been sacrificed too."

"I don't want Mother's fine linen cut up for me," Duncan protested. "It's about the only nice thing of hers that's left."

"No, suh, we got all her silver hid," Louisa declared. "We ain't never fetch it up outen that ole dry cistern at the barn. Too many trashy folks around, black and white. Mist' Duncan, you' mammy wouldn't want you goin' courtin' without no shirt to you' back. Was she here she'd cut this up herself. When we goin' need twelve yards of tablecloth? Got mighty little to eat on what little-bitty cloth we got."

"Let Josuff cut some shirts of this, Duncan," his father said. "It's mighty heavy. Be hot in the summer, but it ought to wear forever."

"All right, I'll agree. But I'm not going courting, Louisa. I need anything else on earth worse than I need a wife."

"Every man need a wife. You fetch us a purty gal here and we git this ole house alive ag'in."

"When I go courting I'll ride my own horse with money in my pocket, and that day is a long way off."

"Us make a good crop this year, you have money in you' pocket. You leave this goods lay right here. I make old Josuff sharpen those scissors good. Get three-four shirts out of this, I reckon."

"Cut one for Father then, too."

"No, no, Duncan—I'll get along with what I have."

"You ain't got nothin', Marse Hugh. Does you go to them speech meetin's, I feel shamed for true," Louisa argued.

Duncan laughed without mirth. "Hard times, sir, when the servants are shamed by us! You'll have a new shirt if you're planning to attend any more speech meetings."

"Young McKee, down at Selma, wants to set up a meeting here to take some action about financing a railroad from Decatur to Selma, before the new legislature meets in the fall. I've had two letters from him. He's a fine young chap—got wounded at Shiloh, never could return to the army. Now he's got this *Southern Argus* going down at Selma, running on faith and a prayer. He's one of the worth-while people who are going to save Alabama. I'd like to have you meet him."

"You told me Villerand had ideas about building a railroad."

"Villerand will work with the Union men, but not with the rest of us. Duncan, when you are properly clothed, why not go down to Selma and talk to Robert McKee? We must depend on you young men if we're ever to restore this state to her former dignity and integrity."

"It's more than thirty miles to Selma, but I reckon I could walk it—if I had some shoes with bottoms in them."

"We can spare a mule as soon as Parmy gets the cotton laid by. I'd hate to see a son of mine riding a mule, but it beats walking," Hugh Wade said.

"Parmy got your saddle hid too, Mist' Duncan. We got a sight of stuff in that ole cistern, with trash and corn shucks on top of it. I wrop the saddle up good in a ole piece of bedtick."

Duncan laughed. "What else have you got hid out there, Louisa? Not the family portraits by any chance?"

"When the Union troops came through here the portraits disappeared," his father said sadly. "I think they burned the canvases in their campfires and stole the frames. They had wagons loaded down with loot. I heard that a squadron of Forrest's men burned the wagons up on the Decatur road. I noticed you'd taken poor little Priscilla Wade down from the wall."

"I couldn't stand seeing her desecrated as she was. That canvas should be burned too."

"I hope I can have it restored sometime. That picture is over a hundred years old. Nobody knows who painted it, back in South Carolina, when that state was a royal colony. Tell Josuff to cut out a shirt for Duncan, Louisa, and can you sew it?"

"Yes, suh! My hands mighty rough, but I make it, you-all git me some thread."

"Duncan, you might go in town and get some thread. Horning will surely credit us for a few hanks of thread."

"Then maybe I'd better go now. It looks a little like rain."

Across the fields was the short way to town. Duncan tramped off through the overgrown meadow, and up the little rise past the tangled burying ground. He saw the bay horse coming and stopped, waiting.

The Villerand girl wore red this morning, with a linen skirt over her habit. She was bareheaded and her dark hair shimmered in the flat, white sunlight. She pulled up the horse as she rode near. "I was coming to see you," she said flatly. "Help me down."

He lifted her from the saddle, feeling the soft, vibrant body against his own, and a tremor went over him that made his breath quicken and his face burn. She drew back, shook down her skirts and pushed back her hair.

He said, "I'm honored to have a visit from you, but you know you've no business riding out here alone."

"I should know. I've been told times enough. You're all dressed up today. That's a new suit, isn't it?"

"Manufactured by Uncle Josuff and Louisa. I'm now on my way to buy some thread so Louisa can make me a shirt from my mother's tablecloth. Allow me to help you back into your saddle and I'll escort you to the road if you'll ride slowly. From there you might be safe if you ride fast enough."

"I never ride the road. It's forbidden. That's why I take this back way through the fields. Anyhow, I want to talk to you. Let's sit down here. I like to sit here on this wall. The dead are so peaceful and understanding." She pushed her way through the ground myrtle and periwinkle and took a seat on the crumbling bricks. "Sit here by me," she ordered imperiously.

He obeyed, brushing the moss and dust from the bricks out of consideration for his new apparel. "What is this momentous subject you wish to discuss with me? It must be important if to ride over here you risk having a good horse stolen and maybe worse things happen to you."

"It *is* important." She pulled off her gloves and smoothed them between her palms. "I want to talk about you. You're in danger, Duncan Wade. It worries me."

He laughed. The curve of her brows was sober, but there was a sweet fullness to her lips that softened her matronly air. "I've lived with danger most of these last five years," he said. "I managed to survive a few million Yankee bullets, besides being half drowned in several rivers and having a horse blown to pieces under me. What is this dire danger that brings you over here—unknown to your mother, I'll bet a horse?"

"The danger of jail. Maybe of being hanged," she stated levelly. Then she flared up, red spots burning in her cheeks. "If you are going to be as stubbornly stupid as my family and make fun, I won't tell you any more."

"I've never been hanged," he mused. "It would be quite a new experience. Who is planning to hang me?"

"You're laughing at me. I think I'll go home." She rose, flirting her skirt down angrily.

"I'm not laughing. My curiosity is aroused. You tell me I'm in danger of being hanged, or at the least clapped into jail, and if you know that much, you must know the crime I'm supposed to have committed."

She dropped down again, mollified. "You haven't committed it yet. But you will. Maybe today if you go into town. And you mustn't do it. It would kill your father if you got into any more trouble. He got so worried after Appomattox when you didn't come home that I was afraid he might not live through the summer. I was, really—that's why I've come over here so often."

"Very good of you, Miss Villerand."

"I told you to call me Maggie. You used to call me that once, but you used to call me a brat too."

"You were a brat, Maggie—a snooping, too precocious, irritating brat."

"All right, but I grew out of it. Admit that. And I'm fond of Uncle Hugh. That's why I came. He and Papa detest each other for some reason I was never able to find out, but it never affected me, or Juliet either."

"So, because you're fond of my father, you don't want me involved in this mysterious crime, whatever it is? What do you anticipate I'm going to do—knock poor old Hod Horning in the head and rob his till?"

"Nothing so utterly silly. I'm afraid you might kill a Yankee. Listen now, and don't interrupt or get mad. When I was in town one day last week—Tuesday—or was it Wednesday?—no matter—anyway, a soldier called me a name and pushed me off the sidewalk into the mud."

"Why, the goddam——" Duncan was on his feet, eyes blazing, fists tightened.

"See?" she said coolly. "That's what I mean. I told you not to get mad. Anyway, a lieutenant stepped out of a building and knocked the soldier down. Then he apologized to me for the soldier's bad conduct."

"If I'd been there I'd have broken the scoundrel's neck."

"I know. That's why I came—to warn you. Just in time too, since you're going to town today. If you should see a Yankee insult a woman you'd fly into one of your rages and likely end up in jail—if you weren't beaten up or maybe hanged."

"One of my rages? Do I have rages?"

"Don't you even know what you do? You were mad enough just then to kill a whole squad of Yankees. I remember when you used to pick fights at all the dances. Juliet would get so embarrassed the way you acted, Duncan. So I think if you do go to town you should try to control your temper. It would please them no end to knock your teeth out or something— and if they could find an excuse to hang you it would be another black blot on the South in their dirty books."

"So you don't want me beaten up or hanged? Very noble of you, Miss Maggie Villerand. So you'd like to see me stand by while some woman gets pushed into the mud. Would you admire any man as cowardly as that?"

"Lieutenant Wilkins will discipline his own soldiers. He was very nice to me, he was really. He comes from Delaware."

"So, if I should see a young woman being manhandled by those scalawags, I'm to put my hands in my pockets and yell for Lieutenant Wilkins from Delaware? What kind of a fellow do you think I am?"

She sighed. "I know the kind of fellow you are, Duncan Wade. That's why I'm uneasy. I know what would have happened if you had been in town that day. You wouldn't have hit that soldier on the jaw the way Lieutenant Wilkins did. You'd have throttled him with your bare hands."

"Very likely. And afterward I'd have stamped his filthy face into the mud."

"And after that you'd probably have been hanged for murder. You can't be hanged, Duncan Wade. I've got plans for you, myself."

He grinned at her indulgently. For a little she had stirred him as a woman, but now with her chin tipped up and her lips parted a little she was naïve and cute, again the child he had teased and laughed at.

"Could a man be so bold as to inquire as to those plans?"

"You aren't going to get into any more trouble," she stated coolly. "You're going to stay here and run this plantation and get rich. And then some time I'm going to marry you."

A hard lump surged up into his throat and tightened there. She was so young, so sweet—and, he realized, so altogether dear! Not like Juliet, who was imperious too. There was gentleness in Marian with no tinge of cruelty, such as he had known in Juliet. Now that fatuous boy who had suffered torments of love for Juliet seemed a pathetic and slightly ridiculous figure. Now he felt old as the ages, fatherly and protective, but intuition warned him against voicing any of this to rouse her to young fury.

He said gravely, laying a hand on hers, feeling her quiver at his touch, "I am greatly honored. And now that our future is all arranged, may I go along to town if I promise not to kill any Yankees or be hanged before you can marry me? And you'd better get along home too before they miss you."

She got to her feet and stood looking at the ground, flicking her gloves together. "Duncan Wade, I'm not talking nonsense," she said. "I may amuse you now, but it won't be that way forever. Promise me if you get into any trouble you'll call for Lieutenant Wilkins. He's not like the rest of them. He's a gentleman."

A queer, unreasoning resentment made Duncan tingle. "His charms seem to have affected you profoundly," he said. "But would it be wise to tell him that I'm to be saved from the gallows so that you can marry me? He might have ideas himself."

Her eyes turned steely as bayonets. "You can still be as beastly as ever!" she snapped. "Go along and let them lock you in their filthy jail. See if I care! And I hope you rot there!"

She jerked the horse near to the wall and sprang into the saddle, disdaining his help. Laying on her crop, she galloped away. Duncan watched her go, unhappily. Always, as with Juliet, he said the wrong thing! But what could he have said? What could any man say who had nothing to offer, no promise even to himself for the future? Heavily he tramped over the rolling meadow, briers piercing his feet through the thin soles of his shoes. He climbed a tottering fence dragged down with honeysuckle vines and took the dusty, weed-grown road.

The way was empty and still; birds bathed in the soft dust; a rabbit ventured from the bushes and skittered back again. Off to the north three Negroes and one white man chopped cotton, their shoulders bent, hoes moving in languid rhythm. A woman in a sunbonnet and dragging skirts carried a jug of water across the field. Between the cotton rows the earth steamed, lush and black in the crushing sunshine. The air smelled of growth, of burgeoning trees and blackberry bloom, of honeysuckle and crushed grass: the rich, dark smell of a rich, dark land.

Thousands had fed on the breast of this land, could again be fed on it. To the north where the soil thinned on the slopes, rising to the low mountains where the bony tail of the Appalachians slept under an evergreen blanket, there were other riches buried that had been barely scratched at. Coal, iron, even gold made up the rigid ribs of those hills. To east and west shouldering down through their valleys moved the great rivers, the Black Warrior, the Tombigbee, the Cahaba, the Alabama. For generations the wealth of the land had been floated down those rivers to Mobile and the sea. Duncan remembered riding a cotton barge down-river. He had been a boy then, excited by the paddle wheels of the little steamer that pulled the string of flatboats, by the billowing wood smoke and occasional sparks that poured from her crooked stack.

His job had been to wait with a bucket ready to haul up water on a rope and douse any spark that fell near the cotton. Now they talked railroads. Steel rails had already been laid on a few stretches, but the war had destroyed most of these; time would be needed to rebuild them. More roads would open transportation to the roiling Tennessee River to the north, a highway to the Mississippi and the open Gulf. Trains would go shouting through the quiet farming country at speeds to make the quiet water highways a thing of the past. It was good, of course. It was progress. It would link the slumberous South with the noisy, pushing North. New cities would be built, money and power would move in. With the money and the power would inevitably come strangers.

Duncan Wade, looking about him at this quiet rural Alabama, was not sure that he would like a new, hectic striving country.

Peace was all around, at this hour, and for long he had known so little peace.

VIII

HORACE HORNING and Emanuel Hale welcomed a visitor. Their trade curtailed by the shortages of goods and a woeful lack of money throughout the county, there were long days when only idlers and men seeking audience for their personal or political grievances came into the store. Some days nobody came in at all.

On such days Emanuel Hale tipped a chair back against the outside wall of the building and dozed for hours, shifting his seat as the sun crept around. The burning heat of it on his bald head always wakened him in time to move before his naked scalp was blistered. For all its long exposure that expanse of skin was still as white and glistening as an egg, in sharp contrast to the weathered and aging brown of his face.

Horning liked to do his napping inside. Sunlight made him squint and brought sweat down his face, blurring his glasses; so, when his partner was on watch outside, Horning took his rest on an old bundle of hides in the darkened room at the rear. The hides smelled to heaven, but Horning had grown used to the reek, and when his wife fumed at the smell of his clothes at home he turned an ear made deaf from long practice. There was no call to be alert in business any more, with the people impoverished, transportation practically at a standstill, the railroads—what few lines existed—still in desultory operation, and most of the river boats burned or sunk.

The air was humid and heavy and clouds moved down from the north threatening rain. Emanuel Hale had his rest broken by a lingering mosquito. He slapped at it peevishly several times, decided finally that he might as well go inside or put on his hat, when he looked down the quiet street and saw Duncan Wade approaching.

The legs of his chair came down with a thump and he got to his feet grunting. "Well, well, young feller! Come in out of this sun. I see you got you a suit made. Looks pretty good considering the kind of stuff you had to make it out of." He took the coat Duncan had carried over his arm the last hot mile and held it out by the shoulders. "Old Nigra's a pretty fair tailor. Kind of weak on the buttonholes, but they don't show too much."

"Louisa did the buttonholes," Duncan said. "Her hands were mighty rough from chopping cotton and the thread tangled."

"Come along in. I reckon Hod's asleep back yonder some place. No business now—two or three days running. Nobody's got any money and everybody's scared to use their credit for fear taxes will take their crops again and they can't pay what they owe. Things were bad last year, but this year they're scrapin' bottom. Somehow or other some credit and confidences have got to be loosened in this county or everyone will go bankrupt."

"There must be money somewhere," Duncan said as he followed the old man into the dim interior. "All the wealth that was in Alabama couldn't have vanished completely."

"Well, five hundred million dollars' worth did, so Robert Patton estimates. Property values alone, slaves and real property—he says we lost that much by the war. All the state capital is gone, state bonds are mighty near worthless, banks busted, and Confederate bonds ain't worth the wind it would take to blow 'em away. Paper the privy with 'em, all they're fit for. Anything I can do for you, now you're inside our busy mart of trade? Got a few plowpoints yesterday, now that plowing season is over. Got some new coffeepots too, if any coffee ever comes to boil in 'em. Next coffee I get ahold of I'm going to boil me up a gallon, black as your shoes, and drink all of it. Lay awake for a week, I reckon, but it will be worth it."

"You can sell me some white thread. On credit. Louisa's going to make me some shirts out of one of my mother's linen tablecloths."

Hale looked appalled. "Now look—you don't want to do that! My Lord, I remember when we ordered that linen for your mother back in '58. Imported, every yard of it, Duncan. Took two bales of cotton to pay for it. Finest stuff we'd shipped in in a long time, but Hugh said Florence had to have the best. You come back here with me."

"A man without a shirt is socially handicapped," Duncan remarked. "Also he's likely to get sunburned and flea-bitten."

"You wait now." The old man pushed open an inner door and a shape stirred in a corner. "Get up from there, Hod," Hale ordered. "We've got a customer."

Horace Horning struggled up and opened a shutter, blinking at the rush of light. "Who is he? Don't let him get away! Oh, it's you, young Wade. Got your suit sewed up, I see. Not bad, not bad. Little bit warm for this weather, I reckon."

"He needs a shirt. Where's that piece of stuff they brought back from that election rally George Houston had? Good piece of muslin, Wade, loaned it to Houston to drape around their speaker's stand. Got a few tack holes in it and needs washing, but it's good solid stuff. Where'd you put it, Hod?"

"Folded it up and laid it somewheres. Ain't but four yards in it. Can you cut a shirt out of four yards of goods?"

"Ought to be able to. There wasn't but ten yards in that bolt of goods and he got a suit of clothes out of it."

"And a pair of pants for Josuff too."

"That was wide goods. This ain't but a yard wide. They draped it around a speaker's stand to get George Houston elected to the United States Senate, but it didn't do him any good to get elected for he ain't never seen the inside of that chamber yet—never will, I reckon, not till Washington celebrates a series of important funerals. Andy Johnson, God A'mighty how he hates all Southern planters and anybody else that started life with more than six bits! Thad Stevens too—so poisoned inside he don't dare bite his own lip! Where you figure you put that goods, Hod? Stir around and see if you can find it. Sell it to you cheap, young Wade, secondhand like it is, but it's good stout stuff."

"Here it lays. Been a coon it would have bit your fingers off. Pretty dirty, Wade. Reckon you can get Louisa to boil it up and bleach it?"

"Tell her to put some peach twigs in the kettle." Hale took the dingy length of material from Horning and shook it out. "My Lord, when I remember all the fine stuff I used to sell to Florence Wade I feel like going out and butting my bald head against a stump! I don't figure good times like that will ever come again in Alabama."

"Not in our life time." Horning nodded. "Be worse before we see better, I'll prophesy. I doubt if they even let the legislature meet this fall."

Hale folded the muslin, looked about and picked up a crumpled piece of newspaper to wrap it in. *"Southern Argus,"* he announced. "Give you all the news along with your purchase. Paper's more 'n a week old, but it takes about that long for mail to get here from Selma, and that's less than fifty miles. Need some thread to sew this with. Hand me down one of them yellow boxes, Hod. Tear in one corner of this, but your old Nigra can cut around that. Now you owe us six bits more. Put it down, Hod, so we won't forget it come cotton-picking time. Know how much tax they're figuring to put on cotton this summer? Fifteen dollars a bale."

"And the Negroes get more than half of the gross value of

the crop," Duncan added. "I suppose the tax comes out of the planter's share?"

"Most likely. The planter, being a belligerent, a traitor to the United States and an ornery, biggity son of a bitch to boot, he don't deserve any consideration," Horning growled. "You ain't been home long enough, young Wade, to learn what a reprehensible tribe you sprung from."

"He'll learn," Hale said. "Sit down, Wade, and Brother Horning here will instruct you, undertake your education. You ain't been rightly schooled as to the kind of no-good stratum of society you was born into."

"I've heard it already," Duncan said. "I walked a thousand miles or more in a Confederate uniform."

"With the buttons? You left the buttons on? That's a misdemeanor. Could be a capital offense."

"With the buttons on. It was winter, by the time they got the red tape unwound and I got out of the army on parole. Everywhere they had a garrison in a town I heard remarks on my ancestry. From Knoxville on I took to the woods mostly, but up in the hills north of here some of the people were meaner than the Yanks."

"Turned their coats when Grant went through, those pinywoods tackies. Turned their coats to save their mules and their meat. Now they're Republicans, that stripe and the Nigras—and Julian Villerand."

"Villerand lost a son in the Confederate Army," Duncan remarked.

"You heard, maybe," Hale drawled, "that that noble Confederate Army got licked? Being licked made it cease to be noble. Now it's pathetic, deluded, impoverished and suspected. None of those characteristics being either stylish or profitable, Villerand can't afford to trot in the tracks of that aforetime noble company. In '61, he kept quiet but now he's arguing that the South was stampeded into a damfool war by Yancey and those South Carolina hotheads."

"My father says Villerand is promoting some sort of railroad proposition. Do you know anything about it?" Duncan dropped on a stool between the two old men.

Horning got up stiffly and waddled to the safe, got out a bottle half full of whisky and reverently removed the cork. "Emanuel and me, we discourse on politics better when we're lubricated," he said. "Better have a snifter, young Wade. This dislocated, deteriorated, disgustingly futile civilization we're existing in now looks slightly less disgusting and degraded when viewed through a slight alcoholic haze." He tilted the bottle, swallowed noisily, passed it to Hale.

"I'd better not drink," Duncan declined. "I have to walk home. I've already been warned not to let my temper get the best of me. With a drink to increase my courage I might be tempted to kick some Union officer in the seat of his nice blue breeches."

"Which would be heinous, outrageous and a justification of the argument that all former Southern gentlemen are now sunk to the level of bestiality." Horning took another pull at the bottle. "Only thing worse would be to shoot a Republican, 'specially a black one. You asked about railroads. If you came home down through the hill country, you saw what the Yanks did to the Memphis and Charleston. Heated the rails red-hot and wrapped 'em around trees. Burned all the trestles and most of the rolling stock."

"God knows we need railroads!" declared his partner, reaching for the bottle. "Somehow we have got to build 'em—did build 'em back yonder B.S.—which don't mean what it used to mean, young Wade. Now it stands for 'Before Sumter,' like B.C. stands for 'Before Christ.' "

"A lot of rich men lost about all they had, in the railroad

promotion business," Horning took up the narrative. "Charlie Pollard got a good start with his Alabama & Florida Railroad, bought the Montgomery & West Point line and planned to connect up with the other roads over at Selma—would have had a system connecting with all the river ports, including New Orleans, if the war hadn't come along."

"I remember," Hale said, "when all the railroads in this state had wooden tracks. Strip of iron nailed along on top of the timbers for the cars to roll on. Pulled 'em with mules mostly. Brought in some little steam engines—'Little Stephensons' they called 'em. But they were mighty feeble, broke down every couple of miles, so then they'd go back to the mules. Folks didn't like the steam engines much, anyway, smoke and sparks blowing back on those open cars they had those days. I went all the way up to Tuscumbia, horseback, back in '32. They'd built that little piece of railroad around the Shoals and I had to see the trains run. Sold that little scrap of road to the Memphis & Charleston later on. Yankee General Mitchel tore it up when he went through there."

"What we need now is a road running north and south." Horning lovingly corked the bottle and returned it to its hiding place. "Take a dry summer and the rivers shoal up; boats are mostly all gone anyway. Trouble with Villerand, he can't think constructively. He won't project to build a railroad any place. He'll try to get the government in Washington into it, or get the right man elected governor of Alabama, get a big Federal loan or maybe promote having the state endorse half a million dollars' worth of bonds. He'll be the agent and collect the commissions. Good pickings for a smart operator on a project like that."

"State's busted so flat now they'd likely have to repudiate any bonds they did endorse. Happened back in '59. Governor vetoed a loan on the Alabama & Tennessee road, but they passed it over his veto. Then they had to cancel the loan because the stockholders didn't pay up and the road didn't have satisfactory collateral to back a two hundred thousand dollars bond issue. The men who'll get rich off railroads in Alabama, young Wade, won't build 'em. Once in a while an honest man like Charlie Pollard, a man with ambitions and good sense, comes along, but it's the unscrupulous fellers with slick, shifty brains who'll milk the profits out of any proposition."

"You catalogue Julian Villerand in that category?" Duncan asked.

Horning spat at a meandering bluebottle fly. "Well, I wouldn't name Julian Villerand a rascal. No, not exactly a rascal. He's what the professor would call an opportunist. Looks around for a weak spot in the economic situation where a little profit might leak out, and there he is with his little tin dipper. Got a sharp nose above that set of red whiskers. Smell an advantage fifty miles against a high wind."

"Villerand came through the war in what you might call comfortable shape," said Hale. "Some of his people left, but so did a lot of 'em. All dislocated and pitiful now. Listened to a lot of highfangled promises, but there was nothing but wind behind 'em. Been taken care of all their lives, the poor creatures, but now nobody's worrying about whether they're hungry or clothed or sheltered except this Freedmen's Bureau, and that outfit is getting irked with the Nigras. Got a bear by the tail when they disarranged an economic and social system that had been established for half a century—now they don't know how to let go. Feed 'em some charity rations, haul 'em in as vagrants and try to make 'em work on abandoned property, figure to vote 'em and disfranchise every Confederate sympathizer and Democrat in Alabama, but nobody loves the poor black man now—not nobody!"

"Josuff says that about half our people would drift back,

but they're afraid of the Yankees," Duncan said. "But we couldn't maintain them now, anyway. We're hard pushed to feed ourselves."

"The poor Negro, young Wade, is a helpless victim of human greed, hatred and stupidity as he stands now," Horning declared. "He didn't want to be snatched out of Africa and thrown into a bondage that he couldn't even understand. Now he thinks freedom is a grand gift, but all the gift amounts to is another form of misery, which he gets for no crime of his own."

"They'll suffer for years," Hale said solemnly. "They'll be exploited, cheated and killed before they find any place they can claim as their own in our social system. God did 'em a wrong when he made 'em black and humble and trusting. White men haven't changed much since Nero's day, not essentially. All the cussedness is mighty close under his skin. The white race won't change either, not to the extent of giving up its love for violences and conflict. Maybe the Negro will change. Anyway, he's going to change or die. That's gospel."

"The Negro," remarked Horning, "has got essential good in him—maybe more than the white race. Take the way he responds to religion—and the loyalty to people he loves. Give 'em a chance and they could be a power for good in this country. Anyway they got what Christ Himself ain't been able to teach the white man—patience and humility. Brought 'em up right smart in a couple of generations. Give 'em time and education and no tellin' what that race could be."

"We won't live to see it—but it might come," Hale agreed.

"Emanuel," said Horning, "you and me ought to get us a couple of pulpits to preach from. Understand, I'm not making a joke. This gospel we've been orating is profound. Trouble is there's been more orating than working in Marengo County this past year. And lofty words don't get to the bottom of what's wrong with Alabama. What's wrong is that no man now, whatever his color, has any trust in any other man, or in the future—and some of 'em are even scared to trust in God, fearing the Almighty might have turned Republican too, lately. Young fellers like Wade here are bewildered. They're the potential of the country, but that strength is going to waste for want of honorable leadership. And men with brains are satisfied to make speeches. What do you plan to do with yourself, young Wade?"

Duncan strode the length of the room, clutching his bundle under his elbow. "There are questions—a lot of questions. And so far no answers. There's the plantation. It made money —it made a lot of money when I was a young boy. Would it make money again without the people who worked on it? That's Question Number One. Number Two is: Can they take the place away from us? My father refused to sign their oath."

"He couldn't take that oath unless he lied. You have to swear that you gave no aid or sympathy to the Confederacy. Hugh bought bonds with every penny he could save or borrow. No man signed their oath unless he evaded the truth—not in this part of the country."

"Question Number Three: If we keep the place where can we get the money to bring it back into production?" Duncan went on.

Horning sighed, got up and opened the door into the front of the shop. "Young Wade, take your bundle of goods and shackle on home! 'Manuel and me are old men. Old men are reckoned to be wise, but we ain't God. We ain't even God's stepsons. We've been abandoned on our own doorstep like all the rest of the lost children in Alabama. Go holler those questions of yours down a well. You'll get as good an answer there as any place I know in this county."

"No," Hale objected, "that's poor advice. Go talk to young men, Wade. But I can tell you who's got your answers. Andy Johnson has got 'em, or Stevens, or Congress, or Governor

Patton, poor helpless tool of Congress that he is. God help him!"

Duncan went to the outer door, smiled back at the two elders, who were regarding him sadly. "Don't forget I owe you seventy-five cents," he said. "Good-by, gentlemen."

IX

OLD JOSUFF'S legs had lost their nimble strength long since. His knees wanted to wobble under him, his feet shuffled when he walked. He could still lift a hoe, however, and the muscles of his thin arms and long purplish fingers were as wiry and quick as ever. Some of his teeth were gone and his cheeks had fallen in; his lips stretched, giving him an amiable, simian grimace, and under the bristling gray brows his small black eyes twinkled with monkeylike eagerness.

Cotton was laid by and old Josuff was glad. No more dragging his heavy feet down the loamy rows, soil getting into his broken shoes, the sun laying a hot hand on his bent back. No more drinking warm water from a stone jug; no more itching with the peculiar sense of degradation that a house Negro suffered when the pressure of circumstance turned him into a field hand.

"Ole Miss, she ain't never sont me to no cotton field!" he protested often.

"Ole Miss, she daid and gone to she last home," weak-witted Parmy would remind him.

Louisa was brusque and acid. "You gittin' sheer of the crop, old man. Git you' pay and git you' rations. Is you ain't suited here, take you' bundle and hit the big road. Everybody done be free now."

But Josuff was afraid of the big road. He had never left the place alone in all his years, and his years went back into a dimness that was now blurred in the old man's mind.

"I done b'long to Mist' Hugh's pappy," he remembered. But he could not arrange time clearly any more, or recall the year of anything, and even the people were vague shadows. There had been black people in all the cabins, he knew, and he could recollect their laughter, the smell of syrup boiling when the cane was ground, the warm sticky drip of it on lavender fingers, drizzling off a biscuit. He could recall the perfume of Miss Florence's hair when she bent over him at his long worktable where he cut out rough Osnaburg trousers for the field hands and cotton shifts, and long-tailed shirts for the young ones. There were other memories, disembodied, frail as mirages, that drifted back into his mind now and then. Cowering on a pallet close to his mother's bed, while a runaway slave from another plantation was hunted and the dogs belled and hooted in the woods and swamps.

He had almost forgotten his mother, a tall, proud woman with quick defiant eyes who had been bought off a ship in Mobile Bay, and mated to a slim black horse trainer whom she had always hated.

That his master, whom Josuff still called Young Marse Hugh, had worked beside him in the field alleviated a little the ignominy of being there himself, but the feeling of shame only gave way to indignation that such things could happen to proud people.

Earning money was strange, mystic and exciting to him. He had never made a purchase in a shop in his life. He had never even entered one except to fetch and carry for his white folks. Now when he ran out of tobacco it was bought for him by Mister Hugh, and the aspect of the transaction that bewildered Josuff and angered him a little was that he had to untie the greasy rag he kept knotted and stuffed in a hole in the wall of his cabin and get out a dime to pay Mister Hugh back.

It never seemed quite right, after having had his tobacco

for fifty years without any question of payment, but he had one moment of triumphant retaliation one day when Mister Hugh inquired, casually, his face red and embarrassed, "Josuff, you wouldn't want to lend me a dollar, would you?"

Josuff, stiffened by perversity and a kind of panic, had replied, "No, suh! I wouldn't want to lend my money to nobody."

Louisa had blessed him out that time, calling him a contrary, ungrateful old fool. She had lent Mister Hugh the dollar herself, but Josuff felt no qualms about that. Nobody was going to get his money, not even Mister Hugh. With it hidden in the wall he became secretive, hostile to his own color, even wary of the white people.

To the three Negroes who accosted him in the lane above the Wade burying ground he gave grudging greeting, half grunt, half glare. "What you niggers want? What you doin' on our place? Git gone from hyar!"

A fat black man, a former Villerand slave who was called "Preacher," approached the graveyard wall. "Brother Josuff," he began unctuously, "us desires a few words with you. Set here a spell."

The other two Josuff had never seen before. He scowled at them as they ranged beside Preacher, who had a big belly mounted on long legs and a greasy, amiable face. "Ain't got time," Josuff grumped. "Got to cotch up that-there mule."

Preacher spread his hands pontifically. On occasions he had held baptizings in the shallows of the river attended by most of the slaves from the places roundabout, each one carefully hoarding his "paper," the pass that permitted him to be off his master's domain and also required him to be back before dark.

"Brother Josuff, you set and discourse with us a brief time and one of these yere boys cotch up you' mule. You too ole a man to be chasin' mules, anyhow."

"That mule ain't let anybody else cotch up wid him," Josuff

argued. "He know me. Young Mist' Duncan, he ridin' that mule to Selma."

"We guarantees to cotch your mule. What-for Mist' Duncan got to go to Selma?"

Josuff could not admit to these unwelcome strangers that he did not know. "Woman up there, I reckon. Anyways, I cut him out a new shirt."

He sat down, still not entirely easy about the motives of these three. Preacher talked fluently about small things. The appearance of the corn and cotton crops, the hard times that were everywhere. All the rich folks poor, all the poor folks gnawin' the rind, makin' out with mighty little of nothin'. Ultimately he arrived at the point of the interview.

"Brother Josuff, I been knowin' you quite a piece of time. Us ain't never been what you could call close friends, but us got confidence in each other—yes, suh, confidence!"

"What dat? How much it cost?" Josuff demanded suspiciously.

"Not a penny, brother. Not one small penny! Us got us an orginization, brother. All the colored gittin' into it. So I says to these boys, 'Brother Josuff, he a good soul. Got good sense. Brother Josuff got to be in us orginization.'"

"What it do?" inquired Josuff.

Preacher spread his big hands on the knees of his faded breeches. There were no cotton-chopping calluses on his palms and he wore a bright brass ring with a red stone in it. It had never occurred to Josuff to wish for any piece of adornment, but now the glitter of that ring filled his vision. He could not take his eyes off of it.

"You admire my joolry, Brother Josuff?" Preacher flourished the ring. "Come a time 'fore long when us wears diamonds, ride in a red-wheel carriage, wear a plug hat. Boy, us goin' to shine! White folks be workin' for us then." He got to his feet clowning authority. "'White boy, fetch me another

bottle of wine and a platter of chitlin's.' Man, howdy, the kingdom comin'! You better go 'long, Brother Josuff, you better
go 'long."

"Go 'long where?" Josuff desired to know, keeping a stiff
face, but his tamped-down excitement betrayed itself in the
twitching of his fingers at a fold of his brown trousers.

"I observe—" Preacher's eyes did not miss that excitement
—"that you got you a new pair breeches, brother. When us
git orginize', you be wearin' a swing-tail coat with brass
buttons on it big as dollars."

"Yeah, man! Gold buttons, brother!" antiphoned a hitherto
silent disciple. "Us gits the white folks cut down to size, me,
I'm goin' to wear gold buttons big as my fist. Gold teef too.
Whole mouthful gold teef."

Josuff's fingers strayed to his mouth and counted his remaining snags. Enough left to pick a chicken bone, but chicken
was only a memory now. So were ham and fat back since the
smokehouse had been stripped by Applegate's raiders.

"You ain't no good for marchin', Brother Josuff. That I
can see," Preacher continued. "You too ole and broke-down.
You can't tote no gun, neither, ole like you is, but you kin vote.
Come election time us is goin' vote all over this-yere county,
and eve'y time you votes you collects a dollar. But you got to
vote right, man; you can't pay no mind to what you' white
folks says. You come to my house tonight after sundown and
you git instructions from the big boss about votin' right."

"Who de big boss?"

"I ain't namin' the big boss. Not yit. When us git orginize',
everybody know who is the big boss," Preacher stated. "You
come tonight and you git you' sticks too."

"What I git sticks for?"

Preacher rose magnificently and shook down his coattails.
The coat had long tails, and one pocket clanked heavily against
the brick wall. Preacher had a moment of panic, explor-

ing the coattail with an expression of dismay. "Ain't broke," he said, relieved. "Brothers, us has one dram for old times' sake. Have a dram, Brother Josuff."

It was raw homemade liquor in the bottle and Josuff drank too deep, strangled and had to be pounded on the back.

"Plain to see you ain't had no dram lately." Preacher tilted the bottle to his own lips. "Brother Henry, explain to the new member about them Freedom sticks."

Brother Henry, ragged and very black, waited for his turn at the bottle. Then he took a dramatic pose. "They gives you four sticks, Br'er Josuff. Painted red."

"What I want with red sticks? How much they cost?"

"They costs you two dollars, but when you see what kin you do wid them sticks you pay ten dollars for 'em. Gladly, brother, gladly."

"No, I ain't. I ain't pay ten dollars for no sticks. I kin cut sticks for myself does I want sticks."

"Not these here sticks, brother—Freedom sticks. You take 'em so—" Brother Henry demonstrated, jabbing an imaginary stick into the ground—"You sticks down one corner, then you walks a fur piece—a fur piece, brother, and sticks you down another stick for a corner. Then you walks way yonder, and when you got four corners marked wid your four sticks then you got prosperity—prosperity, brother."

Josuff still looked unconvinced and baffled. "He ain't know yit what you talkin' about, brother," grumbled the Preacher. "Josuff, does you set them sticks in the ground, all the land what inside them four corners belong to you. Can't no white man, no colored man own it but you. You be rich. You be a landholder and freeholder. Make a crop on that ground, it belong to you. Can't nobody gin a bale nor pick a nubbin."

"Who say so?" demanded Josuff. "Does I go make crop on Mist' Hugh Wade's land, he run me off dis place."

"Mist' Hugh Wade ain't goin' run nobody. Mist' Hugh goin' to be runnin' hisself, us git orginized."

Josuff debated that heresy, inwardly and fearfully. Mister Hugh Wade was an old man too, but he still represented power and authority in Josuff's mind. Did Mister Hugh say "Jump!" a nigger better jump. Josuff's gods could not be toppled so abruptly. That meant confusion and decision, and never in his life had he been permitted a decision of any importance. Freedom had brought too much fear and responsibility, so that already it was a burden on his simple mind. He was torn between admiration and envy of the mouthy brashness of these strangers and a cold terror of them that made all their intentions suspect.

The black grapevine intelligence had not passed Josuff by. He knew that Negroes had been killed mysteriously in the woods, or openly in the towns, and the atavistic intuitiveness of every other black man had smelled the spilled blood. The money in his house seemed terribly in danger, and he had to rest heavily on his feet to keep from breaking into a dead run.

Preacher broke the spell by finishing the bottle and hurling it into the swarming ivy on the wall. "You be to my house, come moonrise, Brother Josuff," he ordered. "You be there. It be to your advantage. Kingdom comin', brother. Praise the Lord!"

He strode away and the two disciples shambled after him in silence. Josuff stood rooted for a long five minutes, not daring to move while they were in sight. Then when the growing corn hid them he shook off the hypnotic numbness that had made his hands cold and sweat run down his legs.

"You mule!" he shouted defiantly, to shatter the oppressive stillness. "You mule—you stand still there, you hyar me?"

The mule, on the upper rise of the meadow, did not lift its head. Its bony tail whacked its hips in wooden rhythms like the pendulum of a clock. Josuff picked up the halter he had dropped in the grass, remembered then and shouted toward the departing visitors. "Done said they cotch that mule!" he stormed, tramping off after the animal. "Mess of lyin' black trash!"

On impulse he returned to the wall, retrieved the bottle out of the tangle, sucked the last drops from it and hurled it, shattering, against the wall. The impact dislodged a brick and from the opening it left, an enterprising blue-tailed lizard thrust his body and explored the soft dust with a scarlet tongue. Josuff threw a rock at it in a frenzy. "You scawpin! You git gone from hyar!"

But the hole in the wall had given him inspiration. No nigger, his native sense told him, would ever go looking for money in a graveyard. He straddled the wall and walked to the unmarked mound where wilting flowers shed their petals. "Miss Florence, she keep my money safe for me," he told the lizard and one curious jay that watched from a cedar bough.

In the meadow again, curiosity and cupidity returned to plague him. He found himself pacing off a breadth of land, setting an imaginary marker to bound it. Doubt and debate fermented within him as he led the slow mule back to the barn. The Freedoms might know about red sticks and nigger making crop on Mist' Hugh Wade's place, but Freedoms and Mist' Hugh Wade were two different kinds of folks. Josuff was in a miserable, chaotic temper when he rubbed the mule down and got the saddle on him. The saddle was dusty from having lain so long in the bottom of the dry cistern and it had to be rubbed off too.

When young Mister Duncan, spruce in a starched white shirt, came out grumbling at the long delay, Josuff had a hard time not to give him a short answer. "Ole mule, he contrary," he grumbled. "Run my laigs off till I cotch him. Too ole for dat, too broke' down. Got to git my rest."

"Go rest then," Duncan snapped, "but get that girth tight

first. I don't want to be thrown, miles from home—not by a damn mule."

"Ought to git you a hoss, Young Boss, and ride like white folks," Josuff suggested impudently.

Duncan threw his gesture of defiance off balance by laughing loudly. "A horse, Josuff? What is a horse? Who owns a horse? General Ulysses S. Grant? General Grant's a great man, Josuff. He set you free. You ought to put his picture up on your cabin wall and bow down to it three times a day. Now, get the hell out of here! Giddap, mule—it's thirty miles to Selma!"

Josuff went, still numb and uneasy, back to his little hut. His bed was tumbled and smelled like a goat's nest, but Josuff was used to that. He sat on it for a few moments, trying to order in his mind the upheaval of his world. Then, in a panic, he jumped up and rushed to the dark corner where he dug at the mortar like a scratching squirrel. A vast shudder of relief ran over him as the bundle came out in his hand. He shut the door, jerked the shutters tight over the one window and made all the wooden bars fast. Then he dumped his hoard out on the bed, piled the coins in stacks and regarded the greenbacks dubiously.

Paper money, he had heard, was no good any more. But he had no idea of tossing this little bundle into the fire as he had seen Mister Hugh Wade do one winter day in the kitchen. He rolled it tightly, wrapped it round and round with a string and tied the whole cache tightly in the rag. Afraid to abandon it for a moment, he opened the door finally and gave a furtive survey to the yard.

At the wooden hopper Louisa was leaching lye, catching the drip in a wooden bucket while Parmy sat, barefooted and half asleep under the magnolia, languidly shelling corn. That meant a hominy boiling, and a boiling of any sort meant toting wood under the sharp goad of Louisa's tongue. Josuff carefully stowed his fortune in his hat and pressed the hat down on his head. He went out boldly and picked a hoe out of the heap of tools in the open shed.

"Brush growin' wild on Miss Florence's grave," he stated. "Got to redd up that place for Miss Florence."

Neither of them looked at him. Louisa shrugged and grunted. Parmy cuffed at a fly. Josuff went through the gate and along the lane feeling taller, more audacious and more secure with every step.

Only the lizard was a witness when he tilted the stone urn on top of the first Hugh Wade's monument, saw the square opening beneath it in the heavier structure of the base. Only the jay bird saw him drop the bundle of money into the square hole and scoop a handful of dirt from the raw grave to cover it. Josuff whistled through his broken teeth as he replaced the heavy urn carefully, so that it sat exactly on the marks where the cement had rotted away.

Then he took a few listless licks at the swarming growth in the enclosure, dropped the hoe on the path and went over the wall to the shade of a huge pecan tree, where he laid himself down with his hat over his face and slept.

X

ROBERT McKEE wiped his fingers on a stiff, dirty apron, looked at his right hand a bit ruefully before he held it out with an eager smile.

"Come in, come in!" he invited. "Sit down here. This cot won't collapse under you. I sleep on it every night." He gave the thin quilt a flirt and two burned matches, a collar button and a handful of tobacco flew off it. "You're young Wade, aren't you? Your father wrote me that you were coming. These meager furnishings are only temporary—at least I hope they are. Fine old gentleman, your father."

"Thanks, I think so myself." Duncan perched cautiously on the edge of the frail-looking cot.

The office of the *Southern Argus* was a corner of an unfinished loft over a drugstore. The desk was a goods box which had been nailed to the wall. A rickety type case leaned in one corner with a filthy towel dangling from a nail. Duncan waited while McKee dumped some trash from a box and straddled it.

"I hope I'm not interrupting anything important," Duncan said then.

"Auction bill. The journeyman printer who sets this stuff is getting over a drunk—just an old habit of journeymen—and the date is getting close, so I was sticking up a few lines myself. Had to whittle out some of the type—I'll show you." He went to the case and brought out a handful of wooden shapes, very black and grimy. "This G is a bit lopsided but it's recognizable. Have to put bold-face type on these bills to satisfy the customers." He sighed and returned the type to the case. "Too many of these auctions now. Too many people taxed out, harried out, selling out for whatever their property will bring and then heading out for Texas."

"Who buys these auctioned properties?" Duncan asked. "Who has any money to buy land now?"

McKee pulled a black, worn pipe from a pocket, got out a limp tobacco sack, filled the pipe and thumbed the tobacco in tightly. "Not you, and not I. Mighty few people who were ever honored citizens of Alabama. Some of the buyers are Northerners out for a bargain—and where can you find a better bargain than black-loam land for five or ten dollars an acre—land that's worth fifty or a hundred? Some of these people are honestly interested in the state and will make good citizens, but a lot are speculators—like some we've got here at home."

"Radicals and Copperheads," Duncan said dryly.

"Not entirely either. There were reputable men in this state who opposed secession, Wade, and as always after the roiling turmoil of a war new economic and social forces emerge. You've heard likely that in '65 the cotton crop in this state sold for forty-five million dollars? That's money in any man's bank."

"Who got the money? Not the planters. I suppose part of it went to pay for the war."

McKee ripped a sulphur match down the wall, nursed the blue flame till it glowed yellow, drew with deep gusty puffs on the pipe. "The percentage of that money that bought shoes for Marse Robert Lee's boys or food to fill their empty guts was appallingly low. Men like your father bought bonds. Others —well, there was a heap of cotton that slipped north after Grant opened up the rivers. The country was full of 'agents.' With transportation almost destroyed, a planter sold where he could for what he could get. The agents had methods of shipping it out, and on the way it was tolled, plucked, short-weighted in other ingenious ways. There was money, there has always been money, but the boys up in Virginia ate parched corn."

"And raw potatoes dug up with a bayonet."

"In wrong hands money can be a power for evil. The planters gave till they were ruined, the speculators grabbed and held on. The same thing happened back in '76 and again in 1812. It will always happen in wars, humanity being the frail and greedy thing that it is. I got a belly wound at Shiloh. I never got strong enough to get back in the fight again. Now I'm so poor I can't even keep my family with me but have to board them with generous friends over at Marion, but I'm dedicated to making this paper survive and pay and become a power in Alabama. I'll have a press some day and good type and a decent chair to sit in. What did you want to see me about?" he asked abruptly. "I'll sell you a five-years' subscription to the *Argus* for five dollars if you've got five dollars."

Duncan laughed. "I've got a lean mule tied out on the common, a little corn he's probably eaten already, and the clothes I sit in."

"The comradeship of ambitious destitution!" McKee laughed. "At least your pants have got a whole seat in them. Fine that poverty is now so universal and patriotic that nobody can look with snobbish disdain on his brother."

There was fire in this young man that made Duncan's blood tingle. He had seen that shining fervor in a few young officers during the last grim year of the war, when courage, unreasoning but indomitable, was about all that the South had left.

"My father wanted me to talk to you. I think he wanted me to be inspired. He thinks that the young men have some kind of a mission in this state and that you are a power in it."

"Question: Are we a state? Andrew Johnson says so, his attitude being that the state never left the Union. But Congress opposes Johnson's attitude and will nullify all his actions. Congress and that stinging adder, Stevens, regard Alabama as a conquered province and all its people as rebels and traitors. Every man who held Southern sympathies will be stripped of his citizenship and all that he owns if Stevens has his way."

"My problem," Duncan said, "is that I can't seem to find myself since I got home. I'm dislocated and confused. You were lucky. You knew exactly what you wanted to do and went at it."

"Yes, I was lucky. The *Times* here took me on when I was able to work again. Then I decided to launch this weekly paper. There were things I could say only under my own masthead. Your trouble, Wade, is that your place in society has abruptly ceased to exist. There's no place for a gentleman's son any more, no horses for him to ride, no slaves to rule—I was going to say no woman for him to marry, but that's not true, thank God! The women have never failed us, they never will. I could say too that the women have never surrendered and probably they'll never do that either."

"We have failed the women," Duncan said. "What have any of our generation got to offer a woman?"

"We offer them mighty tough going, and, God bless 'em, they go along! They've got more courage than we have. You forget that you're no longer occupying a station that allows for elegant gestures. If you've got a girl, marry her and let her take the ragged edge along with you. If she's worth marrying in the first place, she won't whine. My Kentucky gal stuck to me when I was hiding in the hills up in Jefferson County with a price on me, and now I can't even buy her a decent dress, but she's always glad to see me on Sundays."

"You talk like an old man, McKee. You aren't much older than I am."

"When I went to Charleston to the convention that declared for secession I was twenty years old. When I listened to the

harangues in the convention last fall that drafted a new constitution for Alabama, I felt a hundred. Now I feel a little of my
youth returning, I can face a fight ahead—and don't delude
yourself that there isn't going to be a fight, Wade. They're
going to ram Negro suffrage and social equality down our
throats if they have to destroy every court, disfranchise every
white man and trample every tradition and all the pride and
honor we have left. But maybe we young fellows need a fight
—there's a lot to fight against and more to fight for."

"You're pessimistic then, like the old men? You're looking
for military government in Alabama?"

"Well, look what has happened. In January peaceable citizens petitioned Andrew Johnson to remove the troops from
Alabama. The best of the Union Army is mustered out or
killed anyway, and those who've been sent down here to garrison the towns are low-type bounty boys, a lot of them. There
have been violence, looting and an increase in hostile feeling,
but the only action that has been taken by authority is General
Swayne's request that the infantry be replaced by cavalry, his
argument being that infantry was inadequate to control the
situation."

"He'd like us to be ridden down and sabered instead of
being knocked down with the butt of a musket," Duncan said
with dry bitterness.

"Actually I believe Swayne is sympathetic to our problem.
He has said himself that his troops cause as much trouble as
they suppress. But civilian government is bound to be paralyzed
so long as responsible men refuse to take their oath, or to apply
to the President for a pardon."

"My God, am I supposed to beg that illiterate old renegade
to pardon me for fighting for what I believed in?"

"You can't swear that you never aided or supported the
Rebellion. Therefore, according to Congress, you are guilty
of treason, and if you got your just deserts you'd rot in jail.

God, let's talk about something else! Sometimes I get a sickened feeling that the damned Potomac River is flooding Alabama with all the flotsam and filth of intolerance that's floating in it up there. Why the hell can't they leave us alone?" McKee's dark eyes blazed and he strode back and forth in the small space waving his pipe angrily.

"If you put all that in your paper it will probably be suppressed. You say the young fellows have got to fight. Where do we start?"

McKee picked up the smeared auction bill and struck it a flat-handed blow. "We can start here. Stop the exodus of good people from Alabama. What's ahead for them in Texas? Back-breaking, pioneer toil, taming new land, turning furrows in primitive grass that will fight them every foot and defeat them eventually. Unwilling to face hard times at home they're hunting hardship a thousand miles away. Why? Because their pride is hurt, because a lot of them like you can't find themselves in the station that was theirs before the war. That's one job—to sell the South back to her own people before it's taken over by strangers. Money in circulation is what we've got to have. Pay rolls, public works, money in town so the farmer will have a market for what he grows."

"My father said something about your interest in railroads."

"Railroads are our crying need. Open up the country, give us connections with all the ports, north, south, east—give Selma a market for her steel. Selma made good cannon—not one ever burst, we bragged. Selma can make rails and wheels and axles."

"Provided Baltimore or Pittsburgh doesn't bid lower for the order. I worked on the rebuilding of a railroad in Virginia. I was broke, hungry, seemed like a thousand miles from home. They tried working Negroes, vagrants mostly, lost and destitute as I was. I could understand them, but the Yankee engineers couldn't. All the steel that went into the job came from the North and Union officers gave the orders. Why wouldn't that happen here?"

"Because," said McKee, "if we build a road we'll build it ourselves—the farmers, the planters, the men who own timber in the hills. I think Patton would go along and put the state behind us. We ought to call a meeting in your county pretty soon, get a lot of men together, sell them the idea, get the state to endorse bonds and get some money moving—or at least some credit pried loose. Anything that looks like positive action will jar this region out of its apathy of despair."

"Any men who would go along—men the people will trust?"

"The men they called the 'precipitators' at the convention last year? There's Elmore and General Clanton. Clanton and Elmore are able, honest men. Clanton has already given Andy Johnson some plain talk and he's not a fire-eater like Alex White. White inspires men, but he inflames them too—and what we need is to have them forget their hostilities."

"Anything I can do?" asked Duncan.

"Every man can do something. We'll need rights of way from the Tennessee River to the Gulf. Timber for crossties and teams to handle them."

"Our old mule is mighty feeble." Duncan laughed.

"Every mule will count. Laborers too. Now me—I can write. I can write a speech, but I can't deliver one that anybody would listen to. So I'm concentrating on building up circulation for the *Argus*. If we can ever get the mails moving regularly again—that's another reason for rebuilding the railroads— and fast freight, shipping space for cattle so they won't walk their weight off before they get to market . . ."

"I won't have a dollar till the cotton is ginned and sold, McKee, and a penniless man is paralyzed in any situation. I may not have a dollar then if they steal all the crop."

"Why aren't there a few thinkers in Washington—men who have the sense to realize that they're robbing themselves when they loot the South? Can't they see that the planters will come to realize that they're fools to plant at all? But it's bound to pass, Wade—everything passes. Alabama was never wealthy as some states count wealth, but her people ate, they asked no favors, they led a good amiable life. Now that life is gone, but we can't let carping irritation poison a whole population. We've got to put a healthy thing in place of what we had—work in place of leisure, energy instead of lassitude. Sounds like raving, doesn't it?"

"More like editorializing, McKee. We're not afraid of work. My father is an old man and he's got blisters on his hands from the hoe. But when your mule is old, and the harness rotten and half your land grown to sprouts, it takes a lot of words to keep your optimism alive."

McKee slapped him on the shoulder. "You're right, of course. I get carried away by my own enthusiasms. Look here —you need shoes. I've got a pair back here—traded them in on a deal. Let's see if they'll fit you. . . ."

"McKee, for God's sake!" Duncan protested desperately.

"Wait now, don't be an arrogant fool. I'm selling them to you if you can wear 'em. Take your note. Pay me later. I need you. Too many of our young fellows didn't come back. Twenty thousand widows in this state—young ones, most of them. I've got the shoes hid back here—man can get shot these days for a good pair of shoes. You won't be a damn' bit of use to the state barefooted, Wade." McKee dragged a rusty little tin trunk out of a corner.

"A pair of shoes is worth twenty dollars in Demopolis," Wade reminded him.

"These are secondhand. Could be stolen. Can't say, these days. Took them in payment for an auction bill. Here, stick your feet in them."

There was no gainsaying McKee because there was no offense in him. Duncan unbuckled his sad, patched footwear that had known so many weary miles.

"Having spent most of the last five years afoot, my feet are spread like a field hand's," he said ruefully. "There's mighty little of the gentleman left of me now."

"But the man is still intact. Gentlemen we can do without. In fact, a few of these die-hards who hold onto their elegance, obstructing change, fighting progress, we could gladly spare. Ha, they do fit! A trifle large, but they won't cramp or blister. You're not riding back tonight? That's too long a trip for a tired mule."

"No, I'm staying with some friends of my family—the Goldsbys. I'll ride home tomorrow, but first I'll give you my note for these shoes."

"Oh, yes, old Tom Goldsby of the Fourth Alabama. Tom would make a good leader—we've got to get him to come forward. Plenty of men to follow but few to lead. Those shoes cost me two dollars, by the way. Take your word you'll pay me when you can. Never mind signing anything."

Duncan tied the last lace, scowling grimly. "I'll pay you ten, McKee, or I won't have them at all."

"All right, we won't argue. Keep your stiff pride unblemished. At least that's one thing they can't levy taxes on. They're trying to beat it out of us, but they'll never succeed. Can you walk or must you take two steps before the doggone things start moving?"

Duncan strode across the room. "They go all right, first solid leather I've had underfoot since I got that old pair off a boy who wouldn't need shoes any more."

"Hiding up in the hills I went through a winter without shoes. So I know what the lack of footgear does to a man's spirit. Well, good-by, Wade. Talk to your father about this railroad business and I'll come over into your county soon."

"Come and eat greens with us. Louisa dishes up a nice mess of poke salad and hominy."

"Nothing better, with a hot pone of bread to go with it."

"Thanks again, McKee." Duncan clasped his hand, went down the wooden stairs, the shoes making a mighty clatter. In the street the heat struck like a blow and he pulled off the heavy coat. His new shirt was already damp and clinging to his shoulders. The stiff collar rode high, reminding him that his hair needed cutting. He wondered, as he untied the mule and folded the coat over the saddle, if old Josuff knew also how to cut hair.

XI

TOM GOLDSBY did his best to persuade Duncan not to start home the next morning.

"That mule will fall down on you before you've gone half-way. You let me feed him up and rest him today, and you stay over and talk to some of the boys. Bob McKee's all right, but he does go a bit radical now and then. Thinks Andy Johnson and Grant have got good intentions toward Alabama, but hell, young Wade, anybody with clear sight knows that ain't so! Look what's happened already. Even if they've got the best intentions in the world, they're helpless against a hostile Congress. Patton—what's he? Just a figurehead governor set up to fool people. Make us think we've got a government of our own when any ten-year-old boy knows he's just a paper man. One match, one incident, and the whole state government goes up in smoke. And there are a hundred men itching to drag that match down the seat of their breeches."

"I'll nurse the mule along, take it slow. Give me a few ears of corn and I'll make it home," Duncan insisted.

He had heard too much talk already, he was thinking. His mind was cloudy with it and he wanted to be alone, to clarify it, to get an orderly view of his own situation and search out the angles for some sort of future.

Goldsby wanted to talk about the Fourth Alabama and fight over all the battles of the war, but Duncan had been sick of the war for a long time. He had, he suspected, been sick of it since the beginning. With a kind of wooden doggedness he had ridden and fought and seen men killed, he had hidden and starved and slipped away to fight again, hating it all, wanting only to battle through, get it over, get the nightmare of death and noise and fear and stinks behind him.

There was fog lying low over the town and the fields when he rode out of Selma. There were still plenty of signs of the terrible destruction that Wilson's army had inflicted on the town. Houses still had windows out, patched with shingles or tow sacks nailed over. There were houses without chimneys and chimneys without houses. Broken crockery and furniture half burned lay in the weeds along the streets. In a vacant lot a church bell lay belly up like a tragic empty vessel, the rotting ropes with which it had been dragged down still tied to it.

What had been a bank was now a boarded-up shell with auction bills tacked to the planks that blinded it. A fire-gutted church still pointed a blackened spire toward the sky like a shaky finger calling the attention of God to the crimes of His creatures.

I helped do things like this, Duncan was thinking with incredulous bitterness. I rode with men who worked desolation and ravage on towns like this. How could they now face the primitive problem of survival, men who had been caught up in a wild surge of violence, made dramatic by bugles and the deep-throated roar of guns? Wars should go on forever or never be at all. There was too much shock in the readjustment. So peace was the enemy. This was the rebellion road. It had been splendor marching down that road. It was humiliation and agony returning.

The mule shambled slowly but patiently. The awful patience of mules had been an unspoken heroism of the war. A horse caught the spirit of combat, but a mule didn't give a damn. He just kept going till a cannon ball gutted him or his legs folded under him.

Noon was hot and high and Duncan had gone some sixteen

miles when he came to a wooded stretch where buffalo flies swarmed up from the bushes. The mule stamped and jerked his head and tail. When he saw the four Negroes and one filthy white man lying under a tree Duncan was glad that Tom Goldsby had made him fetch a pistol along.

The five sprawled half asleep, ragged hats pulled over their eyes, but they came to life as he rode near, got to their feet and stared at him.

" 'Tain't him," the white man muttered.

Duncan kept on going. Abreast of the group he saw that one Negro was a former slave on the Wade place, a very tall coffee-colored Dahomey boy named Prince. He called, "Howdy, Prince, what you doing out here?"

Prince shuffled nearer, stood sullenly, yellowish eyes guarded and hostile. "Ain't doin' nothin', Mist' Duncan. Waitin' for the captain."

"What captain?"

"Yankee captain—name of sergeant."

"Why are you waiting for a Yankee sergeant? You in the army now, Prince?"

"No, suh. Yes, suh—sergeant goin' pay us. He say come hyar this mornin' and us git paid."

"What's he paying you for? Union headquarters are in Demopolis. You'd have to go there to get paid."

"Sergeant, he say not to come to no headquarters," put in the white man. "He said for us to wait right here."

"Who're you? You in the army too?" asked Duncan.

"No, I ain't in no army. Who I am is my own business, Mister."

"What did you boys steal for this sergeant that you're going to get paid for?" Duncan kept his voice amiable, but he was grateful for the weight of the gun at his belt.

"Ain't stole nothin'. Us gittin' paid for marchin'," Prince said.

"Been drilling nights in the woods, have you? Don't you know the Yanks are fooling you boys? You won't get any pay and you're mighty likely to get shot."

The white man came nearer, a menacing glare in his eyes. "That's a lot of Rebel talk, Mister. You-all ain't runnin' things no more. You snotty Rebels don't amount to nothing around here now."

"Aw, knock him loose from that-there mule!" yelled a very black man.

Duncan held the gun ready, gave the mule a kick in a tender spot. The animal lashed out with both hind feet almost unseating Duncan, but he held on and fired into the ground near the white man's feet. "Get going, you scum!" he ordered. "Next time I won't miss."

They backed away as the mule snorted and circled still kicking out wildly. Suddenly all five dived into the bushes and disappeared as a carriage rounded the fork of the road. It was a handsome carriage drawn by two fat bay horses and Duncan had difficulty sawing the mule into obedience and pulling him off to the side of the road. The carriage stopped and a woman's voice called to him. "Duncan! Duncan Wade!"

She sat on the rear seat of the vehicle, beside a dark, round-faced little man with a jaunty mustache, who held a shotgun across his knees. Juliet!

Duncan felt sudden anger that she had overtaken him riding a mule. The carriage was driven by a white man in livery, a thin man with a set, sallow face and ugly, contemptuous eyes. Duncan took off his hat, bowed briefly and said, "Good morning, Mrs. Destrade."

"Duncan, I heard a shot," she persisted.

"Vermin," he said dryly. "The woods are full of them. Rats and snakes all along this road."

There was a faint stir in the bushes, but the outlaws did not

show themselves. Duncan was satisfied that neither the blacks
nor the white scalawag was armed.

"Duncan, this is my husband, Mr. Destrade." Duncan ac-
knowledged the introduction with a nod. Destrade bowed
suavely. "Duncan is one of our neighbors," Juliet explained.

"You will ride along with us, sir?" asked Destrade. "Mrs.
Destrade is nervous—though I am a very good shot with this
weapon."

"I happen to be going your way." Duncan was not too
gracious, the old obstinacy stiffening him. "But my mule would
not keep up with your team, Mr. Destrade."

"We'll make Andrew drive slowly," Juliet said. "Duncan,
I know what: You can tie the mule behind and ride in here
with us. It will be more comfortable for you."

"I'm sorry, Mrs. Destrade, but this beast would balk. He
wouldn't lead. He'd break the bridle, and we can't afford to
lose a mule."

"Couldn't you tie him somewhere and send someone after
him later?"

Destrade laughed indulgently. "My angel, Mr. Wade knows
that if he abandoned that mule even for a few moments, he
would never see the animal again. Drive on, Andrew, and try
not to leave Mr. Wade too far behind. Just what breed of
vermin did you kill back there, Mr. Wade?"

"The same breed that infests this whole country. Unfortunately I didn't kill anything. There was a covey of five, but
they seemed to be without fangs or teeth."

Destrade's small, dark eyes twinkled. "A great pleasure to
draw the fangs and teeth of such reptiles," he said slowly.
Obviously he was translating his thoughts from another language—French, Duncan assumed. He had the look of a Creole.
"We have drawn many fangs in New Orleans this year. I have
seen them piled in wagons like cordwood, very harmless. This—"

he patted the gun in his lap—"speaks the only language they all understand. Even a man with gold braid on his sleeve understands this language. We shall keep on making ourselves heard in that language in Louisiana. We shall be quite sure that the arrogant ones know that we may be beaten, but that we are not conquered."

"Please," begged Juliet, "let's not speak of horrible things this morning. Mr. Destrade has been telling me ghastly stories all the way from the Athols' plantation, Duncan. If we have grisly times like that in Alabama I shall simply die."

"You will have such times in Alabama, I fear, my dear. You will bow down to your conquerors and your former slaves unless you are more clever than they or resist with violence."

"And don't speak of violence! We had nothing else for years and years. Our poor little Jule!"

The mule, inspired by the company of the team, trotted alongside the carriage, keeping a steady pace. The white driver looked around irritably every time he had to slow the horses, and his rigid body was eloquent with disgust at the whole arrangement. Once when he muttered under his breath Destrade answered him with a blast of quick, angry French.

Juliet said, "How do you happen to be riding back from Selma, Duncan?"

"I had business over there. I rode over yesterday—started the day before actually—but I was late getting away, so I spent the night with the Emerts."

"In that overseer's house? Mr. Destrade, their lovely home was burned to the ground . . . by Yankee soldiers."

"And looted," Duncan added. "Mrs. Emert hasn't any sheets, and all her china was smashed deliberately. She said Wilson's soldiers amused themselves hurling her dishes at the chimney while she stood helplessly watching. They had beaten Emert over the head and tied him to a tree."

"We were so fortunate!" Juliet sighed. "Duncan, we'll be

at home by suppertime and you must stop and have supper with us."

"By all means," Destrade agreed quickly. "You can tell us what the situation is in Selma. I have heard that town was beaten into the ground."

"Wilson's troops found some barrels of whisky that Bedford Forrest hadn't had time to destroy. They went mad, so the Goldsbys said, burned half the town, killed all the horses and mules, committed pretty foul atrocities."

"Please, Duncan! I can't listen to it any more! And you must come to supper, Duncan."

Duncan had started to refuse stiffly, but abruptly the rigidity in him relaxed. Something curious was happening to him. Like the blowing out of a candle he discovered that he was being cured of the old, tormenting ache for Juliet. He had thought himself cured in those grim days after he had torn up her letter, but since he had come home and knew that she was near the old dreams had returned to confuse and weaken him. Now, all at once, she was merely another handsome woman in a black silk dress with a smart little bonnet hiding her hair.

"I will be honored," he said. "Thank you for the invitation." He let the mule fall a few paces behind then, wondering why he had been so impulsive. But the change in his own feelings was definite. Now he had noticed that her eyebrows were arrogant, that her mouth though delicate was a trifle cruel. How had he ever deluded himself into believing that she had a heart? How had he ever been foolish enough to believe her in love with him, though restrained and made reserved by his youth?

This was a chance too, perhaps, to find out what Julian Villerand was up to, what plans he had, if any, what help he expected from the Union with his projects. McKee would want to know how far Villerand had gone, and whether Congress was taking any action on any of his propositions.

Also—and here Duncan put a stern bridle on his thoughts

—he would see Marian again. He told himself that he was not even sure that he wanted to see her. He had tried to thrust the teasing image of her from his thoughts, sometimes reproachfully reminding himself that it was callous not to feel sentimentally about a girl who had flatly announced that she meant to marry him; sometimes indulgently amused by the spoiled, imperious young thing who took a fancy to things and decided instantly that she must have them. Already, very likely, she was dreaming dreams about that Yankee lieutenant who had knocked a soldier flat on her account.

At the county line the carriage halted, the driver got down and tied the team to a tree, slipped their bits and brought out a sack of grain from beneath the front seat.

"We will have lunch here, Wade," Destrade said, as Duncan rode up beside the carriage. "Feed your animal and join us—but keep your weapon handy."

"Mrs. Goldsby gave me a lunch," Duncan said. "I'll wait for you under the tree yonder."

"You'll do no such thing," Juliet protested. "Mr. Destrade had this enormous hamper packed for us at the Athols'. Get the hamper out, Andrew. Do help me down, Mr. Destrade. My feet are both sound asleep."

The white driver laid out the lunch on a clean cloth and retired to a shady spot a little way off with the food Destrade doled out to him. Duncan tied the mule, gave him the corn Tom Goldsby had supplied, accepted a leg of the roast chicken Destrade deftly dismembered, a cold roll and some cheese. Casually he wondered as he ate how the Athols happened to have chickens to roast. Applegate's and Canby's troops must have passed by the Athol place. Duncan did not sit on the grass as Juliet urged, nor did he drink any of the wine Destrade brought out.

He declined it with a short laugh. "One of us had better keep a clear head, and I haven't had a drink since before the surrender—not since some of our fellows broke into a saloon up on the Rappahannock."

"Was it very dreadful up there in Virginia, Duncan?" Juliet had spread her silk skirts gracefully and waited to be served by her husband.

"It was war," Duncan answered, trying not to attack the chicken too hungrily. Five years since he had tasted chicken. A sharp nostalgia struck him like a sudden pain. His mother's table, snowy, shining with silver. Rich tempting smells drifting in from the kitchen where Louisa wielded her basting spoon. Lemuel in his white coat muttering orders at the small Negro boys who flourished fly brushes. The memory burned poignantly, burned out in the quick fire of anger.

So much that was good and lovely senselessly destroyed! At home now his father was no doubt patiently eating the everlasting hominy and corn bread, washing them down with cistern water. And here sat Felix Destrade, untouched apparently by the war, a fat complacent little man pouring wine into a tin cup, smiling as Juliet sipped at it and made a pretty face.

"You think it too strong, my love? Those heavy wines from Portugal have rich body and fine bouquet. You still do not wish to imbibe, Wade?"

"I might get drunk and useless," Duncan said, regretfully tossing a bone away. "Those men I encountered this morning were unarmed, but they could be waiting for somebody not so harmless . . . somebody they called the sergeant. Go easy on alcohol, Mr. Destrade, and let's not linger here too long."

"You are frightening the lady, Wade—" Destrade put away the bottle—"but alas, you are probably most right! Water the horses, Andrew; we still have some miles to go."

"How lucky that we met you, Duncan," Juliet murmured as she helped her back into the carriage. "I'm not frightened at all with my two brave men to protect me." She gave Felix's arm a gentle pat.

The fat little man beamed at her and settled himself with the gun again across his knees.

"You are quite safe, my dove," he said. "Andrew is armed too." As the carriage moved forward he added, "This is like the old time, Wade. I have heard my *maman* tell of the Indians, and how even the ladies wore pistols at their waists when they traveled."

"But how silly for us to need to be fearful now!" Juliet said. "The war is over. True, some of our people have run off, but they'd come back in a minute, I know, if the stupid Yankees hadn't addled their brains with lies. Well, if our 'Phrony ever comes back I'll have her sent straight to the field, the miserable little thief!"

"My dear, I fear you will never see your 'Phrony again. We must accept our lives as they are now; we must not look back."

"One of those boys who stopped me this morning was a former slave of my father—a fine hand with horses," Duncan said, "and I think, Juliet, that another was one of your father's hands. I couldn't be certain. Five years is a long time to remember. There was a white man with them, a dirty rascal with a mean eye."

"If I had seen them, I'd have shamed them all and ordered them to go home where they belong," Juliet stated complacently, pulling on her lace mitts. "You should have told your boy to get straight back to his horses, Duncan."

He laughed and Destrade joined in, giving his wife an indulgent pat on the cheek. "The dear astonishing creatures!" Destrade said. "They would have ended the war early, Wade. They would have simply told the Yankees to go straight home."

"I," said Duncan, "was most concerned at keeping Prince and his ruffians from knocking me out of the saddle and taking this mule. And it would have been no use telling him to go back to his horses, Juliet—there are no horses!"

XII

"SO YOU'VE BEEN over to Selma?" Julian sat like a red-headed Buddha at the head of his table, round little belly pushed hard against the board. "What's happening over there? Are they getting back on their feet again? Any rebuilding going on?"

"Very little." Duncan felt out of place in this handsome room, at a table set with silver and glass, soft light falling from a prismed lamp hung overhead, flowers in a crystal bowl. He was unhappily aware that his shirt was dirty, that he had brought a mule smell into the room with him, along with the hair that clung to his pants.

The big platter of ham on the table, the hot rolls and butter were part of that old time which was past and gone—but not past in the Villerand house, obviously. There was an angry resentment in him that he fought against, but it pushed past his guard as he cut into a pink slice of ham.

"How did you keep them from raiding your smokehouse, Mr. Villerand?" he asked bluntly.

Villerand frowned, sensing some vague hidden insult, then laughed. "We were raided often enough, but when I built this house—back in '37, that was—there were still wandering Indians whom Jackson hadn't forced to go west; also there were white outlaws who followed the wagon trains. So I built some good hiding places. They came in handy when the Yankees overran the county. I even hid the girls in them one time."

"Dusty . . . cobwebs . . . horrible!" Juliet shuddered.

"All we had was a dry cistern," Duncan said, "but they managed to store my mother's silver and my saddle in it. I wondered after I came home how it happened that none of our own people came back and raided it. They must have known about it."

"I still think our people would be loyal to us if they were let alone," Emma said. "I believe they would even defend us if we needed defending. I know Cassius wouldn't let any harm come to us. You'd defend us, wouldn't you, Cassius?"

Cassius waited a breath before he replied, and Duncan saw the man's yellow eyes shift and his thin-lipped mouth straighten. "Yes'm," he said finally.

"I reckon you saw Tom Goldsby and young McKee," Villerand went on. "I got a copy today of that sorry little paper McKee prints. It was a week old. Never will get the mail running on time again, looks like. Must be using ox teams, the time it takes to have a letter delivered."

"That will improve when we get the railroads rebuilt," Duncan launched boldly.

"We've got railroads—and they're all starving to death." Villerand snorted. "Know how much the Alabama & Florida Railroad collected in fares last year? Thirteen dollars! One hundred and sixty miles from Montgomery to Mobile, and they sold thirteen dollars' worth of tickets."

"People haven't got money to ride the trains," Duncan said.

"I travel by boat." Destrade sugared his coffee heavily. "To New York I go by boat. No smoke and no discomfort. Ah yes, you say—very slow. But what is time compared to comfort?"

"Up here there aren't any boats," Duncan said. "They were piled up on the banks all along the rivers as I came down. Stove in and burned."

"Maybe we ought to build some boats." Villerand wa

speaking carefully—evadingly, Duncan knew. "Fetch some more rolls, Cassius. Can't you see the dish is empty?"

"I'm sorry, Mr. Villerand," Emma said hastily. "I was listening and not attending to my duty."

"Good idea, building some boats," said Villerand. "Got the timber up in the hills. Got enough idle Negroes around to build a thousand of 'em. I reckon they're still making boilers in Baltimore or Pittsburgh or some place."

"The rivers are silting in. You'd have to have dredges as well as engines. I thought you were interested in railroads, Mr. Villerand."

"Everybody's talking railroads. That paper of McKee's got a long editorial in it. Build 'em ourselves, he says. Where's the capital coming from? The state's busted, most of the banks are out of business, there's no place to sell bonds nearer than Europe, and I had the word of General Swayne that nobody up north would touch a piece of Alabama paper no matter what was behind it. And with a railroad that wasn't even built there'd be nothing behind it—just hope. Nobody's got money to invest in hope, these times."

Definitely, Duncan was certain, Villerand was talking around the question; definitely he was covering up something.

He laughed dryly. "Hope," he said, "is about all most of us have left nowadays."

"I have never ridden on a railroad train." Emma obviously sensed the impasse, changed the subject deftly. "I'm sure it must be very dirty, all the smoke and sparks and cinders. When I was married and came to Alabama we went from Charleston to Mobile by sailing ship. I was dreadfully ill all the way. I'm sure Mr. Villerand got very bored with me."

"Nonsense! It was a rough trip . . . hurricane season. I was glad to get off that ship myself. Anyway, you weren't very well when we started. . . ."

"Mr. Villerand—if you please!" Emma colored, embarrassed.

"Well, that was September and Juliet was born right after New Year's," he persisted.

"Your daughters are present, Mr. Villerand," his wife said reprovingly.

"Mama," Juliet began hurriedly, "Mr. Destrade has been telling me how dreadful things are in New Orleans now. I told him I was simply terrified to go back there when he is off on a trip. Do you and Papa mind if I stay here until September?"

"Good God, no!" Villerand boomed, but was silenced by a quick little gesture from his wife.

"We are always delighted to have our child with us, Mr. Destrade," she said graciously. "You are very generous to share her so often. Are you going far away?"

"To Canada, belle-mère. Our markets up there are—how you say?—busted. Why should they drink Irish whisky when we make much better? My little Juliet, she is frightened because our Negroes aspire to rule us in Louisiana and to stop that we must do a little shooting. And my Maman—Juliet is a little frightened of Maman also."

Juliet flushed. "Really I'm not, Mr. Destrade. But 'tis very lonely without you."

"I do not scold you, my love. Me—I am a bit frightened of Maman, myself. I am born very long after my three sisters, Wade, so I have four mothers—all very strong in the mind."

Emma rose then, nodding to her daughters, and Duncan felt a pull at his arm. "Come along," Marian whispered in his ear. "Come along, Duncan."

He made a little bow to the other Villerands and followed Marian out of the room. "I must go," he began, "and first I must thank your mother and father for their hospitality."

She twisted a fold of his sleeve in her fingers. "Don't go.

It's awfully dark. Let your mule rest and sleep here tonight."

"Sorry, Miss Villerand. I must get along home. It's only a mile across the fields."

"I told you to call me Maggie. Why are you so stubborn, Duncan? You might be friendly with your neighbors."

"I have been friendly. I've eaten your salt."

She did not let go his sleeve but maneuvered him into the empty parlor. Another lamp burned there, glowing softly through a silk shade. "Sit down in here till Mama comes. She has to attend to the food and lock up everything."

Duncan obeyed reluctantly, perching on the edge of a sofa. Marian sat down beside him. "Juliet," she said, "made all that up!"

"About being afraid in New Orleans? Maybe she is afraid. From what Destrade said things are ugly down there."

"Oh, no—not New Orleans. She made it up about wanting to visit the Athols. She made Felix drive her over yesterday. She knew you were in Selma. Cassius knew and so did Lelia. They know everything. Juliet just wanted to ride back today with you."

"You're letting your imagination run away with you, Miss Maggie. Juliet isn't interested in me. Even if she were, her husband was along. It was merely an accident that they overtook me."

"I don't believe it was an accident. Now she'll beg you to come again—you'll see. She may even ride over to your house and beg you. Papa and Felix are leaving tomorrow for Boston or some other place up north. Oh, she'll have an excuse! She'll say Mama is afraid with nobody but Cassius and Tuby and the field hands. We don't even have an overseer any more. Mr. Simpson enlisted in the Union Army—to get the bounty, Papa said."

Duncan rose and buttoned his coat. "This is all ridiculous," he said impatiently, "and you must consider me a person of little honor if you think I can be seduced by a married woman."

She flushed. Words of such bold meaning were not spoken in the hearing of the Villerand daughters. "I never said that! I said only that she'd try anything—and she will, Duncan. She'll try to keep you in love with her for the rest of your life, and you're a fool if you let her do it!"

"I haven't been in love with Juliet—not for a long time," he said. Not for hours, at least. "I never expect to be in love with another man's wife."

"But Felix might be killed! They're going on the boat from Mobile. The boat might blow up and sink. Boats do blow up." She was almost tearful in her earnestness. Duncan felt a tinge of irritation, but it was touched with compassion for her, so intense, so sheltered, so naïvely ignorant and so sincere in her young intensity.

"Also," he said, lightly touching her hand, "I might be thrown and killed on the way home, there might be earthquakes in Alabama or the Republicans might decide suddenly that the way to get rid of the secessionists is to shoot all of us against a wall—something they'd no doubt be happy to do. Why get all worked up about things that never happen? What if Juliet did flirt a little, a long time ago? It was all very young and very innocent."

"It wouldn't be innocent now. It would be deadly, and I won't have it!" she cried. "She's not going to make you fall in love with her again so you can't fall in love with me! You are going to—oh, yes you are!"

"Hush!" he ordered, his face red. "You don't know what you're saying, Maggie. You'll be embarrassed tomorrow."

"I will not! I will not!"

Emma Villerand came in then, to Duncan's relief. "What are you two children quarreling about?" she asked.

Duncan steadied his breath with an effort. "Miss Marian thinks I shouldn't ride home tonight. Of course you realize, Mrs. Villerand, that I have to go."

"But is there any danger? It has been very quiet around here for a long time."

"I wouldn't think so, but my father would be uneasy if I didn't come. Anyhow, I've spent a good many nights riding in the dark when there was nothing else but danger. May I thank you for your hospitality now and be on my way?"

"Of course. I'll have Tuby bring your horse around."

"You mean my mule." He laughed.

"A mule," remarked Emma with her gift for putting people at ease, "is more dependable and not so excitable as a horse. You were wise to ride a mule."

He said, "Good-by, Miss Maggie," and held out his hand.

She tossed her head and flashed her eyes at him. "You won't always laugh at me, Duncan Wade!" she said furiously and whirled out of the room.

"My poor child!" Emma sighed. "There are so many of them—these bewildered young girls, cheated by war. Fifty thousand young men will never come back to Alabama—and, among them, my boy!"

"I'm sorry, Mrs. Villerand. Jule and I were good friends."

"His name was never on any list, but after General Maury met that bitter defeat we never heard from him. And he did not come back. Wait here, Duncan. I'll have your animal brought around."

"Thank you—and will you say good-by to the others for me?"

"Of course. Mr. Villerand and Mr. Destrade are in the library studying maps over their brandy. They expected you to join them, I think."

"I'd better be on my way, if you will make my excuses."

All the way home across the fields Duncan was uneasy. He

had acted in a cavalier fashion toward Marian, he suspected. Why did he have a perverse urge to oppose her in everything? he wondered. It might be the innate desire of every man to be the pursuer, not the pursued. She was lovely, she had been well reared, she was in every way desirable. He could fall in love with her perhaps if she would retreat in modesty and let him make the advances. Somebody ought to tell her—but what more could he say, in all honor, than he had said already?

If some other man came along, he would probably find himself racked with jealousy. He had known a small flash of it when she had lauded the gallantry of that Yankee lieutenant.

Then, halfway through the weedy meadow, he had an uneasy feeling that he was being followed. The sky was full of stars, but there was no moon and every bush and tree made a darker blot on the summer darkness. His flesh began to crawl between his shoulder blades as of old when he had slipped through the Union lines on scout, and he caught himself sniffing the air, which was an old cautious habit. Men who were fearful, men who skulked, always had an odor about them. Animals sensed it, but the mule slogged along wearily, too tired to be alert as a horse would have been.

Duncan remembered the gray horse he had ridden out of Winchester on a black rainy night when the Valley was lost in mist and the sour old Massanutten Mountains breathed chill gusts from their foggy summits. He had discovered the creeping Union patrol by the nervous flick of the gray's ears, and the twitching of his hide. There had been three of them, and he had not killed them because his mission was to get through unseen and unheard. A shot would have brought a whole reconnoitering squad down on him. He had got past, the gray slipping through the brushy copse on tiptoe like a deer. Now he was glad he had not killed them. He had killed too many men. Sometimes he felt that the odor of death must go with him wherever he went, and when he looked into the mirror the grimness of it looked out at him from his eyes.

People, decent and peaceful people, should be repelled by a man who had dealt in carnage for so long, but death and horror were familiars now. There was no more shrinking in men's minds; there was only a feverish anxiety for survival. And with women it seemed that there was only an eagerness to forget all that was tragic and reach out eagerly for whatever brightness remained. Like the little Villerand. Her young insistencies had a root in the febrile atmosphere of the times.

Somehow, he had to set in order his feelings about her. He gave her credit for rousing him a little from what had been a troubling apathy. Like all planter's sons he had been raised in pride and vanity. Fierce resentments, haste to take offense, violent tempers were bred into his class. It was knowing how absurd and useless this attitude to life was now that had filled him with self-doubt and an angering sort of abjectness, as foreign as the sorry clothes he wore.

Heroes of the war were all pathetic now, and lost. Blue and gray alike faced the end of glory, a glory that was being beaten to death by the stony blows of circumstance. He told himself grimly that Maggie Villerand was too shielded to know what love is. Then the voice of sense argued that love is not of age or of reason. Could it be because he had fallen in love with her a little that he was so instantly on guard with her, so stubbornly determined to save her from herself? He worried at these thoughts unhappily, till suddenly the mule's ears shot upright and the animal stopped in its tracks.

They had passed the yard gate of the Wade place and the barn was a black bulk ahead. And something was moving near that barn. It might be Parmy, waiting to feed and stable the mule, but Parmy would step out boldly. He would not drop and hide in the shadow of the building as this figure dropped and hid.

Duncan slid the pistol out of the holster, dropped from the saddle and left the mule to amble toward its stall. Quietly, keeping to the shadows, Duncan approached the barn holding the gun ready. Suddenly in front of him yawned the gaping hole. The cistern!

It was open, the heavy wooden lid thrown aside, and down there was his mother's silver. And he like a fool had blurted out the secret of the Wades' hiding place at the Villerand table!

He skirted it, sensing movement ahead, stood trying to pierce the darkness, waiting. The hiding figure waited too.

"Come out of there!" Duncan yelled. "Stand up. Come out of there before I fire."

Abruptly there was a scurry, and he smelled the effluvium of fear again—Negroid fear—and with it a hot imminence of hate. He whirled about as a dark figure hurled itself at him with a clubbed length of plank held high. He ducked swiftly when the club descended, struck a down blow with his heavy gun, heard a gulping groan as the attacking shape sagged. Then that shape wrestled and clawed at him, gasping fetid breath, struggling to drag the weapon from his hand. Duncan parried, kneed and twisted mechanically. This had all happened before. This was like a bad dream returning, fury and conflict, the desperate battling hate of a man in fear of death.

His assailant was a black man, tall and sinewy. Duncan jerked his arm loose, brought the pistol down hard on a skull that rang like a bell. He did not want to shoot, still thinking it might be Parmy, gone beserk in a sudden spell of idiocy. Then the Negro pulled free and ran, crashing off into the shielding blackness. Duncan fired twice after him but missed, heard running feet as the prowler fled. Then a light came, bobbing across the yard, and he saw his father's knees and old shoes in the pale lantern glow.

Quickly he stepped out where he could be seen. "Missed him, sir."

"Good Lord, it's you! I heard shots."

"You heard shots and came out here unarmed—and carrying a light so they could spot you without trouble. You'd get well cussed out, sir, for that recklessness in General Johnston's army." He laughed to draw the sting from the reprimand, took the lantern from Hugh Wade's shaking hand. "Look here." He led the way to the open cistern. "I got home just in time to flush a thief away from the family vault."

They stood side by side looking down into the opening where there was a tumble of straw and cornstalks. Duncan held the lantern low. "I don't know if he got down in there. Anyway, he hid against the barn when I came up."

Hugh Wade chuckled. "He wouldn't have got anything but a shirt full of chaff. Louisa and I took the silver out day before yesterday. You know how they are—get a feeling that something's wrong, and, by gad, it's usually true! Louisa didn't trust Parmy."

"I'm quite sure it wasn't Parmy. Too light-skinned—and I know Parmy's smell. Don't tell me where you put the silver, sir." He could not bring himself to admit to his father that he had blabbed like an ass in the house of his father's enemy.

"We got it hid. I sent Parmy and Josuff up to cut sprouts in the fence row while we took it out. I got down there with the ladder, but I wasn't sure I'd ever come out again." Hugh gave the wooden cover a kick. "Ought to have shoved him in, put this lid on and the grindstone on top of it."

Duncan wrestled the heavy lid back, then stooped for something that glittered on the littered ground. "Left his medal," he remarked, holding a flat circle of brass close to the light.

"Now what the devil is that?" his father demanded.

"Some kind of homemade badge. Got 'Union Patrol' stamped on it, pounded in by hand with a chisel, looks like."

"I've seen those things on some colored boys in town. Yanks

hand 'em out for a joke, I reckon. Make the poor boys feel important."

They walked toward the house.

"I had supper at Villerand's," Duncan said. "I got overtaken by Juliet and her husband and she invited me. They had meat on the table and all their silver set out."

"They wouldn't bother Villerand," Hugh Wade said.

"He's going north tomorrow."

"So I heard. Going after some Northern money, Hod Horning thinks—going to build a railroad."

"But he talked against railroads tonight. Said the ones that were operating weren't earning a dollar."

"Yes," said Hugh Wade, "yes—he would. You were there. You've been to Selma. You've seen McKee. Villerand would do that. That's the way Villerand works."

XIII

LIEUTENANT ERIC WILKINS rode a good horse. He had borrowed it from the captain who had come in from Montgomery three days since, had inspected the garrison indifferently and immediately got very drunk. He was still drunk, sprawled on a couch in the house the army had taken over, his coat off, his shirt damp and filthy, one shoe gone, exposing a dirty foot that dangled to the floor.

Wilkins had made a formal request for the loan of the horse, been answered by a throaty grunt which he decided to interpret as assent. Anyway, the horse was getting restive, being too well fed on confiscated corn, and was about to kick his stall to pieces—which destruction would be the source of acrid argument later from the tart-tongued Rebel woman who owned the stable.

One thing Eric Wilkins had great confidence in was his ability to ride. At the first Burnside's men had had their pick of the best horses of three states, and not one had been too tough or too fractious for the young lieutenant from Delaware. Now he made two troopers groom the captain's horse till he glistened, and did not smile even when they jumped away nervously from the restless heels. Then with superb dignity he mounted, held his seat firmly and unperturbed while the animal danced and circled, snorting.

He heard grudging approval behind him. "That Petunia, he can ride anyhow."

"Oughta—rid through a whole war while we was walking," a second man grumbled.

Wilkins had seen little of the town beyond the streets his men patrolled. Of the country he had seen nothing, having arrived in an army wagon on a dark and rainy night. That had been in early March, and now it was early August, a burgeoning, opulent August, and the land was rich with green and many a black-loamed field was a geometric pattern of growing cotton and corn.

He was not quite sure of the road, though he had made inquiry at the store, ignoring the straight-drawn mouth and lowered brow of the man who told him the way to the Villerand plantation. From the appearance of the girl he had rescued and the carriage that had driven her away he had assumed that the Villerands were people of consequence, though it had taken days of canny sleuthing to learn the girl's name. Nobody in town wanted to be seen in friendly conversation with an officer in blue, and many who were badgered into communication gave false information deliberately.

From a voluble Negro Wilkins had finally learned that the young lady was Miss Maggie Villerand, that her folks were "big rich" and that the Villerand plantation was down toward the river. The storekeeper's attitude indicated to Wilkins that a Union trooper's wish to visit the plantation boded no good for somebody, and also, Wilkins suspected, that the owners of Horning and Hale's establishment would be neither surprised nor disturbed if that ill befell Julian Villerand himself.

Wilkins took the road after he had got the horse under control. He went out at a leisurely pace past the fields and through a stretch of swampy land where he kept cautiously to the middle of the road. For five years he had been under arms, separated from home, and now in this vanquished land he was a lonely, suspected and despised stranger. He was beginning to wonder if it had been worth while. He had fought for freedom for the

Negro race, and now the men of that race whom he had seen loafed and pillaged, got drunk and fought one another. These moments of disquieting disgust came oftener now, and the drunken captain had not helped Wilkins' thinking that perhaps the whole struggle which had consumed his young years had been a futile piece of bravado and violence, with no sound basis of statecraft or patriotism beneath it.

He wondered if the colored men were any better off now, detached from the life they had known, their potentialities undeveloped, their minds untrained, turned loose in an apathetic and what was rapidly becoming a hostile world. Slavery was degradation. The few Southerners he had been able to talk to admitted that; also he had heard it expounded that slavery had long been an economic burden on the land. Yet the land and the black people had been geared and adjusted to each other for so long that, like any other disassembled piece of machinery, the result was chaos, the more tragic because the human element entered into it.

The lieutenant pondered all this as he trotted over a wooden bridge and along a grassy lane bounded by fences which stood intact and by cedar trees standing in dark pools of their own shadows. If this was the Villerand plantation, it had escaped the atmosphere of discouragement and decay which blighted the other places he had passed. There were no sprouts or thistles in the pastures and the cotton looked thrifty. Corn stood high farther on. He saw three fat cows grazing. A handsome chestnut horse trotted the length of a meadow, nickering excitedly. Obviously Mr. Villerand had known how to protect his property through a war.

A grove of huge trees of a species Eric Wilkins had never seen before hid the house. When he came near he saw that it was long and low, half-storied above with dormers in the roof and a veranda running all the way around it. A gate barred off the lawn and the drive, and he had already dismounted when he discovered that an ingenious contraption of rope and weights permitted a rider to open it without leaving the saddle.

The captain's horse had been infected with the high spirits of the capering animal in the meadow, and Wilkins had trouble getting mounted again, so that he was hot, irritated and disheveled when he rode up the drive. He had to mop his face and smack horsehairs from his smart blue breeches.

It did not help his embarrassment to come upon a young woman sitting on a bench with some sewing in her lap, a person he halfway suspected of laughing at him. He got down, removed his hat and made a bow he hoped was not too awkward. These Southern beauties, he had heard, set great store on gallantry and courtliness.

"Miss Villerand? I am Lieutenant Wilkins of the United States Army."

She studied him impersonally. "Oh, are you the man Captain Gilbert was to send out? We expected you yesterday."

He was puzzled. "I have no orders from Captain Gilbert, Miss Villerand. This is a personal call."

She looked annoyed. "Captain Gilbert promised my father to send a man out every day to keep in order these hireling Negroes we have working on a ditching job. My father had to go north, and our overseer deserted us to enlist in the army."

Wilkins frowned. "Captain Gilbert has been—er—incapacitated for a few days, Miss Villerand. No orders have been issued to my knowledge, and I am second-in-command. The army does not supervise labor. You would have to get in touch with the Freedmen's Bureau for that."

"Then why did that stupid captain make such a promise? And I am not Miss Villerand. I am Mrs. Destrade. Whom are you calling on, if this is a personal visit? Are you a friend of my sister?"

"Does she have dark hair and gray eyes with sparks in them? She'd probably say with some spirit that I'm no friend of hers." He tried to laugh lightly but did rather badly at it.

"I see." She turned a silver thimble round and round on her finger. "Then whom did you come to see, Lieutenant?"

The horse was determined to eat grass and Wilkins was having an awkward time keeping his head up. He got slobbers on his sleeve and he dabbed at the smear impatiently.

"I came to see your sister—if she will see me," he blurted unhappily.

"Oh, very well." She got up, gathering the sewing under her arm. "I'll call Tuby to attend to your horse, Lieutenant. You are a lieutenant, aren't you? I'm not familiar with the Federal uniform."

"I'm Lieutenant Eric Wilkins, Mrs. Destrade, and if I'm not intruding——"

"I'll ask if my sister wishes to receive you." She started up the path and Wilkins followed, not knowing what else to do. The horse jerked his head from side to side when he reached for the green mouthfuls, and Wilkins muttered angry adjurations at him as they approached the high front steps where flowering bushes bloomed on either side.

At the foot of the steps the young woman faced him. "This is all a trifle odd, Lieutenant. You say that you're not a friend of my sister, yet you wish to see her. I don't care for riddles, they never amuse me. If you are one of those wretched officers they send out to snoop and pry and make our servants dissatisfied, I must ask you to leave immediately."

An unhappy flush burned Wilkins' face. "Mrs. Destrade, I came here on no official mission. I made a very unfortunate impression on your sister in town one day. I came here in the hope that I might erase the impression. This is the first leave I've been able to manage since that day."

She nodded. "Oh, you must be the officer who knocked an insulting soldier down. We heard about you. But from what I heard you got the rough edge of Marian's tongue. Is that a violation of some of your Yankee regulations? Surely a woman has a right to be offended when she's roughly used, under any government."

"Also the right to have the wrong amended, don't you think?" he pleaded earnestly. "I tried to make apologies that day, but she wouldn't listen. I thought if I could call on her in her own home—— I don't like leaving things to rankle when they might perhaps be healed."

Juliet laughed. "My dear young man, you're as transparent as a glass of water! Marian is a pretty girl—a high-tempered girl, I'll admit, but pretty to look at. You wanted an excuse to see a pretty girl again, didn't you?"

He grinned, relieved. "I'll confess, Mrs. Destrade: I did want to see her again. I've been anxious to come for some time. Do you think you can persuade her to see me?"

She shrugged and flung out a hand. "My sister is an unpredictable person, Lieutenant. I'll see what I can do." She raised her voice. "Tuby! I see you asleep back there. Come here and take this officer's horse."

A lean Negro wriggled out from under a clump of shrubbery and came shambling up to take the bridle from Wilkins' hand. "Reckon he drink like any hoss, suh?"

"Of course," Juliet said. "Just because he's a Yankee horse doesn't make him any different from another horse. Don't let him slip his bridle and wander away, Tuby."

Eric breathed easier as he followed Juliet up the steps. At least he was not going to be dismissed immediately. A serving-man unlatched a louvered door, and Wilkins observed that this man had a bruised cheek and a swollen eye. Some African fracas or other. The troopers were always breaking up Negro shindies.

Juliet motioned to a chair in the long, dim hall. "If you will sit here, Lieutenant, I will speak to my sister. But I warned you, she has a mind of her own, and you said yourself that her eyes were full of sparks."

Eric was sure he had waited hours, though the tall clock opposite him had actually ticked off only twelve minutes, when the Negro with the swollen face returned and leaned against the wall.

"How I go for to git a white man arrested and flung in jail, Cap'n?" he asked.

"You have to go to town and swear out a warrant, boy. What did this white man do that you want him arrested?"

"He beat me up."

"What were you doing that he beat you up? Minding your own business?"

"Yes, suh. I was goin' about his place to see a friend of mine, and he hit me on the head wid a gun—shot at me too, but he wasn't no good shot. Missed me a mile."

"Sure you weren't prowling around to steal his hams or shoats? We've had plenty of complaints about you fellows. What's your name?"

"Cassius, suh. And I wasn't after no hams, neither shoats. That man ain't got neither no hams nor shoats."

"What's the rest of your name? You're a citizen now. Every citizen has two names. You were a Villerand slave, weren't you? You can take the Villerand name."

"No, suh, I ain't take Mist' Julian's name. I belong to him since I come here, but he ain't like no nigger to take his name."

"You'd better get a name then if you want to go to law. Sounds to me like you wouldn't have a case if you were prowling around the man's place."

Cassius smirked. "Does I git me a warrant and a jury, I got me a case, Cap'n. Any nigger git a verdict now ag'in a white man if he git him a jury. Can't no white men be neither judge nor jury 'less they swear the oath, and them that swears the oath, they friendly to my color."

Wilkins frowned. "Any jury that would uphold you, if you were marauding on another man's property, Cassius, would be a jury of scalawags, black or white. I don't like what goes on in the courts here. General Swayne doesn't like it too well, either. The general is a gentleman and a reasonable man. If your race keeps going on the way they're doing, the Army is bound to take over. Then anybody who gets tried will be tried in a military court. You'd better stay away from the law unless you know what you're doing."

"I know I got beat over the head, Cap'n—that's all I knows," Cassius grumped, as he shuffled off.

Wilkins sat watching the slow hands of the clock move, and when a half hour had inched away he began to get angry. So she thought she could ignore him callously, did she? He would, he decided grimly, stay till dark. He would sit right here till morning. No, that was an insane idea. Captain Gilbert would be yelling around headquarters if his horse wasn't back by sundown. A brash lieutenant who overstayed his pass and made too free with authority could get himself transferred to Louisiana, where hatred for the Union forces was bitter and more violently demonstrated than in Alabama. At New Orleans more than one man in blue had been found floating face down in the Mississippi River, a bullet in his back.

He walked out to the front veranda and stood looking off across the lawn where roses were in bloom and a white-starred vine climbed fragrantly on the pillars and railings. He was glaring at nothing, his back very stiff, when a whisper of skirts sounded behind him. He turned to see her standing just inside the door, her ivory shoulders bare, a blue skirt billowing over a wide crinoline.

She looked him up and down with sober eyes. "Why don't you go away?" she said bluntly. "You know we haven't a thing to talk about. Shall I tell Tuby to fetch your horse?"

He gave her a slow smile, though his heart was scudding. "If this is Southern hospitality, Miss Villerand, all I can say is that it has been vastly overadvertised."

"I told Cassius that I was too busy to receive callers today. Didn't he tell you?"

"All he told me was that he wanted to have some white man arrested for beating him on the head."

She flushed angrily. "You won't let him do that? If anybody beat Cassius, he deserved it. There have been times when I have itched to beat him myself. He probably got into a fight. Well, come in, Lieutenant, if you're determined to stay." She opened the door without enthusiasm.

"I'm determined to stay until you say you forgive me, Miss Villerand. I'm a very obstinate man at times—and this is one of the times." He managed a smile as he followed her into a big low-ceiled parlor, full of elaborate furniture.

"Why should you feel this terrific desire for forgiveness? You have done nothing offensive."

"Perhaps for making a nuisance of myself. I came out here to tell you that I would like to be your friend."

She considered this gravely. There was a boyish sort of charm about this naïve young man from Delaware. At least he admired her—that was in his eyes, plain to see. And only last night in this very room Duncan Wade, whom she had vowed she would make fall in love with her, had been aloof and hateful, making her feel like a fool, like some cheap girl flinging herself at a man who didn't want her. Maybe she had been wrong all along. Maybe Juliet had the right idea that men prized only what was withheld, or what was greatly desired by somebody else.

"There would be difficulties, as no doubt you realize," she said. "I fear many people would misunderstand my friendship with a man in your uniform, Lieutenant."

"On the other hand, you might convince some of them that not all men in the Union Army wear horns and hoofs, Miss Villerand."

She giggled at that. "Do you know something? When I looked at General Swayne I thought that all he needed was a pair of pointed ears to look like Lucifer, the fallen angel."

"People forget that we are merely men, homesick most of us, sick of war and hate," Wilkins said a trifle wistfully.

"That soldier you knocked down was a bully and a beast. Why don't you control men like him if you want us to respect your army?"

"I did my best to impress upon him the error of his ways," he reminded her.

"There are so many like him and so few like you," she said. "To redeem Southern hospitality, Lieutenant, I'd like to offer you a glass of wine, if you'd accept it."

"I'll be very happy to accept whatever is offered of Southern hospitality, Miss Villerand."

"Wait here, then. I'll get it myself. I know where Father keeps the keys, and I don't trust Cassius an inch where wine is concerned."

She rustled out and Wilkins relaxed, his elbows on his knees. She wasn't angry, but she wasn't being coquettish either. These Southern beauties, he had heard, had no aim in life but to make men aware of them, captivate and then discard them.

In the back hall Marian encountered Juliet.

"Good Heavens, hasn't that Yankee given up and gone yet?" Juliet asked in a whisper.

Marian tilted her head. "He's still here. I'm getting some wine. Southern hospitality must be maintained." Anyhow, she was thinking, she sort of liked him. "He's really a gentleman," she said archly.

"If a Yankee can be a gentleman."

Marian's eyes flashed. "Listen," she snapped. "He is a gentle-man and I like him—and you stay out of that parlor."

"Oh, for pity's sake!" Juliet sighed scornfully.

Back in his own, small stuffy cabin Cassius closed the door and barred it. Then from under his bed he dragged a rusty little trunk Mrs. Villerand had given him long ago. At the bottom of it, from under a clutter of old clothes, items salvaged from the Villerand trash and a rag tied around half-smoked cigar butts, he brought out a tobacco sack and dumped the coins it held into his palm. Not enough yet. Hard to save much money from six bits weekly. Boss got to pay me more money, he decided. Freedom Bureau say sumpin about that. He'd have to wait for his vengeance till the boss got back from up north and he made him pay more money.

White man's justice cost money. He could wait, Cassius knew—wait implacably, unforgetting—anyway till he had five dollars. Needed a name too. Got to git an important name. Name that would sound good and important in court. Not Villerand. Cassius was canny. He knew that there were quarters in which the name of Villerand was not held in respect. He wanted a name that was respected—and also feared. Name of a big general. Name everybody in Alabama was scared of. Grant! General Grant. Licked the secesh, didn't he?

On the back of his door a broken scrap of mirror was nailed up. Cassius walked to it and grinned mirthlessly at the battered face reflected there.

"Howdy, Mister Cassius Grant!" he said.

XIV

ROBERT McKEE rode into the Wades' yard in Bard Leonard's wagon.

"Found this feller over in town, said he was bound to see you, Mister Wade," Bard said. "So I fetched him over. If you don't want him I kin take him back."

Duncan was at work tearing down an unused slave cabin. With the crop laid by he had applied his restless energy to trying to restore the place to some semblance of its former dignity. He was up on the roof of the cabin, ripping off the curled shingles when the wagon rolled into the yard. He slid down the roof, dropped from the eaves and wiped his hands on his thin cotton pants.

"So you got here, McKee," he greeted. "You find us pretty dirty. Tearing off a roof that was rived and pegged on fifty years ago is a filthy job."

"Those rafters look as dry and sound as new, if they are fifty years old," McKee observed. "They cut prime timber in those days and took care how they cured it."

"Boy we had named Prince lived in that cabin with his wife. Old Zeba, his mother, was my nurse—my father's nurse too. She died and never knew that she was free."

Hugh Wade, who had been sitting under the pecan tree pulling nails from lumber and straightening them on a block, got up and came forward. "Glad to see you, McKee. You should have let us know you were coming so we could have greeted you with proper elegance."

"He means, in our other pants." Duncan laughed. "We haven't any other shirts. Louisa washes these, and if it rains so they don't dry, we go in our underwear. Come into the house. At least we can wash. You come too, Bard. I reckon Louisa has got something in the pot for dinner."

"Don't mind if I do." Bard swung off the wagon seat promptly. "Got a nubbin anywheres I can use to bribe this-here mule? I give him a bribe every day, coax him to live one day longer."

"Josuff brought in some fresh beans and onions," Hugh said. "Parmy always plants as many vegetables as he did when we had forty hands to feed, so there should be plenty. No meat, though."

"I've got a trade on for a sow," Bard said as he followed them in through the rear hall. "Does she have shoats this fall, I'll swap you one for some of that-there lumber, need it to build me a hogpen. When they burned me out two year ago they burned me out complete. Stood 'em off from the house with a shotgun, but all the other buildings went."

There was a high-backed washstand in the hall with a big, cracked china pitcher on it and a rusted tin wash pan. Applegate's marauders, Louisa had told Duncan, had smashed the bowl that matched the pitcher. "And the slop bucket too. Set it up on a post in the yard and shot at it."

Hugh Wade apologized for the coarse towels he offered. "Louisa boils and bleaches them—best she can do. All my wife's good linen went to the army hospitals after '62."

"What little we had," Robert McKee said, "has been used up for shirts and bellybands for young ones."

The high-ceiled parlors were bleak now, the carpets gone, the curtains pulled down and carried away. What furniture remained was scarred and shabby. Duncan remembered the Villerand parlor with its overopulence of plush and gilt and polished wood, and clicked his teeth on the bitterness of comparison. At least these rooms were cool. Hugh pulled up chairs for the visitors and unostentatiously provided Bard with a cuspidor.

Duncan made an exploratory mission to the kitchen, came back to report. "Louisa is flustered but proud. She insists that we dine in elegant state in the dining room. Father and I have been using a table on the back porch this hot weather, but for Louisa's sake we must wait on style and dignity. So there will be a slight delay while the scene is arranged to humor tradition. What has happened in Selma, McKee?"

McKee stretched his long legs, brought out a black pipe. "Folks are mightily stirred up over there about this Fourteenth Amendment to the Constitution that Congress wants to cram down our throats. That's about all you hear."

"Alabama will never ratify," Hugh declared. "We swallowed their Thirteenth Amendment, abolishing slavery, and put a clause in our own new Constitution declaring slavery outlawed, but the people gag on that villainous Fourteenth and it will never pass in our legislature."

"They say even some of the Northern states will refuse to ratify," McKee said. "New York for one, I heard."

"You'll have to enlighten me," Duncan declared. "I'm an ignoramus in this political swamp. I can't seem to get caught up on what has happened while I was engaged in making it possible for it to happen. While I was taking part in the glorious defeat of the Confederacy, there wasn't much time to read the papers."

"Yeah, me too," Bard drawled. "What is this-here amendment and why are we agin it?"

"You explain, McKee," Hugh said. "I read a draft of the thing down at Horning's store, but I got so mad I forgot half that was in it."

"Congress voted for it awhile back and submitted it to the states," McKee said. "Andy Jackson is against it. He has sense enough to realize that the South could be crowded too far. Those radicals in Congress passed it anyhow, but it has to be ratified by three fourths of the states. It gives full citizenship rights to every person born in the United States, except Indians, which we more or less expected, but it goes further and does worse. It establishes apportionments of representation in Congress according to the number of persons in each state, but —and here's the big but—if any persons are denied the right to vote in any election by reason of having participated in a rebellion against the United States, the apportionment of representation is reduced in proportion to the number of those disqualified males to the whole number of male citizens over twenty-one in the state."

"In plain words—" Duncan kicked his chair back angrily— "we can't vote and aren't counted citizens."

"You, my son," McKee said dryly, "have taken up arms against the Union. You have to ask for amnesty or be pardoned by the President or you are no longer a citizen. And don't you see? It's the Radicals' way to force us to let the Negroes vote or have our representation cut down. They get us both ways. Your old colored man out there gathering up chips is not only your equal, he's your superior. Congress tacked on a sweet little stinger to the amendment too. They empowered themselves to enact legislation to enforce their amendment in every state."

"If that Congress gits to messing round with us agin, telling us what we got to do, by gormy, we'll secede agin!" Bard Leonard shouted. "I ain't a whole man, but I kin fight to keep Republicans from trampling our rights in Alabama."

"We're trampled already," Hugh Wade said sadly. "We're trampled flat. But that amendment will never be ratified by any Alabama legislature."

"They can pack the legislature full of Negroes and Radicals and pass it anyway," Duncan said. "None of us can vote—but before long Parmy and Josuff may vote to elect Parmy sheriff of Marengo County."

"You're going a little fast, Duncan. It isn't that bad yet. You should read the *Southern Argus*. Then you'd know what goes on."

"I told you, McKee, that I couldn't afford to subscribe to it."

"And I told you your credit was good—but we can't get the paper out to the people."

"Villerand said his copy was a week old."

"A lot can happen in a week, but if they don't suppress me entirely I'll be thankful. Speaking of Villerand, you didn't happen to hear what he was cooking up with those promoters in Boston?"

"He talked as though he'd lost interest in any railroad proposition."

"All the more reason to keep an eye on Villerand. He's a clever article, clever and stupid in an odd combination of characteristics. Bullheaded—unscrupulous if it serves him, too," said Hugh Wade, "but not always too smart."

Louisa appeared at the door. "You gent'men, come set. It ain't like it used to was, noway, but it's the best us kin do."

"If you've got a hot pone for me, Louisa, with ashes on it, I'll praise your name to glory," McKee declared.

"Law, suh! I done bresh all the ashes off my pones. Ain't no ashes git on my Ole Mistis' table."

Duncan felt a choking lump in his throat when he saw the board spread. The heavy linen cloth had been cut and a shining length hemmed to fit the foreshortened table. In the middle an oleander bloom stood in a glass bottle. The plates did not match —they were the few the looters had found too heavy or too old to carry away. The hominy steamed in a heavy soup tureen.

"Put on plenty pepper," advised Louisa. "Plenty pepper and you don't miss the seasonin' too much."

"My sow fetches a good litter and we'll have seasoning," insisted Bard. "Good fat pot liquor that'll stick to a feller's ribs. That missionary preacher from up no'th, that got the Higgs farm, he's got two cows. Yankee money bought 'em yonder, I reckon. All I can do, come a dark night, to keep myself from sneakin' over there and milkin' one of 'em. Churn me up a little dab of butter. Scairt I'll do it some time when his folks has all gone to preachin'. Don't no real folks go to hear him preach—just darkies and trash."

"Agitators—do-gooders! The country's getting infested with them!" McKee stormed. "And another pestiferous tribe is this gang of correspondents from the Northern press. They come down here determined to discredit the South, fabricate stories of violence and outrages, never talk to a single person of dignity or reputation."

"No person of reputation would talk to them," Hugh said. "They hang around on street corners just waiting to hear somebody abuse a Yankee."

"I reckon they hear plenty," Bard remarked, reaching for the beans.

This is change, this is democracy, Duncan was thinking. Bard is a good neighbor. My mother went to his house when his wife died, bringing food and flowers. His son, Tal, dead himself now, helped carry my mother to her grave. But neither Bard nor any member of his family was ever before this seated in her parlor or at her table.

Bard was at ease. Duncan was himself the detached, dislocated person in the room. His place was gone. Bard's was unchanged. He was content with less because he had never known much more. But Bard was lonely now as he himself was lonely.

He said impulsively, "Have some more hominy, Bard. Sorry there's no coffee."

Bard chuckled. "What's coffee? Reckon if any ever does come to town it'll be a dollar a pound."

"Hale and Horning got a shipment of coffeepots. Reckon there's hope."

"If we can hold on to our cotton . . . if we can raise enough to pay the taxes so they won't sell us out . . ." Hugh sighed.

Bard took his leave after dinner, promising to come back for McKee the next day.

"I have to ride that little train, Bard, don't forget," McKee said. "It's supposed to run at four o'clock, one wheezy little engine and two flatcars with benches on them." He laughed.

"So we're back to railroads," Duncan said when they were seated on the back porch. "What about your plans, McKee—any further along?"

"You mean, that meeting we discussed? That's what I came to talk about. There's a railroad reconstruction act coming up which will be passed by the legislature, we hope. It will provide for state aid to railroad construction, probably for state endorsement to the amount of twenty thousand dollars a mile. If a group of responsible and reputable men get together, they could promote a road north and south, under those conditions. Cotton's still high. A railroad north would open rich country, iron, timber—even gold up there, they say. We ought to make plans, support the act and be prepared when it passes to apply for a franchise to build."

"What was that meeting called for August the second in Selma?" Hugh Wade asked.

"That was political. To elect delegates to a National Union Convention in Philadelphia where Southerners can get together with Democrats of the North."

"Any hope that it will help the situation here?"

McKee thumbed tobacco into his pipe. "It won't get anywhere. The Radicals won't let it. There will just be a lot of empty speeches and resolutions. Wade, I wouldn't volunteer the statement that there's hope for anything to happen in Alabama."

"Except rain, death and taxes," Hugh put in.

"At that meeting you're talking about—your railroad meeting—only men who have capital to invest would be of any use. Where are you going to find them," Duncan asked, "unless you take in the carpetbaggers and speculators?"

"Men who own property will be needed, men who have credit in their own community. As long as the land remains there's potential wealth in this country—and land stays around forever."

"All we've got left is the land, and they may take that away from us if some scalawag or carpetbagger with influence should take a fancy to this place."

"We'll hope that won't happen, Mr. Wade. Land is all you have, but you could give a right of way, take stock in the company. Let's look over your boundary. Of course a survey would have to be determined by engineers, but we could get an idea of what's suitable."

"A man wouldn't want his best fields cut up with a railroad —that's natural." Hugh got to his feet and followed the younger men down through the yard. "We're badly grown up to sedge and sprouts already, as you can see. It took forty hands to run this plantation ten years ago. Now our people are all gone but old Josuff and Parmy, and Parmy's a feeble-minded boy. Twenty of them left in one night, thinking to follow Canby's troops. Some of them are still hanging around in Demopolis, I know, living in a miserable camp, depending on the Yankees to feed them."

They tramped up the lane and over the wide meadow to the east, where already dewberry vines caught at their ankles and a bright-eyed woodchuck blinked at them and dived swiftly into a wide burrow.

"Over yonder—" Hugh pointed—"where those trees are, we join Villerand."

There was a path beaten through the meadow, Duncan

noted, and his heart gave an odd, disconcerting jerk as he realized that this was Marian's riding path, the way she took on her visits to the Wade place. She must have jumped the high rail fence that joined the two properties. She might have been thrown there, he was thinking. Perhaps she would never come back to Wades' again. She had been furious when he left the Villerand house, he knew.

"Straight through here—good grade, logical terrain," McKee was saying. "It would make a division between your place and Villerand's, but perhaps that wouldn't matter too much."

"Wouldn't matter at all. The less I see of Villerand the better I'm pleased," Hugh stated.

"Riders over there," McKee observed. "Looks like the army has taken over."

They had come close to the boundary fence. Duncan leaned his arms on the top rail and frowned at two riders who were cantering in leisurely fashion down a bisecting lane beyond Villerand's orchard. He glimpsed a flash of red skirt and, following, an officer in Union blue.

"Young Maggie, fraternizing with the enemy," his father drawled.

"Good-looking horses," McKee said. "That bay has the look of a Kentucky thoroughbred. Who's the lieutenant? Know him?"

"I couldn't say. I've got no friends in the Union Army." There was more bitterness in Duncan's voice than he intended and he caught his father looking at him sharply.

"What a wonderful chance to pick a Yankee officer out of the saddle!" McKee laughed, sighting an imaginary rifle. "There was a time when I would have dumped that lad in the dirt and spoiled his pretty clothes."

"Not from this distance." Duncan got his breathing under control, put down the queer, quick anger that had burned him.

"We waited till we could see the eagle on their buttons. Fire too soon and you gave yourself away."

"You weren't hiding in gullies in Kentucky. Up there we potted them like shooting squirrels. Now I don't even own a good gun."

"Tom Goldsby gave Duncan a pistol. It came handy the other night when we had a prowler around the place."

"Got him buried somewhere, Duncan?"

"No, I clubbed him when he came at me, and he ran. Then I shot and missed. I wasn't quite sure that he wasn't our boy Parmy. Then when I was certain, he dodged too quick for me."

"We've killed men and it doesn't keep us awake at night," McKee mused. "This strange, fierce madness of war! I hope my sons never see what I have seen, never have to sight a weapon on some fellow they don't know and aren't even mad at, and take away his life. That Yank riding over yonder doesn't know we've been standing here figuring how easy it would be to spoil his gay adventure with a pretty girl. He's lucky that he can get a girl to ride with him—not many would, in Alabama."

Suddenly, for no sensible reason, Duncan itched to flay Mc-Kee with hot words, to defend this girl who flaunted her giddy red habit beside the hated Union blue. He set his jaw hard and hot water came into his mouth. He turned away abruptly and started back to the house.

Why should he give a damn what Marian Villerand did, or whom she chose to ride with? All her life she had had what she wanted, done as she pleased.

The trouble was that he did care. He cared more than he wanted to admit, even to himself.

XV

THE AUGUST DAYS were blazing hot. Men's tempers flared. There was little inclination to work, but under the crushing glare of the sun the cotton grew and flourished. Even with poor seed and worse cultivation it looked like a good crop in Alabama.

In Washington Congress and the President were at cross purposes over the disposition of the seceded states. Vindictive Radicals hoped for drastic reprisals, humiliations that would not be forgotten. Rumors drifted like pollen on the hot winds along the Tombigbee, the Black Warrior, the Alabama rivers. Ratify the Fourteenth Amendment, and Congress would pass a law limiting suffrage to men owning two hundred and fifty dollars' worth of property. Alabama took that with a grain of salt. Already Governor Patton had gone north to Missouri to buy corn for the hungry in the state.

Cassius—Mister Cassius Grant—bided his time. The boss had come back. Cassius had almost four dollars in the greasy tobacco sack hidden in the tin trunk.

Julian took the road that led westwardly toward the river. He felt expansive, optimistic. He had talked to smart people in Boston, in New York. When he passed the boundary of his own property he pulled the horse up for a moment, frowned at the Wades' two-hundred-acre expanse of meadow, neglected, overgrown. He swore aloud. "Damned, stubborn old fool!"

The horse jerked at the bit as though he inquired what he was supposed to do about the obstinacy of Hugh Wade, even though he agreed. Beyond the wasted field was an expanse of cotton, and Villerand regarded that, deciding it was spindly, not even likely to make a bale to the acre, just what a man would expect of a snobbish, impractical old fool like Hugh Wade. The narrow wagon road led down toward the river where once the barges had been moored. It was grown deep with grass. Nothing had been hauled out that way in a long time. Probably nothing ever would again.

Villerand turned the horse in at the wagon road. It dipped through a marshy stretch that should have been drained long since. Insects swarmed up, making the horse dance and jerk his head, and Villerand cuffed desperately at gnats that tried to drown themselves in his eyeballs. The wagon road emerged on the Wade lawn. He had to duck to avoid the limbs of trees that sadly needed trimming. Grass was deep here too, and where flowers had bloomed only a few starved volunteers showed color among the weeds.

"Cut off his right hand, live on cowpeas, eat grass, before he'd give in!" Villerand growled.

The front of the house was blank, closed, silent. He rode around to the rear. A very old Negro man came out of a cabin and stood blinking. His feet were bare, his shapeless clothes tied around his middle with a worn bridle rein, buckled and twisted.

"Howdy, Josuff. You still alive?" Villerand greeted this figure.

Old Josuff stretched his mouth in an almost toothless grin. "Jes' restin', Marse Julian. Crop laid by, a man gits hisself a little rest."

"How much crop you got, Josuff? More 'n you can handle picking-time, I reckon?"

"No, suh, no, suh. Us gits it picked. Young Master, he come home. Riz from the dead, he did. Us gits us cotton picked."

"Devil of a lot of work you'll get out of him! Where is your master?"

"Mist' Hugh? They up on the hill choppin' sprouts outen the graveyard. Young Mist' Duncan he tole me: Josuff, you go rest. Bad niggers on the road last night. They come a-poundin' on my door. They lef' when Young Master come out wid a gun."

"You got a gun, Josuff?"

"No, suh. Just got me a razor. I hone it up good and sharp, but young Mist' Duncan, he run 'em off."

"I'll ride up yonder. I want a word with Mister Hugh."

Villerand rode through the back yard, past the empty slave cabins, some of them already torn down and the lumber neatly piled. A blackened washpot stood in a ring of sooty bricks. A big rock beside the path had a litter of pecan shells around it, and the rusting steel scale stood under a shed roof waiting for cotton-weighing time. Not a chicken scratched, not a calf bleated. Two doves circled down from the barn roof and did their tilting cakewalk in the sun beyond a scuppernong arbor.

A few tomato vines grew in the garden patch, and late beans wilted in the heat on the poles. Starvation, thought Villerand. Not enough provender in sight to feed a gopher! In the middle of the garden Louisa's broad rear was bent over some cucumber vines.

There was a gate, but it stood open. Nothing to bar out any more. Villerand rode through and up the lane to the little rise, where there was a sound of chopping. He saw the brick wall then, remembered the day he had helped to carry Florence Wade to that spot, and bitterness rose in his mouth like brine. There was her grave—lost in weeds and trash already. He wouldn't have let her die, he said to himself again, but if it was willed that she must die, he would have set the proudest monument in Alabama over her grave.

He saw Hugh Wade backing out of the enclosure, dragging

an armful of brush. Hugh straightened, breathing gustily, mopping his face, as Villerand rode up. "Evening," he said, no welcome in his voice.

"Good evening, Mr. Wade," said Villerand formally. "How are you?" He did not get down. He did not want Hugh Wade to witness the breathless scramble that occured now whenever he attempted to mount a horse without a block handy. From the saddle he felt adequate, even a trifle masterly, and he did not want to surrender his advantage by becoming merely a short man on foot in the presence of the two tall Wades. He said suavely, "Riding this way, so I thought I'd drop by and see how you all were making out."

Hugh said, "Very well, sir, thank you." He turned back to his green brush, piled and trampled it.

"Getting some swamping-out done, I see," Villerand remarked, refusing to feel dismissed. "Filth and trash grow mighty fast this hot weather. Hard to keep ahead of the sprouts."

Duncan, sweaty and flushed, stepped over the wall, mattock in hand. He laid down his tool and came up, scrubbing his hands on his cotton pants. He said, "Good evening, Mr. Villerand. I didn't thank you for your hospitality that night. I hope Mrs. Villerand made excuses for me?"

"Glad to have had you. Glad to have young folks around. You come over often. I reckon your father was mighty glad to see you come home. I know I'd run up a flag and shout hallelujah if my boy came walking in. But I reckon he never will. Figure to stay here on the place now?"

"Yes, sir, I'm staying. We're doing a little cleaning up out here today. Mighty hot work. Yes, I'll stay. Pa needs another hand on the place."

"Needs a lot of 'em, I'd say. Too much land for a man to handle with little help. That's so, ain't it, Mr. Wade?"

Hugh Wade lifted his head, squared his shoulders. His face

was pale and damp with heat and weariness and he was soiled and shabby, but there was still a superb sort of dignity about the old man that made Julian Villerand, splendidly mounted as he was, look inferior and a bit insecure.

"We'll plant it and we'll keep it," Hugh said grimly.

Duncan felt a little puzzled. He had always known that there existed a stiff, unspoken unfriendliness between his father and Julian Villerand; that it went back to old antagonisms which had never been explained to the younger generation. But now the hostility seemed somehow pointed up, and he saw that it was his father who was on the defensive, not fearful but rather on guard.

Villerand cleared his throat with a harsh, almost beligerent roughness. "Half this place would make you a good living, Wade. And half is all you can work, you and this young feller of yours. No sense in letting the rest of it go to wilderness, wash full of gullies, the way it is."

"We'll manage, Mr. Villerand," Duncan said quietly.

"Look, young feller!" Villerand's face swelled and reddened. "I've been trying to trade your father out of this east two-hundred ever since 'way back yonder when the war began. Joins me over there. I can handle it, but you can't. I knew freedom was coming, knew you were bound to lose your people. Back yonder I even told Mr. Wade to set his own price."

Hugh Wade's eyes burned under his ragged brows. "I set my price, Villerand. My price for that two hundred acres is two hundred thousand dollars."

Villerand laughed. "That ain't a price, that's a fairy story. There are thousands of acres of land in Alabama now that can be bought for five or ten dollars an acre. Away back when this plantation was making five hundred bales of cotton every year, when you had niggers to chop and pick it and teams to haul it, maybe this land was worth good money. Now, all this waste acreage is just a liability. Taxes high and no cash coming in to pay 'em. You can sell off what you don't need and use the cash to save the rest."

"If the land is a liability, why do you want to assume that liability, Mr. Villerand?" asked Duncan. "You have plenty of land."

"I just naturally hate to see a good piece of property go to ruin. And you don't deny that you could use a piece of money. Buy you a team and some tools, hire some of these vagrants that the Freedmen's Bureau is farming out to the planters. General Swayne—he runs the Bureau—he's a pretty decent feller. Friend of mine. Your house leaks too, don't it? Noticed some shingles had blown off on the front when I rode around that way."

"If my father says we're not selling, we're not selling," Duncan said firmly.

"I say we're not selling," Hugh repeated.

"You never took the oath, Wade." Villerand was getting testy. "Don't you realize that they might take a notion to confiscate this property?"

"They've let me alone so far. I'm not uneasy."

"You wouldn't stand a show in any court—reckon you know that?"

"What courts we have now are mockeries of justice. Packed with men of no property or responsibility."

"Just what I've been trying to tell you. We're all at the mercy of the Union Army and a lot of no-account politicians. On the other hand, there's too much wild and reckless talk on our side. Elmore and White—all those hotheads shouting white supremacy, run the army out of Alabama—doing us more harm than good."

"You don't believe in white supremacy then?" Duncan asked.

"Why, naturally I don't reckon that my stable boy Tuby belongs on a jury along with me, Wade. But if the law put him there, I reckon we've got a responsibility to teach Tuby enough so he knows what it's all about. I don't hold with burning schoolhouses just because some people decided that it was for the good of the country to teach Negroes to read. What it comes down to now, as I see it, is: Which is the law—the law of Alabama or the Constitution of the United States?"

"Then if you were in the legislature, you'd vote to ratify this Fourteenth Amendment, Mr. Villerand?"

"Well, that's a question I couldn't answer off hand, not being in the legislature. Not much chance I'll ever be elected, though you never know who can be elected any more, in this county. Some of the Northern states will reject the amendment, I'm told. Tennessee has already ratified it."

"That must have been because of the Union sentiment in East Tennessee and so many folks elsewhere refusing to take the oath. It couldn't have been voted otherwise. With so many white men disfranchised in Alabama, the same thing could happen here."

"You ought to get you a pardon, young Wade, and get your disabilities removed."

"To my mind," Duncan stated, "a pardon implies a confession of guilt. I haven't been guilty of anything except loyalty to my beliefs and convictions."

"But you're hamstrung, way you are now. Young men ought to be in shape to take over the responsibilities in this country."

"I'm not selling any land, Villerand," repeated Hugh Wade again, going back to his brush piling.

"You're spiting yourself, Wade. I'm willing to pay ten dollars an acre. Plenty of good land going for that on the block, even for less."

"Then the smart move for you would be to bid in some of that land, I should think," Duncan suggested amiably.

Villerand pulled up his horse, jabbed a foot awkwardly back

into the stirrup. "Raised you up another impractical fool, didn't you, Wade?" he said angrily.

He rode away and Duncan calmly picked up the mattock, climbed the wall and began a vigorous attack on the tangled undergrowth on the graves. Hugh trampled his brush pile as though there were an enemy beneath it. When his father came back to pick up more brush Duncan rested on his tool for a breath, wiping sweat from his face.

"There must be something stirring if Villerand is so hot after that meadow over there," he said.

"He may have some kind of a project cooking. McKee said that flat over there was the obvious place for a north-and-south railroad survey. Villerand just got back from the north. Were you thinking what we could do with two thousand dollars, Duncan? I admit I was briefly tempted, but I overcame it. But I could see your mind working."

"You're too clever, Mister. You'll be having second sight like Louisa next, knowing what goes on before it happens. I was thinking how nice a fat team of mules would look going down those cotton rows hitched to a new wagon. And a few vagrant thoughts about some decent clothes for you."

"My clothes will do. I'd rather wear rags to the end of my days than sell a foot of land to Julian Villerand."

"I've never been quite certain why your hackles always rise when Villerand comes around. Did it have something to do with Mother?"

"He wanted her," his father said. "Not that I blame him for that. She was a very great lady. I was proud that she was mine, proud and humble. But because she turned him down and married me, Julian Villerand has lived with one idea in his mind ever since—that some day he would humble me, condescend, show himself the better man. This war gave him a chance to see me brought down, in circumstances I'd never known before. He'll never give up—not till I'm laid up here beside her." He sat down on the wall and leaned on his knees, pushed back his hat and his damp hair. He was very weary, Duncan saw, his eyes looked sunken and faded. "I used to worry," Hugh went on, "when you were sort of off your head about that oldest girl of his. I was glad when she married that man from Louisiana. She's like Julian—she'll get harder as she gets older. Now the little one—she's different."

Duncan kept a careful silence. There was too much confusion in his mind about Marian Villerand. When he tried to put her out of his mind completely, some small endearing way of hers would creep back to soften him and tear down all his grim purposefulness.

"Your mother was always fond of that child," his father continued, "though she and Emma Villerand were never friends. Not that Emma was sly and tricky like her husband, but she was always aloof and hard to know and Julian gave her everything he could find to buy—and that was a backhand slap at me too. If your mother had a new bonnet, Emma got one from Paris costing four times as much."

Duncan said, "I'd better get at the job. Near to suppertime."

He strode back through the tangle and prodded an inert form with his foot. "Wake up, Parmy. Bad luck sleeping in a graveyard—hants might get you."

Parmy grunted, slobbered and dragged himself to his feet. He wore Duncan's old Confederate tunic, buttoned up to his chin. It had faded to a sickly yellow on the seams and the buttons were tarnished black. It was filthy and stank of sweat, and Parmy loved it and wore it even on the hottest days. He picked up a hoe now and held it in front of him. "Persent arms!" he shouted. "That's what the sojers says."

"Who told you? Have you been out drilling with those trashy Yankee Negroes?"

Parmy looked frightened for a moment, then slyness made his flat eyes opaque. "Ain't seen no Yankee niggers."

"If I catch you out in the woods with that scum, I'll run you off the place, you hear me? Then the Bureau will catch you up and put you to work on some other place and you'll work—with maybe nothing to eat."

Parmy understood that. He knew that he was free and must be paid for his labor, but what he had heard of the Bureau, the "through office" the colored people called it, scared him. Generals and captains, he had been told, rode around grabbing up Negroes and making them work far from home, and then strange Negroes beat you up and took your money. He grabbed at Duncan's sleeve.

"No, suh, Mist' Duncan. Don't you run Parmy offn this place! Parmy got to stay here long as us lives."

"Get to work then. Clear out all the trash in that corner. And if anybody comes around here at night, talking this soldier business, you come running to the house."

"Been comin' round already. But I ain't goin' out no nights. Parmy skeered out in the woods at night. One time they cotch me, but I run home—run all the way." He fell to whacking at a weedy tangle, making the dust fly.

Duncan uprooted a cedar sprout, carried it to his father's brush pile. "Parmy's talking military stuff," he said low. "Have they been getting him out with those gangs, drilling in the woods?"

"How do we know what they do after dark? No patrols any more. Parmy's weak in the head and easily intimidated. If a man in uniform with an air of authority ordered him to burn down our house, he'd probably be afraid not to do it."

"And if you ordered him to go out and cut that officer's throat, he'd likely do that, too. Come home grinning, wiping the knife on his pants."

"We are deeply indebted to the Negro race, son. In time we can repay that debt by helping them to raise themselves to the level of responsibility. But in the meantime we have a duty to protect them from being exploited and misled, and protect ourselves from them and them from one another. It's a big undertaking. I'm glad Tom Goldsby could spare that gun."

"The trouble is the Yanks can't realize that there's a middle ground of reason and sense where the black race is concerned. They think they can raise their intellectual level overnight."

"I don't believe that. Their purpose now, at any rate, is to keep the Negro a pliant, ignorant and superstitious tool, make him vote, pillage or even kill, to suit their purposes. Our good fortune is that in spite of all the pressure upon them so many of the race are decent and faithful."

"Do you owe Julian Villerand anything, Pa?" Duncan asked abruptly.

"Not even good will, son. The little girl has been friendly and a comfort to me. Emma came to your mother's funeral riding in a carriage when all the other neighbors had to walk."

"Someday I'll put a monument here—but it may be a long time away," Duncan said.

"A good son is a noble monument. I think she'd be content with a monument like that."

"I'm not conceited enough to believe that anything I may do will be remembered long after I'm gone, but a marble shaft will stand for a hundred years or more. I saw some up in Virginia that were dated in the 1600s."

"At least you're faced with a challenge, Duncan. You find an old civilization in ruins; it's your job to rebuild it."

"I'll do my best, sir—with what I can lay my hand on for the job."

"Keep out of fracases, Duncan. Arouse no animosities and avoid controversies. Your temper flares as mine used to do Now I know that a cool implacability serves me better."

"The way you talked back to Villerand."

"There's a difference between courage and recklessness. We learned that from this war. We plunged into it rashly; we had to fight through on courage and grit. Now we have to find more courage to live life as we find it. We'd better head for the house now. Louisa will be getting supper ready, needing wood maybe. Clean that hoe before you hang it up, Parmy, you hear?"

"Yes, suh." Parmy fell in behind them with alacrity.

Halfway down the slope Hugh turned and looked back up the hill.

"I think she would be very proud to have a marble monument," he said.

XVI

SHE HAD no business riding into the yard that morning. After a long effort Duncan had at last succeeded in putting her out of his mind. He had convinced himself that all his dreams about Juliet were forever dead, and that Felix Destrade was welcome to her. He had even made himself forget how she used to look, with the sparks of laughter in her eyes and the proud lift of her head, in the days when there had been gaiety and music and coquetry in all the big houses along the river, days when for the most part he had hung on the fringes of her admirers, worshiping from far, filled with young fury that he was considered too young to join her train.

Now this was the devil to pay to have his face begin to burn all over again and all the stony indifference he had been confident of desert him abruptly. It angered him too to see the quick wistfulness that showed on his father's face when the handsome bay horse stepped lightly over the litter of chips and sawdust they had made sawing up timbers from the wrecked cabins. Hugh Wade had always loved a good horse and now he let go the saw handle and came up, to lay a fond hand on the neck of the bay, a gesture that twisted the heart of his son and filled it with new bitterness.

"Well, well!" Hugh exclaimed. "We are honored, Miss Juliet. Two pretties. You and this horse both get more beautiful every day."

She held down a hand to him and gripped the callused fingers hard. "And you are a worse flatterer every time I see you, Mr. Wade. Help me down. I don't ride often now and I'm terribly awkward at it. I brought you something. Be careful—it might break."

She was out of the saddle as lightly as a breath. She reached up for a parcel, carefully wrapped in a white cloth.

Duncan took his time brushing the sawdust off his clothes, moving nearer. "Good morning, Mrs. Destrade," he said woodenly.

"Oh, my word! Why so formal?" She laughed. Then she commanded, "Help me with these, Duncan . . . eggs."

"Eggs?" repeated Hugh, his face changing. He wanted no gifts of charity from the Villerands. That was evident from the stiffness of his neck.

"Listen, Mr. Wade." She sensed his attitude. "These are your eggs. I was riding through your meadow—there where the thicket is, on the edge of the wagon road—and I saw the hen fly out. And it was a brown hen. We haven't any brown hens; ours are all domineckers. It must have been one of your hens that strayed, one that the soldiers couldn't catch."

She opened the cloth, kneeling on the ground, and ten white eggs rolled gently about. Duncan saw his father's eyes quicken. Good Lord, he's hungry! he thought with a flash of defensive anger. The flavorless vegetables they had had to live on all these weeks, the tasteless hominy, he himself had accepted, grateful that they filled his belly so long used to the scanty army fare. But his father was old—and so thin!

He said hastily, "It might have been a stray hen of yours, Pa."

Hugh Wade nodded, obviously eager to accept that idea. "Louisa did have a lot of brown hens. But we should let her hatch these eggs . . . that is . . ." He frowned and flushed, remembering that such crude matters as the mating of chickens were not spoken of in a young lady's presence. "I'll have one boiled." He hastened to repair the breach. "I haven't had a boiled egg since Mrs. Wade was taken sick."

"I hope they're fresh enough to boil," Juliet said. "They spoil so quickly this hot weather. We can go and try anyway, can't we? Well, if you did try to hatch chickens, Mr. Wade, somebody would probably steal them. Tuby locks our chicken house every night, but Mama says the hens disappear just the same. I hope Louisa hasn't let the fire go out."

Hugh Wade followed her to the kitchen. Duncan picked up the hammer and began pulling nails out of the planks with quick, irritated jerks. So Marian had been right, when he had thought her only jealous, childishly jealous, he knew now. Juliet wasn't going to let him alone. He might tell himself that this was only friendliness, he might think that Julian Villerand had put his daughter up to breaking down Hugh Wade's stubborn animosity, but his heart knew better. He asked himself sternly what difference it made to him, and was angry that no answer could be found in his mind.

He heard laughter coming from the kitchen, Louisa's high-pitched cackle rising above the rest, and felt left out and annoyed and ashamed that he could not face this episode with the detachment on which he had prided himself. He gave a nail a furious, vehement jerk. It came loose suddenly, flew up and struck him in the eye. A pain like flame shot through the eyeball. When he pressed his hand over it quickly there was blood on his fingers.

Nothing to do but go into the house for hot water, though he hated parading an injury before her—like a little boy showing off his sore toe. Louisa looked up first and squeaked.

"Lord-a-mercy, Mist' Duncan, what you done to yourself?"

Juliet and his father were hunkered down before the fire, her black habit trailing out on the floor, both intent on a long-handled pot that bubbled. Juliet looked around and sprang up. "Duncan—you've hurt yourself!"

"It's nothing," he protested. "Rusty nail scratched me. Give me a clean rag and some hot water, Louisa."

"Sit down here. Let me look." Juliet moved a stool out with her foot, while his father came close worriedly.

Louisa brought a bowl of warm water, leaned over him, her body close and warm. "Ain't put your eye out anyhow," she comforted.

"It's your eyelid—and a cut on your eyebrow," Juliet said. "Keep your hand down, Duncan, so we can see."

"Can't bear the light," he mumbled.

Louisa slapped a warm wet rag over the injured eye. "Let it bleed. Heal quicker."

"Those old square iron nails are sharp as knives, some of them," Hugh remarked. "Cut my hand on one not long ago."

"Cobwebs and soot stop it," Louisa volunteered.

"Hold still, Duncan. I have to see where the blood is coming from," Juliet ordered. "Oh, it's in your eyebrow—the cut. You'll lose some hair and have a scar, I'm afraid. Louisa, is there any whisky in the house?"

" 'Fore God, Miss Juliet, where us git any whisky? Dem Yankees drunk up everything on the place and busted what they ain't drunk."

"They even drank Mrs. Wade's cologne," Hugh said.

"I don't see how we can put a bandage on that cut, Duncan." Juliet dipped the cloth and rinsed it, folded it and pressed it gently down. "We'll have to tie something around your head to keep the light away when we get the bleeding stopped. If you'll get me some scissors, Louisa, I'll cut the hairs away from this wound. They'll stick and pull when the blood clots. It was a lucky thing it didn't hit your eyeball. You must have closed your eye quickly. Now don't move. This may hurt a little. Louisa, you wipe the blood away while I cut."

Hugh Wade had wandered to the door while the women's ministrations were going on. He turned back frowning. "Visitors," he said. "More Yankees."

Duncan started up, but Juliet pulled him down. "You must not move till I tie this around your head. If they're Yankees they won't leave till they get what they came for."

"There's nothing left for them to take," said Hugh, starting out.

Juliet deftly draped a width of clean cloth around Duncan's head, knotted it behind. "Now you look like a pirate," she said. "Why don't those miserable Yankees stay away and leave us alone? I heard my father talking this morning. He said they were all so furious about some stupid amendment or other that they'd likely come down on us like a ton of brick."

"Thank you for your assistance, Juliet." Duncan got up, headed for the door.

"Can you see out from under that bandage?"

"Yes, I can see. I'd better find out what those fellows want."

"Probably more taxes or something."

"If they tax away our crop this year, we won't plant another seed!" he declared hotly. "We're not getting blisters and calluses to plant cotton for scalawags and thieves."

Juliet followed him to the door and they looked out at the young officer who had come riding into the yard, followed by a buggy in which were two scurvy-looking white men.

"Why, it's that lieutenant who came to see Marian!" she exclaimed in a low voice. "His name is Wilks—or something like that. But who are those men with him?"

"Friends of Marian's too?" Duncan asked dryly.

"The lieutenant rescued her from a soldier who had insulted her. She said he's a gentleman if he is a Yankee."

"Obviously," Duncan said, "this is no social call."

One of the white men had alighted from the buggy and taken an official-looking paper from his pocket.

"You'd better go inside, Mrs. Destrade," Duncan advised.

But she pushed past him, holding up her trailing habit, and said, "Good morning, Lieutenant."

The officer bowed, removing his hat, and to Duncan's eyes he looked thoroughly uncomfortable. "Good morning, Mrs. Destrade."

The man from the buggy did not take off his hat. "Which one's Duncan Wade?"

"I'm Duncan Wade." Duncan stepped forward. "Who are you?"

"Liveright. Deputy Sheriff. Got a warrant here for your arrest, Duncan Wade. Didn't need a warrant—could have jest come and took you on this charge, but the plaintiff wanted a warrant. Anyway, this-here paper makes it all tight and legal."

"What charge? What am I accused of?" Duncan demanded, aware of Juliet's indignant eyes, his father's suddenly shaking hands.

"Assault with intent to commit murder on the person of Cassius Grant," droned the deputy, spreading out the document.

Duncan looked at his father in perplexity. "Who the devil is Cassius Grant?"

"Never heard of him," Hugh returned.

"When am I supposed to have assaulted this person I never heard of?" Duncan asked.

The lieutenant reined his horse closer. "Let me have that paper, Liveright, you know you can't read it."

"I larnt the charge off anyhow," the deputy protested. "It's my business to serve this-here on the accused party."

"Give it here," Wilkins snapped. "Mr. Wade, you are accused of beating a certain Cassius Grant over the head with a pistol and shooting at him while he was endeavoring to escape from you. I'm sorry, but you'll have to go with us, Mr. Wade."

"So they send the army along now, do they?" Duncan said. "Just when was this alleged crime supposed to happen?"

"On the night of August fifth, it says here. While the plaintiff, Cassius Grant, was making an innocent and friendly visit to your premises you attacked him, inflicting grievous injury with the intent to commit murder."

"August fifth? I was in Selma on August fifth. No—that was the day I came home. My God, I did beat up a nigger that night! He was stealing my mother's silver."

"Cassius Grant?" Juliet repeated, frowning.

"The man is employed in your home, Mrs. Destrade," Wilkins told her. "He made inquiries of me about legal procedures when I was in your home some weeks ago."

"You mean *our* Cassius? But his name isn't Grant!"

"He took that name. He came to town yesterday and swore out this warrant. Sorry, but you'll have to come with us, Mr. Wade."

"You mean you're taking my son to jail for running a Negro thief off the place?" demanded Hugh, his face purple with fury. "I saw where he'd opened up our cistern. I heard Duncan shoot at him. Unfortunately he missed."

"Fortunately perhaps, Mr. Wade. I should hate to have to arrest your son for murder."

"I can't believe it was our Cassius," insisted Juliet. "I know he has been sullen and lazy lately, but I can't believe he's that wicked, Mr. Wade."

"Look here, Miss Juliet." Hugh pulled out the brass medal from his pocket. "Ever see this? We found it out there by the cistern where the Negro dropped it when he was after the silver."

"Half the Negroes in the county got 'em," said the deputy. "They give 'em out when they was drillin' 'em. Makes a Negro feel important to give him a badge."

"Cassius did have one. He said it meant he was a Union

patrol," Juliet said. "If he was after your silver, Duncan, you certainly had a right to beat him."

"Ain't nobody got a right to beat a free Negro," the deputy argued, "neither shoot at him."

"If it was Cassius and he swore to those lies, I'll go home and beat him myself!" Juliet stormed. "I'll wear out this crop on his worthless hide."

"Please, don't do it, Mrs. Destrade," said Wilkins with a bleak, rueful smile. "I should hate to have to send an officer to serve a warrant on you."

She stormed at him. "How can you bear to be mixed up in such foul business, Lieutenant? Duncan, I remember now. That night you were at our house you said something about the hams, and Papa told you he had a hiding place, and you said you had only the cistern. Cassius beat you home to get the silver. You must have Cassius arrested, Mr. Wade, for trying to steal your property. You should go straight to town and have him put in jail."

Hugh laughed harshly. "No court in this county now would issue that warrant, Miss Juliet. And probably no officer would serve it if it was issued. You will give my son time at least to change his clothes?" he asked. "And he has just badly injured an eye. It will need treatment."

"I got to go with him if he goes inside," the deputy said.

"I won't change my clothes. These clothes are good enough for their filthy jail!" Duncan said hotly.

Louisa, who had stood watching, began to wail, her apron over her face. Old Josuff came up and stared, rheumy eyes harrowed and feral. "What dey do wid Young Master?" he inquired.

"They takin' him to jail. 'Count of that no-good Cassius," Louisa told him.

Duncan clasped his father's hand, bowed briefly to Juliet, started to the buggy. Juliet put her hand over her mouth, stifling a cry. The deputy climbed in, shifting the heavy pistol he wore ostentatiously. Then Juliet galvanized into fury. She ran to the mounted officer, stood at his stirrup, her eyes blazing. "Never come near our place again, Lieutenant Wilkins!" she ordered. "If you show yourself there, you will not be received."

"I'm sorry, Mrs. Destrade. I am only acting under orders. Drive on, Liveright."

Hugh Wade stood like a figure in stone till the buggy was out of sight. Then his clenched fists beat the air. "Damn them! Damn them to hell!" he cried in bitter agony.

"That no-good yellow nigger!" Louisa stormed. "All his own color despise him. Tryin' to steal my Mis' silver!"

Josuff said nothing. Quietly he went to his cabin. There he sat on his cot stroking a shiny razor over a leather strop. . . .

"You must have Parmy saddle up for you and go straight into town, Mr. Wade," argued Juliet. "I'll ride with you and we'll get a lawyer, the best lawyer in this county."

"My dear—" the old man got control of himself—"it's no use. There isn't a lawyer in Marengo County now who can even enter their courts—not one of any reputation at all. Even if I had money to pay—and I haven't any . . . There's no law any more—only bribery, thievery and corruption. Damn it, why didn't Duncan shoot to kill? We could have buried the black scoundrel then. I'd gladly have buried him myself."

Juliet began to cry and beat the air with impatient fists. "But we must do something! If you won't go, Mr. Wade, I'll go myself—alone."

"No, no, Miss Juliet. You mustn't go. I won't allow it. You'd be insulted, perhaps even attacked, by the riffraff that hang around the courthouse. You'd better go home now. Josuff, I want you to walk across the field with Miss Juliet. Go as far as Villerand's fence—and don't you ride off and leave Josuff you hear?"

"Josuff's in he cabin, Mist' Hugh. I'll tell him." Louisa bustled off.

"You mustn't ride over here alone again—you or Marian either," Hugh continued. "It's unsafe. I forbid it, though I thank you for coming today. I'm sure Duncan would thank you too."

"I won't go," she insisted. "If I do I'll get Papa's gun and shoot that wretched Negro dead!"

Hugh Wade's drained face changed. Decision came into it, and a hard, bitter look. "About Cassius, Miss Juliet—it would please me very much if you act as if nothing had happened. Don't speak of this at all. Keep him puzzled and worried."

"He'll strut and grin, the nasty yellow thing. He may even brag. And if he does, I'll cut him to pieces with this whip, Mr. Wade."

"No, you won't. You'll keep still and hang onto your pride. You won't let a free-issue rascal know that he has any power to hurt you or any friend of yours. Are you listening, Miss Juliet?"

"Yes, I'm listening, but I don't like a word of it."

"But you'll do as I say because you want to help Duncan."

"I don't know if Duncan wants help from me. He never looked at me. He didn't even say good-by."

"He was holding onto his temper and his pride. If he hadn't been fighting mad, he wouldn't have missed when he shot at that Negro. Wades don't miss when they shoot."

Then Louisa came back with Josuff. Hugh Wade turned to them. "Louisa, you and Josuff listen to me. No talking about this—not even to Parmy, you hear?"

"Yes, suh, Mist' Hugh. Parmy, he down to the river fishin'. He ain't know."

"You, Josuff, you understand? Not a word where it can get back to Cassius Grant. Cassius Grant! My God, why didn't he call himself Cassius Lincoln—or even Cassius God Almighty?"

"I ain't had no words wid that nigger no time, Boss," insisted Josuff. "You knows I don't go off this place 'less it wid you or Young Master."

"Go along with Miss Juliet, Josuff."

"Mist' Hugh——" Josuff came close, then thought better of what he had been about to offer impulsively. He had started to say that he had money, if it took money to get Mist' Duncan out of jail. Canny, cautious cupidity held his tongue. He was not going to turn loose his money, not for nobody.

He trudged heavily across the meadow after Miss Juliet's horse, grumbling a little. "Too hot for ole man like me to walk 'way over hyar."

"Go back then," she ordered. "I'm not afraid. Anyway, what could you do to protect me? You haven't even got a stick."

"Got my razor," Josuff announced smugly.

When Juliet had taken the horse over the boundary fence and trotted off down through the peach trees, Josuff sat down for a while and dozed, the sun hot on his thin shoulders. Then feeling hunger pangs growing within him he struggled up and headed down the meadow.

At the brick-walled burying ground he stopped and looked around slyly. No one was in sight. The mule fed in the field beyond, the jay bird came and squawked a challenge from a cedar bough.

Josuff tilted the stone urn on the monument, moving it slowly so it would not fall. Mindful of snakes and lizards, he peered into the opening before he put his hand in, dug among the debris there and finally sighed, content.

His money was still there.

He felt a faint pang of conscience at letting Mist' Duncan go to jail when maybe those white men would have taken money and let him go free. Josuff was a trifle vague in his mind about the power of money, but instinct told him that it was enormous, that men had been killed for it, white folks lost their homes for it, Negroes got mighty biggity and ornery because of it.

He eased his anxiety by conjecturing that there might be ham and chitlings in that jail. Yankees had got all the hams there was. It was a Yankee jail, wasn't it? Maybe Mist' Duncan would git him a bite of ham and some red gravy.

XVII

THERE WAS FOG in the low places when the air cooled and a swirl of vapor half hid the moon. Summer nights were short and not dark enough to hide the Negroes who prowled like cats, always in groups that kept close together, to defeat by solidarity the menace and threat of vindictive white men, hants, plat-eyes, hooty-owls and snakes.

They kept to the roads, walking always in the middle, talking loudly and at times belligerently, both to affront their enemies and to reassure themselves.

"Us topman now. Us ain't got to be skeered of nobody," Preacher blandly assured the half dozen who followed him. "This-here the Union League you boys gittin' into. White people into it too, but us topman. They can't get nobody elected 'less us joins up and votes. Brother Cassius, how come you lose your badge?"

Cassius disdained to answer. He said loftily, "Brother Forsyth, my name Mister Cassius Grant. And I ain't brother to nobody."

"How come you ain't call yourself Cassius Villerand? That a fine high-soundin' name, brother."

"I ain't borrowin' no name a white man done wore out. Where this meetin' at? I done walked two miles already."

"Bide you time, Mister Grant, bide you time. Ain't much furder. Does us git orginize', and git our rights, us all ride in carriages, smoke big black seegars, drink plenty good liquor. This-here the Wade place. Mighty gone to rack. Be worse of now, they done got young Wade up yonder to the jailhouse."

Cassius ignored that. He had no wish to share his personal quarrels and triumphs with people who before the upheaval of war had been mere field hands and hostlers. He felt a trifle degraded at tramping down the road with them now, but the captain who bossed the Freedom Bureau had sent the word and Cassius had no intention of being counted out when the promised rewards were distributed. What the Union League might be he had no idea, but this, he had been assured, was the black man's day, this was Kingdom Come and Jubilee rolling in a gold chariot with the proud white boss licking the dust from the chariot wheels.

His feet hurt. Miss Emma Villerand had been in a big way all day, finding cobwebs and dust and making all the colored servants live hard and groan inwardly while she ordered them about with brooms and mops. Cassius comforted himself that Miss Emma would be out in the field one of these days, dragging a heavy cotton sack, while some haughty colored boss, preferably Mister Cassius Grant, shouted orders and short-weighted the cringing white workers at the scales.

"Ole Brother Josuff, he ain't show up at no meetin's," Preacher complained. "I done carried him the word, two-th'ee times myself. Then I sont Prince to tell him be on hand, and young Mist' Wade, he come out with a gun and tell Prince to git hisself gone right quick. Brother Josuff, he git too ornery and us goin' bust in his face some these days."

"Josuff ain't no quality man," Cassius declared. "He just a ole white-folks' nigger. All white-folks' niggers does is carry ales and make trouble."

"Ain't carry no tales to me," Prince stated. "All he say, git gone or he cut my th'oat with a razor."

Cassius breathed easier. He was hoarding his glory. He had made his mark on a legal document and seen white men duly constituted with authority ride out to avenge his black eye and

bruised head. Legal retribution had been all written down on a
paper with fancy printing on it and seals at the bottom. Now
Duncan Wade was in jail and no jury, Cassius had been assured, would turn him loose. Cassius walked with a prideful
stride and proudly disdained to peer fearfully at the shadowy
clumps of bushes along the road.

The meeting was held in the cellar of a half-burned church
down near to the river. Bed Forrest's horses had been quartered in the churchyard and feed had been stored in the cellar.
Rats leaped and ran as Preacher lighted the lantern that swung
down from a beam.

"Us wait outside till the white boss git hyar," Preacher ordered then, concealing with bravado his own instinctive unease.

There were old gravestones in the churchyard. Some of the
disciples protested against waiting in a burying ground and
went back to the hot, odorous interior. Mosquitoes, attracted
by the light, came in swarms to this banquet of warm, human
meat. Preacher set some disciples to gathering bark and kindled a smoky smudge, even removing one of his own soggy
socks and laying it on the fire.

"That stink the skeeters out. When us git orginize' good I'm
goin' wear solid silk socks anyhow."

Cassius did not mingle or join in the laughter and the loud
talk. He leaned aloofly against a tree in the darkness and oc-
cupied his mind despising these simple-minded creatures, his
black brethren. When they were voting, he had already decided,
they were going to be voting for him. Men of his race had
already won office in other states, he had heard at the Villerand
table. He himself could be a legislator, he could even be a judge,
maybe sit up in a courtroom with a big brass spitton handy,
and sentence white men to hang for abusing Negroes. He
intended to fly high and tread heavily on anyone who had offended his dignity by giving him orders or treating him with
insulting indifference. Mr. Julian Villerand, locking up all his

liquor, acting friendly with Democrats and all the time plotting with folks up north to steal Alabama money, like as not. Build a railroad—ha! Mr. Julian wasn't buildin' no railroad. He was fixing to rob everybody, Cassius was certain. Let him get hauled up in Mister Judge Cassius Grant's court and he'd get learned to carry water on both shoulders!

The proceedings of the meeting, which finally got under way, did not interest Cassius greatly. He had heard all the talk before. All promises. All boasts. You boys got to learn to read. How you goin' to be big top-man like the white people when you couldn't even vote without some white man tell you where to mark? Cassius got bored. Nobody handing out any money, no liquor except some rotgut stuff, eat a man's guts up. All low-down, field-hand blab, beneath the dignity of a man who intended to be a judge. Quietly he slipped away at last alone. Most of the participants were too drunk by then to notice his departure.

Hugh Wade had not slept at all.

When the house was quiet and the doors barred, he had oiled and cleaned the gun Duncan had brought back from Selma and loaded it with care. Then squatting before the fireplace in the dining room, he reached high into the chimney and brought down a shower of soot. His mirror was cracked and swimmy, but he saw clearly enough in it to cover all the skin of his face and neck with the black stuff, even into his ears and up into the edges of his hair.

The old hat which he dragged far down covered the rest of his graying locks. His shirt was grimy, his hands were blackened. He put on an old dark coat that had been Duncan's and was now too tight for either of them, but it had deep pockets that held the gun. He kept his hand on the butt of it as he slipped silently out into the night.

He had been lucky, listening outside the kitchen. Parmy and

Josuff had been talking about a meeting while Louisa fed them, Parmy insisting that they ought to go, that some bad niggers might come and do them bodily harm if they failed to appear. Josuff had refused angrily to have any truck with such trash, and Louisa had threatened Parmy with short rations and two days' hard labor digging yams, if he set foot off the place.

Josuff had settled the matter finally. "It costs two dollars. Ain't no black trash gittin' my money."

Parmy was silent. "Parmy done wastes all he money anyway," Louisa had stated disgustedly. "Done spent it all on liquor and candy."

Hugh went quietly across the yard and into the lane. The night was murky, with coolness coming down from the hills to the north turning the breath of the earth into scarves of drifting vapor. A night for growing, his planter's heart knew. On such nights you could almost hear the cotton and corn stretching higher, opening leaves to the night and the dew.

On the slope a rabbit leaped out and ran for the security of the burial plot. There in the cedars an owl complained in soft, liquid flutings. Hugh Wade kept to the thickety growth that was head high along the cornfield. Honeysuckle bloom was a heavy fragrance on the air, and the old man breathed it with a brief return of old happiness, a delight in the riches of summer, but the grimness within put down the relenting softness. He had no time to remember old days or happier nights. There was a place where he must be, and a time when he must be there, and he thought he knew the time and the place—though when he reached the place he could wait grimly for the time.

A smell of peaches ripening came from Villerand's orchard beyond the fence. That orchard had been Julian's boast for a long time. Hugh thought about his own trees, long neglected, the old fig tree in the yard gnarled and brittle, the apple trees gnawed by cavalry horses and broken by storms and never removed because there was no one to wield an ax or drag away a log . . . no one with strength or time for work save what was imperative for survival.

Where the path into the orchard began was a handy tangle of sassafras sprouts overrun with briers and vines. Into its dark shadow Hugh Wade crawled and lay low. A grasshopper grew jittery under his hand and he freed it silently. He eased the hand back to the gun in his pocket, cautiously got the weapon ready. He had no intention of shooting from ambush. That was a guerrilla trick which honest men despised. But he did not intend to be seen till the right moment.

The coolness that came ahead of dawn made his bones ache and he fought a desire to sneeze, pinching his nostrils hard with numbed fingers. Suddenly he hated being old, being awkward and clumsy at times with his hands, being unable to see with his former sharpness. He flexed his hands, warming his trigger finger, controlling each muscle with such tension that his chest tightened and ached with it. A bird stirred in the trees beyond the fence and let out a thin, sleepy four-bar trill, then was silent again. Apprehension began to trouble Hugh. What if daylight came too soon? People would be stirring. Field work got under way early on these hot days.

Then, when he had begun to get too taut, to consider the possibility of failure, of having to creep ignominiously back to the house in haste lest he be seen, he heard the crunch of footsteps on the path across the meadow. Uneven, lurching footsteps. A man half drunk plodding dizzily toward the fence.

Carefully, curling his palm around the gun so the hammer would not catch on a twig, Hugh eased himself out of his hiding place, lifted himself on his elbows and sat up. The approaching figure was plain now against the thinning purple of the night sky. A hundred yards. Fifty. The Wades did not miss.

By the height, the narrow head, the insolent carriage even in semi-intoxication, Hugh knew that this was the man he waited for. He started to rise, stiffly, when from a clump of bushes a few feet away another figure erupted, springing at the approaching man with a kind of animal cry, half howl, half snarl.

"You damn' nigger you!"

Good God! Hugh gasped. Old Josuff!

Hugh scrambled up. The two were struggling. There were oaths, grunts, then a throaty cry, a gurgle. The tall figure went down. Old Josuff staggered a few paces. Hugh got him by the arm. On the ground Cassius Grant writhed for a moment, his body contorted, then was still.

Josuff was sobbing, panting, slobbering, scrubbing his face with his hands.

"Done cut his th'oat, Mist' Hugh!" he whimpered. "Done cut his th'oat from year to year!"

Hugh slid the gun back into his pocket with a swift surge of relief. Now he need not kill. Now the thing was done with black man's violence but with no evil on his part save the evil of intent. He trembled all over so that his teeth clicked and his stomach surged, and cold sweat broke out on his skin. His voice was a croak. "Who is it, Josuff? Whom did you kill?" Although too well he knew.

Josuff was shaking too. "You know who him is, Mist' Hugh. That yellow scound'el, call himself Cassius Grant. Him put Mist' Duncan in that jailhouse."

"He needed killing," Hugh agreed, still holding to Josuff's sleeve. They were two old men, sickened, spent, holding each other up. "Yes, he needed killing."

"What us do now?" Josuff asked in a small, weary voice.

Hugh shifted his weight, looked down at the dead Negro. There was more light in the sky now. He could see the body clearly, the white shirt stained with the blubbering blood, the narrow contorted face that still wore a sadistic, evil grin.

"What were you doing out here anyway, Josuff?" he asked

"I done followed you, Mist' Hugh. Dat Cassius a bad nigger. I knowed you goin' try waylay that Cassius. I feared you mought git killed."

"How did you know I came here to wait for Cassius?"

"Mist' Hugh, you bound to kill that nigger. What he done to Mist' Duncan, you been bound to kill him. If he ain't kill you first, you bound to kill him."

Hugh scrubbed perspiration from his face, though the mist that crept up from the marsh was sharply cool. "We have to do something with this body, Josuff," he said nervously. "Daylight's only an hour away."

Josuff quickened. "Mist' Hugh . . . us tote him down to the big road and leave him lay there. Anybody mought kill a mean nigger like that Cassius."

"No, it wouldn't do. They'd suspect me first of all. We'll have to bury him, bury him deep. But we can't bury him here. A new grave here, after what happened to Duncan, would hang me higher than Haman."

"Us could bury him in us buryin' ground," Josuff suggested. "Ain't no nigger goin' search a buryin' ground. No white folks neither. Mist' Hugh. If I cotch up that mule reckon us kin lift him?"

"We've got to lift him. And hide this blood here too. Some hound may come sniffing around. Hurry and catch the mule, Josuff. The burying ground is safest. We can pile brush over the fresh earth."

"You fetch a spade while I cotch the mule, Mist' Hugh." Already Josuff was executive, more than a partner in this before-dawn adventure.

Fortunately the ground was soft where the vines and weeds had been lately cleared away. Josuff grunted and wheezed as he dug, and when he tired Hugh took over and labored, his heart pounding, till the long trench was deep enough. Then they dragged the body off the somnolent, uncaring mule's back and rolled it into the grave. Josuff hacked and slashed at the briers that remained in the plot, and piled brush over the mound, while Hugh rode the mule back to the boundary fence and scattered dirt and rocks over the drying pool of blood on the ground.

Day was lime-green and gold above the eastern horizon when he got back to the brick-walled enclosure. Josuff had done well. There was no sign that a body had been lately interred there.

"Come a rain and can't nobody find that nigger," gloated Josuff, shouldering the mattock and spade.

"If anybody has seen us, Josuff, say I couldn't sleep and came out here to work. You came to help me. Remember that if Parmy or Louisa ask any questions."

"Dat woman, she bound to want to know where at us been, if she woke up," Josuff grumbled. "Breakfas'time 'most now."

The old Negro trudged off down the lane, but Hugh Wade stood still for a little under the cedar trees, his hat off, his face drained and gray. Then he stopped and patted the smoothed and ordered grave where his wife lay.

"I had to do it, Miss Florrie," he said hoarsely. "I had to bury a scoundrel near to you. But you'd have told me to do it, Miss Florrie. You'd have killed him yourself if you could, now wouldn't you, Miss Florrie? Of course you would!"

XVIII

OF ALL TIMES to have a row going on in the house Julian Villerand was profanely voluble that no time could be worse than this day.

After making that long wretched trip up north, spending too much money and getting seasick, to persuade the Stanton brothers to come down and look over the possibilities for promotion and investment in Alabama, he had finally got them here as guests in his house and now the devil was to pay.

No butler to serve breakfast, the girls carrying on a long quarrel upstairs, and now here came Marian down, dragging him into the library to demand that he put Cassius off the place.

"How can I run him off the place when he's not even on the place?" he demanded angrily. "Tuby, you sure he ain't drunk out there in the quarters? You boys always lie to cover up for one another."

"No, suh," Tuby jittered, his eyeballs bulging like two boiled eggs. "Mister Cassius, he ain't been nowhere round since before dark last night."

"*Mister* Cassius!" roared Villerand. "I'll mister him when he shows up."

"Tuby—" Emma came to the door—"you will have to put on a white coat and carry jugs of hot water upstairs."

"Mister Cassius' coat's too big for me," Tuby protested.

"It can't be helped. Roll up the sleeves. We can't have these Yankees believing that we don't live nicely down here."

"For God's sake, Mrs. Villerand," pleaded her husband, "don't be calling them Yankees to their faces!"

"I suppose," she said with resignation, "I'll have to call them gentlemen. It was not so awkward with that Swayne man—you could call him 'General' without offending your own instincts, or keeping any inner reservations. Cassius may come back at any moment. He often stays out all night lately."

"Well, he's never stayed away through breakfast before."

"He's ashamed to show his face," Marian declared. "He knows what we'd say to him—trying to steal the Wades' silver and then having Duncan arrested."

"My dear," her mother argued, "we don't know that Cassius had any idea of stealing the Wades' silver."

"How do we know old Hugh had any silver to steal?" her father asked. "He'd have sold it long ago, dog-poor as they are! And nobody with any sense would shoot at a colored man in times like these."

"He wouldn't have sold it—not ever," Marian declared. "Not Aunt Florence's silver. He'd have starved first."

"That young Wade always was a hothead. Might have shot one of their own people—and God knows they've got mighty few left! Bound to get in trouble sooner or later. Safer in jail than anywhere, to my notion." He followed his wife into the dining room. "Why did Juliet take a notion to ride over there yesterday, anyway? Came back with a wild tale, got the place all stirred up."

"Juliet has a very dull life here. I thought it quite all right for her to ride Marian's horse for an hour or two, though Marian was highly indignant over it. They've been having hard words ever since."

"Well, tell 'em I've had enough of it. Why do we have hominy for breakfast, Mrs. Villerand? In Boston we had meat and potatoes and even apple pie. Those fellows won't know how to eat hominy. I doubt if they ever saw any."

"Then I fear they'll have to learn, Mr. Villerand." Emma sighed. "There isn't an Irish potato left, fit to cook. The old ones are all sprouted and bitter and the young ones aren't large enough. I had Tuby scrabble out a hill yesterday. They're no bigger than marbles."

"Papa," persisted Marian, coming in behind him, "you have to do something about Duncan Wade—you simply *have* to. It's outrageous."

Julian Villerand had already waited too long for his coffee. His temper flared; flushing, his face grew as red as his beard. "What the devil can I do?" he shouted. "He got himself into this business. Let him get himself out of it!" Confound guests anyway, who kept a whole family waiting around for a meal to be served!

"He did not," Marian insisted. "Cassius got him into it. And that wretched Eric Wilkins helped."

"Well, Miss, I can say this: It's no time to antagonize the Union Army. If Alabama don't ratify the amendment, the Army's going to take over. General Swayne didn't say as much straight out, but he implied it, and it was plain what was in his mind. I'm trying to do something for Alabama, something big and important. Employ a lot of people, turn loose a lot of money—money that's needed to put this country back on its feet. The Army and the Freedmen's Bureau are in the saddle already. If that dam-fool legislature balks—and looks like they're going to do just that—they'll not only be in the saddle, but they'll have their heels on our necks."

"You could get a lawyer. You must know some good lawyers, Papa."

"I'll not get any lawyer. I'll not risk what I've got started now just to mix in a crazy boy's fight with a Negro. My Negro, too! If I'd known about it I might have got that warrant myself."

"If you had," his daughter said in a deadly level tone, "I'd never speak to you again!"

"That will do, Maggie. That's no way to speak to your father," Emma interposed. "Apologize immediately and go to your room. But first go and tell Lelia to stir up some batter cakes. Surely even Boston people will know how to eat batter cakes."

"Probably," Marian remarked saucily, "they'll eat them with their knives."

"She gets worse behaved every day," her father snapped. "Why all this whooperoo about that young Wade? He ought to know Negroes prowl like tomcats. Likely one of those half-witted old people Wade's been able to keep has some whisky hid. Shooting around in the dark—might have shot his own father!"

"But they're our neighbors—and think of having such people in that disgusting jail! And of course all the children were friends in spite of your dislike of Mr. Wade. Duncan was rather a nuisance around Juliet before the war, but it was just a puppy-love affair. She never took him seriously. And I must say that you're to blame for Marian's impertinence, Mr. Villerand. When I refuse her anything or reprove her she knows she can go straight to you and get her way."

"Well, she won't get her way if she thinks that just to get a brawling boy out of jail I'm going to jeopardize the good feeling I've built up in the right quarter."

"He's not a boy exactly. Duncan must be past twenty-five now."

"He can rot there till he's fifty for all of me. Where you reckon that damn Negro went? I've paid him regular every week, gave him that old blue coat of mine too, and I know he steals my seegars—I miss them every day."

"The coat hangs in his cabin. Tuby says all his good clothes are hanging there. Or should I say *your* good clothes, Mr. Villerand? You've spoiled Cassius too. He has been growing very insolent. I had to speak sharply to him yesterday when I was trying to get the house in order for these guests of yours."

"Maybe you made him mad and he took off. Well, there are a lot of idle Negroes. Find another one without much trouble."

"I don't know that I would care for a strange Negro in the house, Mr. Villerand. We do have daughters."

"Juliet said anything about when Destrade would be back? He was mighty vague when I left him in New York. He's got money . . . should get it to working for him instead of hiding it up the chimney the way those Frenchies do. Live on soup, Juliet says. No wonder she doesn't want to stay down there with that old lady."

"It's the conditions in New Orleans, I think. They're really dreadful from what Mr. Destrade says."

"If Destrade had a good home for Juliet, she wouldn't be any more concerned about what went on outside than she is here. Tight—that's those Frenchies. Won't put out a shinplaster if they can squeeze by on a two-cent piece. Not that I don't like having Juliet at home, but after all she married him."

"I know people wonder—and probably talk," Emma said. "Have you asked Mr. Destrade to take a share in this project of yours—whatever it is? Of course I know nothing whatever about business."

"Can't pin him down. Slippery as a fish. Got more than a hundred thousand dollars salted away. Why haven't they got a family? Because young ones cost money!"

"Really, Mr. Villerand! You amaze me! Ah, good morning, gentlemen!" Emma was instantly the hostess as the two Boston men came into the room. "I hope you slept well?"

She was not much impressed with the brothers Stanton. They were redheaded, stocky, hard-faced and, Emma decided, "pushy." She had met carpetbaggers before, but these were extraordinary examples of the breed. General Swayne had been a Yankee, but he had had the manners of a Southern gentleman. The Stantons jerked out chairs and seated themselves at the table, not waiting as gentlemen would till she herself was seated. The smaller one tucked his napkin under his chin and reached immediately for the butter.

Ignoring her presence, they began talking business instantly. Something about the Northeast and Southwest railroad, partially built before the war, wrecked by the Union troops who were trying to destroy the Confederate line of supply.

One, she discovered, was called "J.C." He was the more voluble.

"What we got to work on, Villerand, is this next legislature. That railroad assistance bill they passed last year is a puny political sop to you boys down here—twelve thousand dollars a mile! For finished, complete and equipped construction! Why, the rights of way alone ought to cost that much, if it was handled right. Of course, to interest anybody up home the rights of way would have to be owned by the right people in the first place, and that's where you come in, Villerand."

Emma gave her husband a quick, appraising glance. He looked harassed, she thought, uncertain. He answered her glance and she thought she caught a faint tinge of fearfulness in his eyes. Emma, for all her bland and calm serenity, her apparent ignorance of what went on in the world of masculine affairs, was innately a shrewd thinker, gifted with discernment that had not atrophied from being long unused.

As a Southern lady she deferred to her husband, pretended to admire and support him even if she had long since lost her illusions about his sagacity or mental attainments. Julian had always been a schemer, bullheaded, more than a little insensitive, often downright stupid, she knew in her secret heart, but his ventures till now had been small, personal and cautious, though even in these he had never let ethics or moral values influence him too much if there was an advantage to be gained.

She was glad that her daughters had refused to appear at the breakfast table; grateful that they were not seeing their father as she was seeing him, out of his depth and uneasy, like a man about to bargain with a beast and uncertain of the strength of its claws.

"First thing has to be done, Villerand," said the Stanton who was called "D.N.," "is to get a new bill passed. Cotton ought to go high this year. There'll be money in circulation, and money on the loose makes men think big and talk big. Get that bill changed so the state will endorse mortgage bonds up to twenty thousand a mile, and cut out that proviso that all the rails and axles and steel and stuff has got to be purchased in Alabama."

"If those materials are available in Alabama," Villerand amended.

"Might be possible to see to it that they aren't available," said the other Stanton. "You can't get Northern capital interested if there's no business going to heavy industry in the North. Get the right kind of bill passed, get your rights of way in the hands of the right people who can make a little profit on that part of the deal, and we may be able to find financial backing for you. Got to find somebody who will buy those bonds, first of all. The whole world knows that the South is flat busted. It will take smart work to peddle those bonds. Even if the state endorses them, it will take a year, Villerand—maybe two."

"In two years somebody else can get ahead of us," Villerand argued. "Milner, maybe. Or some group of local men. McKee, over at Selma, is hammering on that. Editorials in that little old paper he prints every week."

"Get your rights of way and survey tied up and nobody can get in ahead of us," D. N. Stanton insisted. "Most of what you hear is just talk, and you can always get the military to squelch it if it gets to be a nuisance. Trouble with the South, it was built on talk! Oratory and high-flown notions of grandeur, and nothing solid to back it up. Talk investment in the South to any concern north of Washington and they think all you've got down here is moonlight and magnolias and all your propositions are so much perfumed wind."

Emma felt her skin prickling and a hot protest rising in her throat like a painful swelling. Her South Carolina heritage of pride and assurance was causing her blood to boil against these strangers who outraged her hospitality by their crudenesses, their insults, their repellent manners. She pushed back her chair, trembling a little, keeping her voice cool and steady with an effort.

"May I be excused, Mr. Villerand? I'm sure that you and these . . . gentlemen—" there was a flagrantly obvious pause over that word—"will wish to discuss your business privately, and I have duties elsewhere." She waited an instant, wondering if the Stantons were going to be offended by her scorn, but apparently they were too selfishly obtuse for delicate nuances of tone to penetrate their thick skins.

Julian rose and bowed a little, and she left the room too quickly, not wanting to witness any longer her husband's sorry role in this conference. The Stantons merely sat and stared. D.N. reached for more syrup.

In the back hall Emma stopped and got control of herself. It was bad enough to know that such men as those in there had power of decision over anything in Alabama, but to have them in her beds and at her table and see them making a dupe of her husband was intolerable. For they *were* using him, she was confident; dishonesty and corruption had an effluvium and her nostrils and sensibilities were delicate. She could smell evil, and there was nothing a mere woman could do about it. Criticism, she had long since learned, made Villerand only more perverse. Like all small men his self-assurance was overgrown and mixed with a pugnacious obstinacy.

Juliet came down the stairs, an empty cup in her hand. "Are they still here?" she whispered.

Emma nodded. "They are talking business in there with your Papa."

"Mama, they'll make a cat's-paw of Papa! They'll use him and discard him, and meanwhile he'll probably have ruined himself with all the people who really matter in this county. He'll be a scalawag and we'll be a scalawag family. We'll never be able to hold up our heads again."

"There's nothing I can do, Juliet," Emma said wearily. "They have abominable manners, and I've the feeling that they are utterly unscrupulous—maybe even wicked. But your father is convinced that what he's doing is for the good of the state—though I do feel that he is more than a little worried."

"You ought to put your foot down, Mama. Papa listens to you sometimes."

"I've never interfered in his affairs. He wouldn't listen if I tried. Of course you don't have to stay here, Juliet—you have a husband and a home to go to."

"I haven't any home! Only that mildewed, chilly old house and *Maman*—not to mention Thérèse and Annette and Angèle! They talk about me behind my back, knowing how little French I understand, and even the servants are impudent. But Felix Destrade thinks it is all perfect. You knew I didn't love Felix when you persuaded me to marry him, but of course you couldn't know how ghastly life with him would be. I wish divorce wasn't such a disgrace!"

"Juliet, you don't know what you're saying!"

"Oh, yes, I do! I know very well and I think about it constantly. Because there is such a thing as love, Mama, though it's not supposed to be ladylike to talk about it. Sometimes I think I'll simply rebel and refuse ever to go back there—not till his mother dies, at any rate. But then those vinegary old maids would still be around, waiting on Felix Destrade hand and foot in that revoltingly obvious way they have of implying that I'm absolutely useless."

"Juliet, I hope I'm not hearing what I suspect from your words: that you think you have fallen in love with someone else than your husband! You could learn to love Mr. Destrade. I find him very agreeable."

Juliet began to cry, and Emma knew a shocked and incredulous sort of misery. For what she was seeing in her daughter's face was a young, tormented anguish. Rapidly Emma ran over in her mind the roster of all the young men of their acquaintance. Nowhere was there a clue . . . unless . . . but she would not let herself believe that Juliet was so silly as to revive that troubling, long-ended, very young affair with Duncan Wade.

She asked abruptly, "What were you and your sister quarreling about this morning?"

Juliet stiffened instantly, and her eyes turned stony and remote. "Oh, that, Mama." She tossed her head. "Nothing at all! Merely some more of Marian's silly jealousy."

Emma Villerand had to be content with this.

XIX

THE JAIL was hot, airless and crowded, but it was clean. Every morning a jailer with a filthy mustache half concealing a mouthful of broken teeth strode in importantly, strutting on bandy legs, supported by an iron-jawed sergeant in a uniform too small for him.

With shouts of abuse he herded all the prisoners, all white men but one, into the corridor, handed out buckets and mops and hunks of lye soap, strong and brown, and ordered them to scrub the place clean and wash themselves before they would be given anything to eat. The food was soupy peas with a little fat meat, grayish corn bread and water. On Sunday they got a little molasses and some army hardtack.

"Might as well be back in the army," grumbled a tall young man from the upper end of the county. "We ate better than this in the Nineteenth Alabama."

"We didn't," Duncan said, sopping up the last greasy bit on his tin plate with his bread. It was good to taste even a bit of fat again. He realized now how much he had missed it. "That last winter above Richmond, we boiled acorns one time, and one time we came across an onion patch and dug them all with our bayonets—they lasted about thirty minutes. What are you in here for?"

"They say I hid out some cotton to dodge the taxes. Then when they came for it, with soldiers, I burned it—so they say," answered the other, with a wry grin.

"Made a nice hot fire, didn't it?"

"Plenty of smoke, anyway. They find a sheet up your chimney?"

"No, Applegate didn't leave us any decent sheets," Duncan said, missing the import of the remark. Having stayed so close on the place, he knew little of what went on in the county.

"Thought maybe you got caught out riding with some of the boys," said the other, who had said his name was Lindsay. "You haven't joined up with the Black Cavalry, then?"

An older man who shared their cell looked about nervously. "Don't talk too much. Never know who they've got planted in here."

"True, you might be an informer yourself," Lindsay said.

"I'll ask you to take that back, sir," said the older man stiffly. "I am a man of property. I've still got my land. Ask anybody up Linden way about Cephas Strong. One of my Negroes swore me into this trouble. Swore I was robbing my hands of their share of the crop. The scalawag government took my cotton, but they said I had to pay the Negroes anyway, so they threw me into jail."

"Apologize," Lindsay said quickly. "What I want to know is, when do we get a trial and what chance has a man got when the judge can't even read the lawbook or sign his name?"

"I heard they've got a colored man, judge, over in Selma," Strong said, mollified. "Goes to sleep on the bench most of the time, spends the rest of it eating goobers. My brother-in-law tried to post bond for me, but they wouldn't accept his bond because he'd had two boys with Forrest up at Black Creek."

They talked, sitting on the still damp floor. Then they leaned against the wall and dozed. The heat was punishing, the cramped quarters were torture for active men. The guards were too obtrusive at times, then for long periods the prisoners were ignored, except for the shambling Negro who brought their meals. Duncan, dull and dizzy from the heat and the forced inaction, found his brain playing him strange tricks.

When he grew drowsy it was hard to separate dreams from reality. He had been locked up only two days when he would have sworn that he heard Marian Villerand's voice in spirited argument with somebody outside. He told himself that this must be part of his dream, remembering the anger in her voice and eyes the last time he had seen her, in her father's house.

There was no word from his father and that worried him too. Hugh Wade was frail and Duncan had never known his father to be impetuous, but he knew how quickly the traditional pride and spirit of the Southern gentleman could flare into incredible violence.

"You never told us what you're here for," Cephas Strong reminded him on the fourth day, which Duncan remembered was Monday.

"I beat up a citizen of African lineage. He was engaged in a larcenous piece of business on our place, so I dented his thick skull with a pistol. Unfortunately he survived."

"They should not be allowed to survive," Lindsay stated viciously. "I have some friends engaged in the education of scoundrels of that type, black and white. So far the lessons they have been teaching in the upper Tombigbee country have been very effective. Dark nights, terror, mystery, a touch of the fantastic—amazing how meek an obnoxious character becomes when something unexplained, sudden and terrible gets after him. Even the white trash are learning the fear of God—and to my mind they're ten times worse than the poor darkies."

"Farther south they've got the Order of the White Camellia," Strong said, "but if a man gets mixed up in that masked, night-riding business and somebody happens to get killed, he's likely to find himself hanged. Somehow the attitude of these people who were our enemies has got to be changed. Those bitter, vindictive rascals in Washington are in command now, but it won't last forever. Retaliation down here will only intensify their hate for us. I'm for peace myself."

"And what has a peaceful attitude done for you, sir, may I ask?" Lindsay's black eyes flashed. "Here you sit, eating slop the same as the rest of us, outraged and persecuted, your dignity lost, your rights disregarded." He was, Duncan thought, as alert and arresting as a stallion, and probably as dangerous. Lindsay turned with apparent nonchalance and aimed a casual kick at the wall. "Notice how thin this is?"

"Easy on that," Strong warned. "They'd like a good excuse to shoot all of us."

That afternoon the surly guard opened the door of the cell and poked his head in. "You're wanted, Wade," he growled, "up front. Keep your arms folded and your hands on your elbows, or I'll put the shackles on you."

Lindsay laughed. "We'll pray for your soul, Wade. Don't kick too hard when they pull the rope. Very undignified for a Southern gentleman."

"Shut up, you!" ordered the guard, shifting the rifle he carried nervously. "Straight ahead—no funny business, Wade, or you'll get it."

Duncan walked with what dignity he could muster into the office at the front of the building. His clothes were dirty. He had had no chance to shave for four days. His hair was growing too long and hung lankly about his ears. The office was hot and filled with blazing sunshine. After the dim gloom of the cell Duncan blinked as he entered, then opened his eyes wide and painfully in startled surprise.

The jailer slumped behind a battered table. Two soldiers sat with chairs tipped back against the wall. In the middle of the room holding up her skirts from the rough floor stood Juliet Destrade. Duncan stared stupidly for a moment, his astonishment freezing him, before he became aware that Julian Villerand was there, looking hot, annoyed and stuffy.

Juliet said, "Good afternoon, Duncan."

Duncan felt a quick, prickling resentment; anger at circumstance that forced him to appear in such sorry state before these people, anger at himself that he could not feel any appreciation of their coming. There was irritated condescension in Villerand's eyes, but Juliet's look was troubled.

"These folks came to see you, Wade," said the jailer. "Stand here. State your business, Mr. Villerand."

"Let me speak first," Juliet said hastily. "I want Duncan to understand. Papa is willing to give bond for you, Duncan, so you can be released from this dreadful jail."

"Our jail ain't so dreadful, lady," the jailer protested. "Our prisoners get treated good—get every consideration."

Duncan looked at Villerand and their eyes seemed to strike flinty blows like steel on stone. "Why do you wish to give bond for me, Mr. Villerand?" he asked.

Villerand gave a contemptuous sound, half laugh, half snort. "I don't," he said bluntly, "but I've been heckled and tormented by my women till I'm willing to risk it to get a little peace at home."

"Better be thankful you got a friend, Wade, 'stead of arguing about it," the jailer suggested.

"I'm not arguing. Mr. Villerand knows that I was falsely accused, and by a man in his employ. He's trying to salve his conscience. I will not accept bond from you, Mr. Villerand. If I did, it could be construed by you as an admission of my guilt. I'm guilty of nothing except trying to protect my father's property from a marauder, which is the lawful right of any man. I demand that I be tried fairly. Then I'll be acquitted of this trumped-up charge. I want nothing else from you or anybody."

"Duncan, don't be stupid!" Juliet pleaded. "Marian and I have wept to get Papa to agree to this. Marian even ran off and came here alone to argue with these people—it was dreadful. Mama had to forbid her to leave the house today."

So it *had* been her voice he'd heard! The thought warmed an icy region in his heart.

Villerand drew himself up and glared. "While you're talking so biggity, Wade, you might tell me what's become of my colored boy. He ain't been seen since the night after they brought you here to jail."

"How should I know anything about Mister Cassius Grant? I've been locked up here since he swore to that warrant."

"You know, Papa, that Cassius was polishing floors for Mama all that day when Duncan was brought here. I went straight home, after the officers came for Duncan, but Mr. Wade had asked me not to mention the arrest, so I said nothing till Tuby came running in to tell you about it. Cassius probably disappeared because he was too cowardly to face what he had done."

"Maybe he did, lady," said a soldier, "and maybe somebody decided he wasn't going to appear against a white man. Happens all the time." He tossed away a toothpick and glared at Duncan. "You had friends took care of that boy for you, didn't you?"

"I did not. I didn't even know the fellow was missing. Maybe you failed to pay him as much as he thought he deserved, Mr. Villerand."

"That's a lie! He got wages regular. He left all his clothes. He didn't plan to run away. You boys better look into it. Some of Wade's Negroes might have had a hand in it."

"We have one old colored man so feeble he can hardly get around and a weak-witted boy who's afraid of his own shadow," Duncan said coldly. "May I be returned to my luxurious quarters now, jailer? There I prefer to remain till Mister Cassius Grant appears in court against me."

"Look, if I give bond for you, Wade, you're out. You can't help yourself," Villerand said. "That's the law."

"You won't give bond for me, Mr. Villerand, knowing that I refuse your help. Thank you for the effort, reluctant as you were to make it. And thank you too, Juliet. You realize my position, I'm sure. I demand to be cleared legally of this mischievous charge. Nothing else will do."

"I think you're being obstinate and stupid, Duncan. It's unkind to refuse help from your old friends and neighbors."

"I don't want help. I want exoneration. I want these charges against me dismissed. The man attacked me before I struck a blow at him. He had a heavy piece of timber. He meant to kill me. The law that says a man may protect himself and his property is as old as the Bible, Juliet."

"Might be some charges you can't talk yourself out of, Wade," Villerand threatened. "If my boy don't show up, there might be some hell popping around here. All right, Hank, lock up the ungrateful hound! Feed him bread and water. I don't give a damn."

He strode out. Juliet followed, looking back ruefully over her shoulder.

The guard gave Duncan a peremptory prod with his weapon. "All right you, git goin'! You had your chance and throwed it away."

"My chance will come in open court, fellow."

At the cell door the guard jangled his heavy bunch of keys, flung the door back, then gave a yell of consternation. Duncan stared, dismayed.

In a corner of the cell sat Cephas Strong. His hands and feet had been tied with strips torn from the ragged mattress. A gag of the same stuff had been thrust into his mouth and tied behind his ears. But above this his eyes twinkled sardonically. In the wall was a gaping hole. The rotting mortar and plaster had been kicked loose, the floor was littered with debris, and in the brick outer shell was an opening through which the sun streamed in. Lindsay, the young planter from the northern end of the county, was gone.

The jailer came running back when the guard shouted, and four soldiers appeared immediately, crowding into the corridor outside the door.

"Looks like you lost you a man, Hank," a soldier jeered. "Now we gotta go hunt him for you, by damn! Couldn't have got far."

The jailer aimed a kick at Strong. "You could have stopped him. You could have hollered anyway."

"How could he holler with that gag in his mouth?" Duncan asked.

"You shut up!" The jailer turned on him. "I bet you was into this too. Get them rags off him! Hell, anybody could have busted loose, tied up like that. Lock 'em both up somewheres."

"We ain't got any empty cells, Hank. All crowded."

"Throw 'em in anyhow." He turned on the military. "You boys go git that Lindsay. Don't fool around while he gits away. Shoot to kill if you have to."

"We'll get him—'less he had a horse hid out. Could of had somebody fetch him a horse. General said we'd ought to have cavalry here—us boys can't catch up with a man on horseback."

Duncan and Cephas Strong were shoved roughly into a dim cell already crowded with four men, who voiced loud and instant complaints.

"Shut up, you bastards!" The guard whacked about him indiscriminately with the rifle. "Keep back away from this door and no talkin' or you'll get the business end of this gun."

When the lock had clanged and the guard had hurried off, the six imprisoned men eyed one another warily, scarecrow figures all, in soiled, sweat-soaked clothes, faces ragged with untrimmed beards.

"Welcome, gentlemen," said the oldest of the four. "Perhaps we can manage to sit down if every man pulls in his feet."

They squatted, three on the single low bunk, three on the floor.

"What happened out there?" asked a lank, gray-faced man with a cough.

"Man escaped. Kicked a hole in the wall. I still don't know why you didn't go with Lindsay, Mr. Strong," Duncan said.

"Rheumatism. Can't run." Strong rubbed the marks on his wrists where the bonds had been. "Didn't want to get shot in the back. He tied me up," he explained to the strangers.

"Of course you fought like hell," a third occupant remarked. "You're Strong from down the river. I'm Davids from Sweet Water. And you—" he looked at Duncan—"would you be a Duncan? You have the look of that family."

"I'm Hugh Wade's son. My mother was a Duncan."

"Thought I wasn't mistaken. All the Duncans have got that go-to-hell look about them. Who got away?"

"Boy named Lindsay from up the county. He must have had a horse hid. Would have known he couldn't get far on foot."

"Wonder how stout this wall is?" The lank man prodded it experimentally with his toe, the effort bringing on his cough again.

"You shouldn't be here, you need a doctor," Duncan said.

"Won't need him long. I shot a carpetbagger. He bought tax title to my little farm. Lays on the railroad survey, somebody told me. Anyway, he come around wavin' a paper and orderin' us to get off the place—I drilled him neat and pretty. They come after me—soldiers. I'll hang, I reckon. Worry about my wife and young ones. Her folks will take care of 'em, I hope. But they ain't got much themselves. My name's Gaunt— fought with Bragg," he added.

"Damn them to hell!" muttered the old man, giving the wall an angry whack.

The guard came back then, shouting threats, promising to

come in and deal out punishment if another sound was heard from that cell.

"Let him come. There's six of us in here," whispered one when the guard had gone.

"I learned a trick or two on patrol in Virginia," Duncan said, "but we'd be shot like rats in a barrel."

"I reckon you're right." Gaunt sighed. "But when you're resigned to bein' hanged, it don't matter much."

"We ought to get him out of here," Davids worried under his breath. "He's got five small children."

"And a consumption on his lungs, from the sound of him," Duncan whispered back.

Dusk fell and no food was brought. A lighted lantern was hung up outside the barred door. Its wan glow showed them to one another, a desolate group, all men who had once been men of substance, if not gentlemen, now submerged, touched by the bestiality of a common civic agony.

Alabama was sick to death and they shared her fever and her pain, fought the pressure of her hopelessness.

The jailer came late and shoved a pan of cold corn bread in at the door, pushed after it a bucket of water. "Gnaw on that," he growled, "and don't let me hear any noise down here or I'll shut you up permanent."

"Mind telling us," Davids asked, "how we're expected to sleep?"

"Sleep like hawgs. Good enough for a lot of stinkin' secesh aristocrats."

"Have some plum cake and muscadine wine, aristocrats?" Duncan passed the pan around.

"Wigglers in that bucket, I'll bet," Strong grumbled.

Somehow they slept. Aching, miserable, twitching and mumbling, they dozed, woke and twisted, one man's foot in another man's stomach, swearing, even sobbing, in the weary way of men racked beyond endurance. Gaunt's cough cracked in the small space like rifle fire. Hate was in the air, the only feeling greater than their wretchedness. It rose above the anguish, fiery, terrible. Duncan could taste it like copper on his tongue when he stumbled up at dawn and leaned against the wall to give the old man, Davids, and the sick Gaunt room to relax their legs.

They had taken turns on the single bunk, two at a time, but only to be tormented by swarming bedbugs. Even a walk to the gallows, Duncan was thinking bitterly, would be a relief. To stretch his legs, to breathe clean open air! He wondered if Lindsay had been overtaken and shot. Not likely, since the garrison infantry had to rely on mounted deputies or borrowed horses. Lindsay would know the country, the good hiding places. He had brought this misery upon Duncan and Strong, but even the four into whose scant quarters they had been crowded wished him well, Duncan knew. He'd have to take off for Texas, probably. Texas must be pretty well filled up with Alabama people by now.

Kirby Smith had held out there longer than any other Confederate general. The last shot of the war had been fired down there on some border bayou.

"Why don't we move around?" Duncan asked later. "Take a rout step and all keep together and we can get the kinks out of our legs. All but you, Mr. Gaunt. You lie still."

They tramped, close to the wall, in the limited space, for an hour, shaking the building with cadence of their tread, till the jailer came and screamed at them to sit down and be quiet or he'd goddam quiet them himself.

There was more pea soup at noon. Then, when the heat had mounted till they were all gasping and weak from lack of air, and Gaunt's white face was contorted by his efforts for breath, the guard came again jangling the everlasting keys.

"You, Wade—come out!"

"Remember, boys, I died gallantly for the Bonny Blue

Flag," Duncan voiced his farewell as the door clanged behind him.

"In there." The guard pointed.

Two people rose from wooden chairs as he went into the office.

One was Horace Horning. The other was Marian Villerand.

XX

HIS FIRST THOUGHT was of the girl. "You've got no business in a place like this," he said abruptly.

Horace Horning gave a little barking laugh. "Gallant feller, ain't he? Why don't you kiss her instead of blessing her out? Most young men would feel flattered to be noticed by a pretty girl. Most of 'em would be glad of a chance to kiss her."

Marian had flushed crimson. All Duncan's feelings about her were seething now in disquieting turmoil within him. She was unpredictable, she was loyal and disturbing and too imperious, and with it all she was dear!

She began, "Duncan——" Then she faltered, moving her hands helplessly, looking as though she might cry. She wore no riding habit, yet there were trash and horsehairs clinging to her black skirt.

"You came to town alone?" Duncan asked, feeling at a loss for anything else to say. "It's not safe for you."

"She came alone," Horning said in a voice of cool reproof, "and she laid herself out to catch thunder when she gets home because of you."

Her eyes kindled. "I'm not going home," she stated firmly.

"Of course you're going home," Duncan informed her. "You'll see that someone goes with her, Mr. Horning? It was good of you to come, Miss Maggie, but——"

"Sit down," ordered Horning, motioning Marian back to her chair. "We've got things to talk about, young Wade, if you're all through flying off the handle and can forget that you used to be an officer with men to yap orders at. You sit down too. I bought me a piece of this jail, and I mean to be comfortable in it."

He let his heavy body down into a chair that creaked, and folded his thick fingers over his stomach. Duncan perched uneasily on a stool that had been a chair before the back was torn off it.

"She knows she shouldn't have come here," Horning began. "She came once before."

"They wouldn't let me see you, Duncan, and I went to a lawyer and he wouldn't even talk to me. He said a nice girl shouldn't bother her head about law and courts and things, and he went all the way home with me, except that I made Diablo jump the fence and left him behind—but he came to the house anyway and Papa threatened to lock me up."

"So she cried for two days and wouldn't eat," Horning took up the tale, "and when they sent food upstairs she threw it out."

"I threw it down the stairs—the tray and everything," she admitted. "Then Juliet said she'd work on Papa—but it wasn't any of her business."

"She was here. Yesterday. Your father too."

"Whole town knows," said Horning. "Heard he offered to go bond for you and you told him to go to hell."

"I was not quite so impolite. I told him I wanted justice, nothing more."

"Smug, ain't you, as well as being a doggone fool? Likely you ain't heard that justice has been hanged and quartered and consigned to an unmarked grave in Alabama. Being rusticated and removed from public events, as you might say, you probably missed that information. Buried Justice right next to Public Honor and Democracy, and nettles grow about the tomb. When a man with your military background and precarious temper gets justice in this county, young Wade, they can rent out hell for lions and lambs to snuggle up in. You need a few buckets of cold water poured over your head so you'll cool down and realize that Justice has give way to Expediency, and you better welcome Expediency if you want to survive. Wouldn't hurt," he added in a judicial drawl, "if they mixed a little soft soap in that water, from the looks of you."

"Don't I know I'm filthy?" Duncan croaked, trying to swallow the angry misery that was too big for his throat. "Do you think I enjoy having a lady see me like this?"

"I'm not a lady, Duncan," she said meekly. "Ladies never do the things I do. I've heard that over and over. Ladies stay quietly at home and depend on gentlemen to fetch and carry for them and fight all their battles. I think being a lady is stupid. I'd rather be a shameless hussy, if being a hussy makes me free to do what I want to do."

"She's excited," Horning remarked amiably. "She don't mean the half of it. Now, young Wade, you keep quiet and listen to me. From now till you get summoned up for trial—which Lord knows when that will be—you're out of this place. See any guards or soldiers around here? There ain't, because half an hour ago I signed up bond to be responsible for your conduct and your appearance when wanted. You're in my custody. Wasn't easy to manage, either, so you be appreciative and never mind the high-flown talk about honor and stuff. You're worth a thousand dollars to me, on the hoof, so long as you remain inside the sacred boundaries of the sovereign state of Alabama, and I mean to see you stick around where I can keep an eye on you and know what you're up to. The plaintiff in your case is still among those missing. He ain't never come back from where he took off to, without adieu."

Duncan got up. "No," he insisted, "no, Mr. Horning, I can't agree to that."

"Oh, thunder! You still all full of elegant notions? Still think you're wearing that red sash you rode off in five years ago—and a plume in your hat? Brass buttons too. I know. One

Southern gentlemen can lick six Yankees. Only sorrow is, we couldn't. We're down and spit on and the expediencies we've been trained up to despise all our lives are our only hope. You're my prisoner, Duncan Wade, and there ain't a damn thing you can do about it—begging your pardon, Miss Maggie. So if you're through spouting fire and looking around for your sword and shining armor, you come on over to the store and I'll lend you a clean shirt and a razor."

"But, Mr. Horning——"

Marian bit her lips and twisted her hands unhappily. "Duncan, please! It's all settled. There's nothing you can do about it."

"I can say that I protest against it! That it's an imposition on Mr. Horning and a travesty on justice!"

"Go on and say it, if it eases that blue-steel vanity in your gizzard, young Wade," said Horning. "Not that I think you're actually worth a thousand dollars. You're too blinded by the arrogance that was the downfall of as pretty a piece of civilization as ever existed on this continent. All the beating you've taken since hasn't learned you a lot of common sense, but there's possibilities in you. Anyway, Bob McKee and this young lady think so, so who am I—just an old calico peddler—to set my judgment up against them? Come along. Ain't any use arguing. No use standing back on a lot of ideas that have ceased to exist. You've got to go with me. Hank Filler wouldn't let you back in his jail if you was to beg him on your bended knee. One of your stripe busted hell out of his jail yesterday and they ain't caught up with him yet."

The sun was a white-hot blade smiting the drowsy town, but on Duncan's face it had the benign glow of a blessing. He breathed the scorched air and felt the richness of it quiver to the deepest vein in his flesh because it was the air of freedom. Marian caught his arm and clung to it and they followed Horning across the almost deserted street and around the corner to the store.

Duncan said, "You shouldn't touch me, Miss Maggie. I'm filthy. I may be verminous, not fit to be near a lady."

But she held on tighter. "I'm not afraid of anything now," she declared.

"You should have been afraid—riding to town alone." He was thinking of those scoundrels who had accosted him on the road back from Selma. On his account this reckless girl might have encountered dangers like that.

"No, they locked up my saddle and all my riding things after I ran away last week. Papa was sending Tuby in with the wagon to buy new cotton sacks, so I hid in the wagon. That's why I'm so dirty." She shook out her skirt. "Tuby was scared to death. He moaned and took on and said Papa would have him whipped, but I told him nobody dared whip a colored boy any more. When we got to the store I got out and went and talked to Mr. Horning. He won't lose any money, Duncan, because you won't run away, and you'll never be brought to trial either, because Cassius will never come back."

He said, "That's a wild conjecture, but I hope you're right."

The blue fire was in her eyes again. "Oh, he won't come back because he knows I'd kill him if he did! I've already spread the word. I've told every Negro on our place I'd shoot Cassius dead if he ever showed up, and I will."

"You mustn't get involved in my troubles. It's dangerous business, threatening Negroes now. And you shouldn't have run away, though of course I'm grateful."

"Are you?" she asked sharply. "You didn't sound like it back there at the jail. Talking back and protesting all the time. Maybe you were disappointed? Maybe you'd rather have had Juliet get you out of jail? She tried, didn't she? She browbeat Papa and made him go, and Papa was in a rage because you were so arrogant and independent, so he said."

"Miss Maggie, please let's not fight over Juliet again. I've told you times enough that I'm not interested in other men's wives."

"Ha!" She loosed her hold and faced him, her bonnet slipping a little over one eye, giving her a gamine look, part elf, part spitfire, part angel, so that Duncan had a perverse itch to box her ears and shake her and kiss her all at the same time. "Ha!" She tossed her head, further endangering the bonnet. "You don't know what she has in her mind. But I know. I heard her say the very words to Mama and Mama turned green and almost fainted. Divorce! She said she wished divorce wasn't a disgrace!"

"That's nonsense. That's fantastic. Anyway, she's married to a Catholic. Destrade would never give her a divorce."

"On some grounds he might," Miss Maggie Villerand remarked sagely.

They entered the store, and Emanuel Hale came puffing up and regarded Duncan with an appraising eye. "I wouldn't believe it," he said; "Not after all the soap and lye gets requisitioned at cost price for Hank Filler's jail. What the devil does he do with it? Eat it?"

"Scrubs floors with it," Duncan said. "I won't shake hands till I'm clean, Mr. Hale."

"Hod's already started a pot of water heating back yonder. Sent for his colored boy to come and shave you too, young Wade. Put you through the mill, didn't they? Anyhow, one customer of ours got away. Young Lindsay. Lit for Mississippi like hell's afire—reckon he made it by morning. Ain't heard or seen anything of that boy of Villerand's, swore you into that rathole. Heard he was seen at some meeting the Radicals had up at old Mount Horeb Church that night, ain't been seen since. Every now and then one of 'em disappears. White fellers too. Well, young lady, you had to get you a man out of jail, but anyway he's a man—some resemblance, anyway."

Horning raised a shout from the back room. "You, Wade—come on back here. Customer might come in. We ain't got so many we want to scare any of 'em off."

The water was warm and there was plenty of it, and Horning even produced a cake of fancy soap. "French," he remarked. "Ordered some one time for Athol's wife. She was having a Yankee general quartered in her house and she said she wanted to show him we lived like quality down here. Smell you up so all the fancy ladies will follow after you, maybe. Here's an undershirt. Don't start arguing now, it's all down in the book. This shirt too. 'Manuel nor me haven't got any pants would fit you, too big in the belly. Soon's you get clean sit here by the window so Tobe can see to get those whiskers off you. Trim you up a little too."

"We've got to send her home, Mr. Horning—Miss Marian —she says she ran away."

"Declares she won't go, but she will. I offered to hire a rig and take her, but she swore she'd jump out and run off across the fields. Might do it. Wouldn't put it past her, high-strung like she is. Looks like you've caught you a gal, young Wade. Nice little thing, but fire and tow. Flies up like a guinea hen if you cross her."

"Couldn't you send a boy out there and tell Villerand to come for her?"

"Reckon I might, if she didn't know he was coming. If she found out, we might have to get her down off the Methodist steeple. You better marry her and tame her down some, young Wade. Somebody's got to." Horning picked up Duncan's soggy shirt and looked at it dubiously. "Reckon it might be possible to boil this garment up in lye and redeem it. You'll have to put Louisa to work on it."

"We can always bury it." Duncan laughed. "I was working when they came for me, hot and dirty. I didn't change my clothes."

"Surprised you didn't put on your swallowtail and fancy cravat. Villerand ain't going to like his girl getting mixed up in this affair, reckon you know? Reminds me—he was up at the courthouse, 'while back, snooping around the tax office. Him and two carpetbaggers he's had hanging around out there. You folks got anything Villerand might take a notion he wanted?"

Duncan jerked up his head, just missing Tobe's poised razor. "Two hundred acres of land," he said sharply.

"Well, you're a free man now till you get docketed for trial. That colored feller never hired any lawyer to represent him— just lit a shuck and ain't been seen since. Of course, somebody that don't like you might press for trial, in case that Cassius ain't here to do it himself."

"What can they do about raising taxes on us, Mr. Horning? No doubt that's what Villerand has got in his mind. He's bullied my father for a long time trying to buy that piece of land. Thinks the railroad survey may run that way, I reckon."

Horning shook his head. "Anything I could tell you would be one man's guess. Look at the property they've confiscated, dispossessed and sold out already. If there's a way to work a scabby trick they'll find it."

"If a reputable company promoted a railroad south from Decatur, my father would give that right of way. But anything those rascals propose would be just another scheme to defraud a lot of people and exploit the state. If I go to the courthouse to find out what they're up to, it might hurry them into springing some sort of legal trick on us before we're ready to meet it. The devil of it is," he muttered sadly between swipes of Tobe's hot towel, "you can't fight scalawags who hold power, unless you've got money."

"Set up straight now so Tobe can trim your hair, and listen to me. I hypothecated a thousand dollars of my credit to get you loose from those scoundrels over there because we need young men with guts. If so be you've got any inward stamina, you can do a lot for Alabama. If you ain't got anything but bellyaches in your interior, I made myself a bad bargain."

"I'll try to see that you don't get the worst of the bargain, Mr. Horning."

"There's one thing Hugh Wade can do right now, and I leave it up to you to talk him into it, sudden and permanent. That piece of property Villerand wants he can mortgage to 'Manuel and me for two-three times what it's worth. We'll set up a credit for you all, so you can meet any taxes they decide to raise on you, to sell you out. And we'll refuse to surrender our lien to anybody whatsoever, no matter what pressure they put on us."

"Good Lord, Mr. Horning, we owe you too much already! What good will it do me to cultivate any intestinal stamina if you're going to carry me around on a chip like this?"

"I'm not figuring on carrying you. I'm figuring on you getting around over some of these counties, along with Bob McKee and some other fellers who know how to put words together, and charming money out of feather beds and sweetening up a few hard-crusted hill tackeys and widows into donating timber and rights of way and signing up for stock if we can build a railroad. And getting the legislature to endorse it and pass that assistance bill, and getting Bob Patton to sign it— when it does pass." Horning let out his breath gustily and sank into a chair. "Got the doggone railroad mighty near built, a'ready, and I'm plumb wore out!" He laughed.

Duncan got up and brushed hairs off his neck and arms. "If you say it can be done, I'm ready to have a go at it. I'll try to get over to Selma and see McKee——"

"Won't need to. He'll be over here in a day or two. Had word from him this morning. Got orders to get you out of jail one way or another, said he needed you."

"So it was really McKee who put you up to giving bond for me? You didn't do it just to please Miss Maggie?"

"Well, she did hasten things up a little, charging in here all covered with chaff and on fire to commit some kind of female violence on the judge and the sheriff and the whole dumb Union Army."

"We have to keep in mind that I'm likely to be consigned to a few years' hard labor, sooner or later," Duncan reminded him.

"That might be taken care of. Some of the boys have been doing a right smart job of dissuading lately. Come a real dark night and I might could get word to a lively little bunch of dissuaders. But don't let them get you into any of that masked business. Captain Gilbert and that young lieutenant of his are itching to run down a few of those night riders and decorate timber with their twitching corporosities. We need you, lily-pure and unblemished. Now——" he handed Duncan a clean, starched shirt—"just one item remains to be disposed of: What are we going to do with Miss Maggie?"

"I wish I knew," Duncan said anxiously. "She's a brave, sweet, spunky little thing, solid gold all the way through. And yet——"

"And yet you ain't right sure you're in love with her? Be simple if you were—you could just marry her out of hand and take her home and let Hugh and Louisa take care of her."

Duncan buttoned a shirt cuff with care. Neither of them had noticed that the door into the shop had been pushed open. "It takes more than love to make a marriage," he said deliberately. "Even if I were in love with the girl, how could I marry without so much as the price of the license or a dollar to pay the preacher?"

Her voice behind him made him jump. "Thank you both very much," she said acidly, "but I don't choose to be married out of hand. I'm not a cat to be dumped into a bag and disposed of because it's a nuisance. And even if you were in love with me, Duncan Wade——" she mocked his tone expertly—"I wouldn't have you if you were the last man left alive! And you needn't bother about me, either of you. My friend Lieutenant Wilkins will see that I get safely home. A woman—" she tossed her head angrily, but there was a suspicious glitter in her smoky eyes—"a woman can be quite certain she is safe if she is under the protection of the Union Army!"

She ran out like a fury, the outside door banged, and Emanuel Hale came into the back room, looking startled. "What busted?" he asked. "She went out of here like a whirlwind and ran off down the street."

"Why didn't you keep her from listening at the door?" demanded his partner.

"Had to sell a customer some buckets he wanted. Couldn't let the business go to pot just to please a lady. Reckon she'll go home? Maybe you'd better run after her, young Wade. Ain't safe for her to be running around alone."

"This ain't any time for him to run after her," Horning argued. "Though I'd bet a calf that that's just what she wants you to do, young Wade."

"She'll be safe," Duncan said dryly. "She's asking for the protection of the Union Army."

"Young Wade," said Horning, "I say you are in love with that gal. If that ain't jealousy I see sticking out of you, like quills on a porcupine, I'm a brass-tailed monkey."

"Well, what if I am?" Duncan demanded desperately. "What the hell good is it?"

No good at all. The old men shook their heads in sad agreement as he took his leave.

XXI

TRAMPING HOMEWARD over the hot, dusty road, he told himself that if this was being in love, it was misery.

There was no sense in it. There had been no wooing, no tender scenes between Maggie Villerand and himself. On the contrary, every meeting with her through this summer had ended in misunderstanding, with Maggie flying into a fury and marching off in a scorning temper. Why, then, did he have this sick feeling of having hurt something tender and defenseless, something he actually ached to protect? That clouded look in her eyes as she flung those last contemptuous words at him had had no fire in it, but the misting of tears. Always before, he had been able to justify himself for angering her, but now a sour pain bore upon him, half shame, half baffled uncertainty.

She had ordered him to fall in love with her, had announced bluntly her intention of marrying him eventually, and then he had been merely amused. Now he felt the stony accusation of cruelty. He had hurt her and sent her dashing out into recklessness and folly. Now he knew how futile his vacillating arrogance had been; he wanted more than anything to comfort and reassure her, when it was undoubtedly forever too late.

Why had he been so slow to waken to the truth? Was it because during all this time he had still been tormented by anxiety for fear he might not be cured of Juliet?

He took the short cut through the fields and along the wagon road which led past the burial plot, and there too misery lay in wait for him. On that brick wall she had sat, flicking the heads of grass with her crop, soberly warning him against the flaring of his uncontrollable temper. He could see her now, bending over his mother's grave, discarding the faded flowers she had put there, heard her saying, "You can't be hanged, Duncan Wade, because you're going to get rich and marry me." And only the grace of God and the rage that had spoiled his aim had made him miss killing a man and offering himself as meat for the Yankee gallows!

There was no one to blame for his stupidity, not even Juliet. She had taken herself out of his life with finality, not even sparing him the ultimate blow while he was off fighting a grisly war. That she had come back again to stir the old dreams alive was doubtless only his own vanity in action. Or had there been a betraying quiver of tenderness in her hands when she dressed his wounded eye? Divorce, Marian had said, flinging the word at him abruptly. All nonsense, he told himself now with too stern emphasis.

Lieutenant Wilkins! He would be dazzled and eager to help a pretty girl in distress, and would promptly forget Juliet's icy command not to show his face at the Villerand plantation again. For the length of the lane Duncan let himself hate Lieutenant Wilkins with fierce ardor.

Parmy, he noted, when he could see through the red haze that blinded him, had not finished clearing the burial place. There was a wilted pile of trash heaped in one corner that should be burned. Parmy was helping his father saw some heavy timbers when Duncan reached the yard.

Hugh Wade let the saw fall—it squealed untended and Parmy jerked at it—and came hurrying to the gate. "Well, sir, well, sir!" he cried, pumping his son's hand. "So they turned you loose? Don't look as though they treated you too badly— even gave you a clean shirt."

"Mr. Horning did that. He went on my bond, so I'm not clear as yet. How are you, sir? I've been worried about you."

"Never need worry about me. A few sparks left under this old ashy top. Louisa, here's our boy come home. All shaved up and handsome."

Louisa came flying, drying her hands on her apron, full of shrill, joyful expostulations. "Tole Old Master I wasn't making no tomato pickle just for him and me to eat. Tole him you'd be sittin' there, spreadin' it on your beans like ole times."

"Where's Josuff?" Duncan inquired later.

Parmy grinned. "Josuff hidin', Mist' Duncan. Keep he door locked, mos' all the time. I tell um, 'Josuff, what you done do you got to hide all the time?' He yell at me, 'Go 'way, nigger, hush you' mouf!' Maybe he come out, you tell um, Mist' Duncan."

"Have they been intimidating the good colored people around here?" Duncan asked his father. "I heard talk in that jail about night riding."

"You never know. They're a shut-mouthed race about their own. Have any night riders been seen around here, Parmy?"

"No, suh." Parmy's flat eyes were evasive. "Nobody come here but ole Prince and Preacher. You tole um git gone. They git."

"I told Prince he was to stay off this place and let you boys alone. What does he want here anyway?"

"Tole us we gotta go to meetin'. Say us gotta pay two dollars."

"It's some League business the Yankees have got up, I think. More devil's work to fool these poor boys and turn them against their white friends. If Prince comes back here, Parmy, you come running, you hear? I'll 'tend to Prince."

"Ain't skeer me none, Mist' Hugh. I ain't got no two dollars."

Duncan walked over the yard to the little cabin and knocked hard on the door. "Josuff!" he shouted. "You come out of there."

There were faint sounds inside, heavy breathing, then the scraping of the wooden bar being cautiously withdrawn. The door opened a scant space and Duncan saw that it was further secured by a piece of rope lashed between heavy iron staples. Josuff's face appeared at the opening, gray as ashes, his sunken eyes narrowed till only the black pupils showed. "Howdy, Mist' Duncan," he croaked. "I'se proud you come home."

"Come out of there, man, and let me look at you. What are you locking yourself up for? We won't let anybody hurt you."

Josuff tugged the rope loose and let the door open the width of his body. The air in the cabin was hot and fetid, the interior dark as night. Josuff looked bleached and very old and sick, his ragged clothes hanging loosely on a body shrunken and bent.

"Come out and let the sun shine on you, Josuff," Hugh ordered. "You'll die, shut up in there all day long."

Josuff looked apprehensively toward the west where the sun was a fiery globe sinking under a canopy of molten light. "Sun 'most gone, Mist' Hugh. Dark comin'."

"You come into the kitchen tonight and get your supper. Louisa's tired of sending food out here to you. Not a thing is going to hurt you, Josuff," declared Hugh. "Not a thing. Your young master's home now."

Josuff swallowed hard and convulsively. Tears came into his eyes and ran down his drained cheeks. He made a grasping motion with a hand like a turkey's claw and pulled at Duncan's shirt. "Sun 'most gone, Young Master," he whimpered. "Do it come dark, I'se skeered. Do it come dark, sumpin come hyar and git me."

Abruptly he closed the door and they heard the bolt slide to again.

Duncan frowned, baffled and uneasy. "What's wrong with him?" he demanded. "Somebody has been at him. Somebody has scared all the sense out of him."

His father's face changed oddly for an instant. Duncan felt a

brief, startled unease, but when Hugh spoke his voice was calm
enough.

"Josuff and I are old men," he said. "When you are old
there are things that matter greatly, yet seem unimportant to
the young. On the other hand there are things that might ap-
pall you, but to Josuff and me they are of no consequence and
not to be worried about. We may even do things you wouldn't
do—that's the privilege of being old. Let Josuff alone. If his
fear is real to him, it's real, even though he imagines it. And
there are plenty of real fears abroad these days. A tired old
man might easily decide it was a blessing to bar a door; he
might even decide that the quiet of the grave is a blessing."

"Whatever you're evading, Pa, by your riddles, I still think
Josuff has had a bad fright from something. No imagination
could put so much raw terror in anybody's eyes. He looks a
hundred years old and half dead."

"Well, one thing is sure: nobody will ever break into that
cabin, no matter who comes prowling around here. Leave him
alone. Parmy carries him food and water. When he feels it's
safe to come out, he'll do it of his own accord. Josuff," Hugh
went on, "was here before I was born. Nobody knows how old
he is; the slave books were burned when that log wing my father used for an office was destroyed, away back when I was a
young man. It was burned in the last Creek raid, and all the
old records with it. Even our old land grant was lost. Luckily,
my father got a new deed made out and recorded."

"That reminds me, I have a message for you from Horace
Horning. Come inside where we can talk."

"Put the tools away, Parmy." Hugh took off his old hat
and rubbed his thin hair with an open palm. "I'd better tell you,
Duncan, that Villerand and his Yankee visitors were out walking the boundary the other day."

"Parmy, you haven't finished cleaning up in the burying

ground," Duncan reminded him. "There's trash up there that ought to be burned."

"I'll get to it," his father said. "Won't hurt anything if it stays there till spring."

Hugh was rather proud of the casual manner he had been able to achieve so far, though he feared he might have trouble keeping the grim secret he shared with Josuff till spring. It might be smart to worry a little, he decided, and not appear too confident of Duncan's unmolested future. Could be some kind of scurvy Yankee trick pulled to go ahead and convict him anyway, even if no plaintiff appeared. The matter of evidence or proof had small weight in places of power now; all that the Yankees needed was the power and that they had seized remorselessly.

This casual attitude did slip with a jolt when Duncan gave him Horace Horning's message.

"Mortgage this land!" he exclaimed. "It's never had a lien on it since my grandfather got it as a grant for fighting the British at New Orleans. True, a lot of the original tract has been sold off from time to time. My father sold the Duncans some acreage and used the money to buy more slaves. That was to improve what land was left—but a mortgage, never! A Wade who put his land in jeopardy would have been counted a disgrace to the name."

"You've got the wrong slant on it, Pa," Duncan argued. "If Villerand got an idea of pressuring you to make you sell out to him, a mortgage would protect you. He could get the taxes raised on you so he could buy in the east boundary at a tax sale. It's being done all the time. If that happens, Horning says he'll find the money to save you, and the mortgage will protect him."

His father scowled at the floor, let his thin yellow hands dangle between his knees. "I am curious to know how Horace

Horning happens to be so well supplied with money," he said. "Could he have been sending cotton up the rivers all this time, fattening himself from the Yankees while he appeared to share the privations of the South? I would not care to have dealings with a man who could have so little honor."

"Pa, we're already under obligation to Horning. He went my bond, and we owe him money besides. He and Hale think Villerand is in with a Yankee outfit to sell railroad bonds endorsed by the state; they think he's scheming to promote a road that might never be built. I don't know where Horning got his information. I didn't ask him, any more than I would ask a man who has graciously offered us help where he got his money. His idea is to protect our land till an Alabama company can be organized to build the road down from Decatur, with all the ownership held in the state. He wants me to go out with McKee and line up some men of consequence to get the proposition going. I told him that for a proposition like this you'd give the right of way. It would make it awkward for me if you balked on the initial project, Pa."

"How could I give away land that was burdened by a mortgage? Not that I would refuse to give it, but I can't help shrinking from the very thought of a lien."

"We'd work that out. Actually there'll be no money involved, unless we need help suddenly from letting the place go to a tax sale. I think, myself, that Horning and Hale are men of integrity. If they profited by the war, so did other people, who aren't so anxious to let go any of their profits to help the state get back on its feet. McKee's supposed to be over here tomorrow. We have to beat the scalawags to this railroad proposition. Their only idea will be to loot the state more than has been done already. Villerand may be merely a dupe; he may think he's doing a public service to Alabama."

"Villerand's a fool. Anybody could sell him down the river, just by making him feel important. Louisa says they've had a big ruckus over there, because the little one came to the jail to see you. She says they've been keeping Miss Maggie practically a prisoner ever since."

"She got away. She came to town today, came to the jail with Hod Horning."

Hugh Wade rubbed his hands together slowly. "I reckon you know that child's in love with you, son. And," he added dubiously, "so, I'm afraid, is the other one. It was plain to see, that day you hurt your eye, the day they came for you. That's old foolishness, Duncan. It ought to die, in all honor."

"It is dead, sir." He spoke with emphasis, more for himself than his father.

"Then it's the little one? Your mother would be pleased. She always loved that child. I loved her too. And young Jule—I was fond of the lad. He never got on well with his father. Before he enlisted he used to come over here, full of grievances. I had to persuade him that it was dishonorable for me to listen to them."

"Suppose I did love her—what right have I got to love any woman?" Duncan flung out with desperation, flung it as it were into his own teeth.

"You're a Wade, an honored name through the history of Alabama, and you're young. Life is before you, years of it. To an old man like me the careless way the young regard the blessing of having a future is distressing. Rank ingratitude, to my notion."

"You forget, sir. My future might be spent in jail."

"We'll face that when it comes and pray it won't." Hugh got up stiffly. "I reckon Louisa has supper ready. Do you think you can stomach our plain food after all the elegant living you've had in Hank Filler's tavern?"

"There were several meals that consisted of thin air and leisure to meditate on our sins, without being distracted by having to chew. The rest of the time we got peas drowned in spring water. Corn bread once, with worms in it, but we did taste grease now and then. Gaunt declared they boiled the dish-rag in the soup."

"Was that Burley Gaunt from across the river? He's a sick man. Shot some rascal that took tax title to his little farm, I heard, some carpetbagger from Illinois."

"He thinks he'll hang, but he may fool them and die first. He has a wife and children."

"They'll get no help. A lot of worthless people are being fed out of Union charity, but a man who takes up for his own is a pariah and a villain and his family can starve in the fields for all they care."

They ate their supper on the porch, and under the magnolia tree Parmy gobbled his food like an animal. There was no sound in Josuff's cabin and no light showed through the chinks. A mockingbird, perched in the old fig tree, burst into an ecstasy of song, and a pain like homesickness ran through Duncan's veins. There was so much now that was grim; men lay in danger of death, hate was like smoke in the air, and in his little hut Josuff cringed in some mysterious dread. Yet the birds sang and in the green rows the cotton bloom fell and green bolls thickened, and eastward, over the Villerand plantation, an eroded moon crept sluggishly up to the dark depths of the sky.

The earth would not be denied, and men with their pettiness and their ambition challenged it but briefly. Green sprouts grew in every untended field and vines clambered fragrantly over moldering structures, as though God might be sick of man and anxious to blot out all the works of men from his sight.

A sick land, but birds sang in it, and, over there where the moon rose, a girl who had flung out of Horning's store with tears in her eyes was likely telling herself that she was finished with Duncan Wade forever.

Duncan got up with deliberation. "I think I'll walk over to Villerand's," he said.

"Good idea . . . though they may not let you see her."

"I can try, at least. Did it take you a long time to realize that you loved my mother, sir?" Duncan inquired.

Hugh Wade studied that. "An hour after I first talked to her I knew that she was the woman who could heal the hurt I'd been carrying for five years—after I lost Jessie. They were both wonderful women. Sometimes a flower springs up over night, son, but most good things take time to grow."

"I've been a fool," Duncan said. "I'm not sure I can undo my folly."

He went out through the yard, then turned and came back hurriedly. "A wagon, Pa. Would they come back for me at this late time of day?"

"Stay here. I'll see what goes on."

Duncan waited a little, then strode out to the yard, hearing shouts and laughter.

Bard Leonard was driving the wagon. His passenger was Robert McKee.

XXII

"I HATE HIM! I hate him! The cold fish!" she had said over and over to herself all the way home, keeping her chin rigid, keeping her voice light, prattling nonsense to Eric Wilkins, not knowing whether what she said made sense or nonsense.

Eric Wilkins had been a trifle perturbed when she went dashing into the garrison headquarters, babbling out a story of having been forgotten by her servant, that somebody must escort her home, that she was terrified, that her family would be frantic when the wagon returned without her! Inwardly she wondered if Tuby would have the courage to go back without her, but a delicately studied dismay, a tear or two and a piteous admission of helplessness were usually effective with a man, she had learned long since, and military men in blue were only men after all.

"I've been told that I was unwelcome at your place," Wilkins said soberly. "However—a lady in distress! You did right to come straight to us, Miss Villerand. Private Rankin, you and Corporal Steede find me a couple of horses, or a rig."

Private Rankin gave Marian Villerand a contemptuous look as he walked past, and reminiscently rubbed his jaw. Trust Petunia to get himself in soft with all the little Rebel heifers! Came a-running, looking through all the enlisted men on duty as though they were so many dirty windowpanes!

"Where would the lieutenant suggest that we find a horse and buggy?" Steede asked at the door.

"Hire something. Requisition something—I'll sign a

voucher." Out of his own pay, Wilkins was thinking. Anyway it had not been Marian, but that proud, cold-eyed sister of hers who had berated him when he was only doing his sworn duty, taking that high-headed young fellow into custody.

Wilkins would never understand these people, he was certain. They had gunpowder in their blood and ramrods for spines, and their notions of honor went back to the days of King Arthur and all his gilded knights. They lived like storybooks, but he knew a pretty girl when he saw one, and if this was surrender, all the more glory to the Union Army.

From somewhere presently appeared an old carriage, dry and dusty, and harnessed to it a gray horse with one blind eye and the lurching gait of a camel.

"One animal your General Bedford Forrest decided was unfit for a military career." Wilkins laughed as he helped Marian into the high seat.

"Oh, this horse belongs to the Armbruster sisters. They drive him to church on Sundays at a slow walk, and pull grass for him in vacant lots. They were probably terrified when your soldiers came for him. They'll be wailing, certain they'll never see old Dobbin again."

"Is his name Dobbin? I never knew a horse had that name except in school primers."

"They're Dobbin people, the Armbrusters. They had a dog once named Fido."

"Are they named Mary and Martha?"

"Oh, no. They're Miss Iolanthe and Miss Seraphina. It's very good of you to take me home, Lieutenant. And don't pay any attention to my sister. She flies off at the least excuse—I think it's because she's not very happily married. Whenever any man pays me attention, she gets jealous and loses her temper."

"She seemed to take it as a personal insult that I was ordered to escort that young fellow Wade to jail. Of course all you people stand together—we have found that out to our confusion and frustration."

"He's out on bond now," Marian said, keeping her head high and her tone carefully impersonal, "but probably they'll put him back in again presently." And lay him low and humble him as he ought to be, the hateful thing! She hated him, but why did her throat ache so, and this pain keep swelling in her chest so that she wanted to cry out against it?

There was a ticklish moment when they passed Tuby on the road. He was poking along dejectedly in the wagon, slumped over, the reins dragging low on the horses' rumps, but he sat up with a jerk when he saw her, his big mouth opened, and his eyes looked ready to burst out of his head. He gave a yell of relief and whacked at the team, but old Dobbin, summoned to a spark of spirit that would have amazed his owners, struck out at a jolting trot and outdistanced the wagon.

At the gate to the Villerand place Marian turned, with a sweetly naïve smile.

"If you'd rather not come in, Lieutenant, I can perfectly well walk from here," she said, devilishly inspired. She could head off Tuby—she had to head him off or corner him alone later and threaten him with dire things if he tattled. Or she could stroll in and pretend she had spent the afternoon in the orchard moping over her mistreatment. They had been treating her abominably, bringing out all the worst in her. As Duncan did. Always with Duncan when she wanted to be nonchalant or gaily scornful, or pridefully indifferent, she ended by saying furious things that later she yearned to take back.

Lieutenant Wilkins was in no mood to surrender his newly won advantage. Probably those old sisters with the thousand-legged names would want a dollar for the use of Dobbin and this antiquated vehicle, and Eric Wilkins meant to have his money's worth.

"I shall deliver you at your door and see that the stupid person who abandoned you in town gets a stout reprimand," he announced in his most military manner.

"It wasn't Tuby's fault really. I did run off and leave him. But there were friends I wanted to see. It was all a misunderstanding, more or less. And we do have to be so frightfully tactful now with our servants since you set them free," she reminded him coolly.

"I had no part in that. If I'd known they were going to be such a confounded nuisance and keep me stuck in the army forever, I wouldn't have voted Republican."

"Well, as slaves they had nothing to worry about. Of course, I'm thinking of *our* slaves. Now Tuby has to buy his own shoes, and he won't wear them except when Mama lays down the law. He thinks he's horribly abused to have to spend the money. He's just now beginning to realize how much it cost Papa to have shoes made for him all these years. You needn't get down to open the gate. Just reach for that rope."

"I know. I found out when I was here before."

She let him help her down gallantly, and waited for him to escort her to the front door. A bold face was her best move now, she had decided resignedly. After all she was twenty years old. They couldn't beat her, a grown-up woman! By all the county standards she should have been married long since.

There was no Cassius to open the door, so it was Juliet who came and released the bolt. She backed off a little, slightly startled at the sight of Lieutenant Wilkins. "Oh—how do you do?" she began, at a loss, getting no further because Marian took over glibly.

"You remember the lieutenant, Sis? He has been my rescuer again. Do come in, Lieutenant. I went to town—with Tuby," she went on breathlessly, "and somehow I got lost from him and the lieutenant was so gallant. He borrowed the Armbrusters' horse and buggy and brought me home."

Juliet's eyes narrowed. There was a look of decision in them, almost of triumph of some sort that disconcerted her younger sister. "You went to town—in those clothes?"

"I was in a hurry and Tuby couldn't wait. I had to have some needles—and of course there weren't any. Do come in and have a chair, Lieutenant. I'll call Mama—she'll want to thank you too. Juliet, for heaven's sake, don't just stand there!"

"In here, Lieutenant." Juliet's voice was stony as she led him to the parlor. When Marian had moved out of hearing she said, "I don't know what part you played in my sister's latest escapade, but I mean to find out."

"I had no part in any escapade. I'm as ignorant as you, Mrs. Destrade," he retorted. "Your sister came into headquarters asking for an escort. I did what I could for her in the circumstances. I had no wish to be received here if I was not welcome."

"Very well, Lieutenant. I accept your explanation. Mama will doubtless be interested in hearing it too. Please be seated."

He did not move. He stood stiffly, holding his cap in his hands, all his buttons glittering. "I really see no reason for me to remain," he said. "After all, your sister is safely home, my errand is accomplished. But if I may say so without being misunderstood, there are men in my command with whom she might not have been safe."

"You see, then, what a problem we have? What a rash, undisciplined person she is? She keeps my mother in an anguish of anxiety continually. Something has to be done about it, and at once."

"But your sister is not a child, Mrs. Destrade. She seems quite capable of taking care of herself."

"Young unmarried women do not take care of themselves in the South, Lieutenant. Such boldness in a young woman is considered unfortunate at least. Perhaps in your country women are more emancipated, not so bound by old traditions of what becomes a lady. My husband says that in New York he saw some women even serving in the shops."

"Very true. My sister—she's just twenty—writes me she means to teach in a girls' school, but down here a girl can't even be seen carrying a package on the street."

"A young girl would always be accompanied by a servant on the street—if she were a well-reared young girl."

"And if she had a servant," he added dryly. "We live in two worlds, Mrs. Destrade. Perhaps some day we may be reconciled so that we will all understand one another."

"I fear that day is far off, Lieutenant. If you will excuse me, I will see what is detaining my mother."

The sound of angry voices in the library across the hall was becoming more obvious every moment. Juliet slipped to the door, opened and closed it quickly. "For heaven's sake, Papa!" she expostulated in a low tone. "That man can hear you."

Julian Villerand was standing in the middle of the floor, his face flushed. He was in riding clothes and he slapped at his boot angrily with his crop. "Let him hear! Send him away, somebody."

"But he's a Union officer, Papa." Marian turned from the window where she had stood white-faced, staring out. "You said only a fool would antagonize the Union Army."

"I'll go." Emma's face was pale too, but her voice held the calm that seldom deserted her. "After all we do owe the man the courtesy of thanks."

She went out, quietly closing the door, and the three left in the room stood like so many statues, till they heard the front door shut and the bolt shot to. Marian followed the departing figure of the officer as he carefully turned the buggy around and rolled down the drive. Then she whirled around, her eyes flashing. "I will not be treated like a half-witted child!" she cried.

Julian strode to the fireplace, took a whack at the mantel

posts with his crop, braced himself belligerently on the rug, his beard vibrating like the antennae of an angry insect.

"Why the devil don't you stop acting like a half-witted child, then?" he shouted. "I ought to take this whip to you. You didn't think I'd go to town, did you? Didn't think I'd hear about your disgraceful capers—hanging around that dirty jail? Whole town is talking about it."

"You were there yourself, yesterday—and so was Juliet."

"Juliet's a married woman."

"She forgets it plenty of times."

"Don't try to excuse yourself, Miss, by picking on your sister! She dragged Hod Horning over there and got that Wade fellow out on bond," he told Juliet. "After he stood up there yesterday and insulted me to my face—made me a laughing stock. As for you, Miss, God knows what all that riffraff and those soldiers around the garrison are saying about you. If you don't care on your own account, you could have a little consideration for your family."

Emma had let herself back into the room. She sat erect in her chair, but her hands twisted upon themselves in little spasms of misery.

"Tuby never lost her," Julian went on, glowering at his wife. "She told him to go on about his business. I was ready to wear him out when he drove in, but he told me right quick how it happened, and I could tell he was giving me the truth. You had it all figured out, I reckon, to drag that officer out here? Suits your ideas of independence to be seen cavorting around with Yankees."

"At least, Mr. Villerand," put in Emma, "the Yankees Marian brings to the house have acceptable manners."

"So you take up for her too, Mama?" Juliet demanded. "Can't you see that she's ruining herself in the county by her behavior?"

"You're jealous," Marian said with a smugness that was

more irritating than anger. "You tried to get Duncan out and he wouldn't have it from you, but when I tried he accepted gladly enough." And he'd sent her, casually dismissed, rankling, enraged, rushing out to restore her self-esteem by enlisting Eric Wilkins in her behalf, she was trying not to remember. "Marry her out of hand," old Horace Horning had said. It made her face burn now to realize that she would have married Duncan Wade out of hand, any way at all, at that moment, if he would have had her!

"This is all quite stupid," Juliet declared. "Here we are, quarreling among ourselves, about quite unimportant things, when what we must decide is what can be done to save Maggie from her own recklessness."

"I don't need saving, thank you very much."

"Certainly you do. Doesn't she, Mama? Papa says the scandal of her actions is all over town already. We can't have that sort of thing."

"You," Marian said icily, "needn't suffer. You can go back to New Orleans and live with your husband as a married woman ought to do. There could be a slight scandal about your actions too, Mrs. Destrade. No doubt people are speculating already."

"That's it!" Julian slapped his boot. "That's what will be done. You'll go back to New Orleans, Juliet, and take Maggie with you."

Marian stiffened, aghast. "I won't go!" she cried. "I will not! I will not!"

"You'll go if I say so, Miss. You'll go tomorrow if your mother can get you ready. You'll stay there all winter too. I'll write Destrade. Tell him I'll take care of all her expenses."

"It will take days to get a letter to Felix," argued Juliet, "maybe weeks. Why do I have to be exiled because of Maggie's shameful performances? Why can't you send her to Charleston to some of Mama's relatives?"

"All old—old feeble people." Villerand's lips puffed out and set doggedly. "Anyway, that's your home, Juliet. It ain't exile to go home." His mind was obviously made up. He was not going to be swayed from his decision.

She wants me sent away, but she wants to stay here, on account of Duncan, Marian was thinking. If I have to go, she's going too! She managed a pitiful whimper. "Please, please, not Charleston! If you're determined I must go somewhere, let me go with Juliet."

"It might be very nice, Maggie," Emma said. "New Orleans is a big city. You could study music, perhaps, or take up painting, or learn French."

"I'll tell Destrade I intend to pay her board."

"But surely, Mr. Villerand, one does not insult one's family connections by offering to pay board!" his wife protested. "You would be furious if Mr. Destrade had ever suggested paying board for Juliet."

"Ha!" Julian barked, his mouth ironic. Ask Destrade to pay board for Juliet and he would scream outrage till they heard him in Montgomery! And he'd never refuse any money for Maggie, Julian was willing to bet on that. "Juliet's our daughter," he said. "This is her home, but I understand that down there everything belongs to the old lady."

"Everything!" Juliet said bitterly.

"Perhaps with Maggie there Mr. Destrade can be persuaded to make other arrangements, so you can have your own home," Emma said.

"He wouldn't, Mama—ever. Especially if you offer to pay money. *Maman* is greedy enough, but Angèle and Thérèse and Annette—they put pennies in the alms basin when they go to mass and boil the coffee grounds over and over. But of course, if you and Papa decide it's for the best . . . I know you're tired of having me on your hands so much. . . ." Juliet dabbed at her eyes.

"We never tire of you, my dear, but after all, if you can help us in this extremity . . ." Emma sighed. "There's really no hurry, is there? It would be awkward, Mr. Villerand, if the girls arrived in New Orleans before your letter."

"I think I'll go down with them myself. I've got some people I want to see in Montgomery—Swayne and Patton and some others. I can explain to Destrade when we get there. We can stop at a hotel till they make arrangements for Maggie."

"You come too then, Mama," Marian pleaded.

"Oh, child, not on that awful boat from Mobile! I get so deathly sick. Besides some one must stay here—the cotton is coming on."

"You shouldn't be here alone, Mama."

"I'll be quite safe with Tuby and the others. You'll need clothes, Maggie, but New Orleans is a better place to get them than here. Juliet can attend to it."

"I think she should still wear mourning, Mama. It's not three years since poor little Jule . . ." Juliet let her voice break. "She does flaunt those colored habits around here, but in a city mourning would be such a protection."

"Very nice! Then I couldn't go anywhere but to church!" Marian snapped.

"Mr. Destrade's mother has worn mourning for seventeen years."

"I haven't buried a husband. If you have your way I'll never have one."

"And if you have your way, Maggie Villerand, no man will look at you—a girl who has no respect for her own reputation!"

"No more of that, now!" ordered Villerand. "Get her things ready, Mrs. Villerand. We'll drive to Montgomery, take the train to Mobile and from there go by boat."

"I hope you're satisfied!" Juliet snapped as they went up the stairs. "Sending me back to that grisly hole."

Marian did not deign to answer. Heaviness was beginning to bear down on her heart. Duncan was free. Temporarily at least. But he did not want her. Eric Wilkins obviously would never understand her. Anyway, he would be moved on ultimately to some other post.

Life here was a desert. New Orleans could not be much worse. Even with fat Felix and the dreadful Destrade sisters. She would, Marian decided perversely, make life interesting for Thérèse and Annette and Angèle, not to mention *Maman*. They would be easy to shock, but they would endure her because of the money. But she would not wear a lot of moldy old crepe and black dresses, no matter what anybody said. They made her look like a crow.

Young Jule had liked gaiety all his short life. She knew the scrapes he had got into, gambling, horse racing—worse things that the servants whispered about! He had gone to war with a scarlet plume in his hat and his boots shining. Mourning would not please Jule at all. And she had no intention of trying to please Juliet. Maybe she could be so difficult and so annoying that the Destrades would send her home. That was something to think about.

XXIII

THE HILLS rose higher against the sky, and the valleys were deep and aloof, full of haze even before the sun went down. Little cabins showed pin points of light when dark fell and feathers of pearl-colored smoke early in the foggy mornings.

Here and there an apple orchard, hopefully planted and lately untended, bent boughs studded with hard little red fruit. Streight's cavalry had gone through these northern hills of the state, punished when they were overtaken by Bed Forrest, fled from or welcomed as the temper of the farmers shifted. Here was a black ruin where a barn had been burned, fences were down and rails carried away. There, another small freehold would lie smug and unmolested. Hogs grunted in crude pens. Women in sunbonnets, feet bare, eyes feral, watched with guarded hostile faces.

Bridges had been burned, never rebuilt. They swam their horses through the shallow Cahaba, splashed in creeks, made camp at night when no other shelter offered, lying out under the stars with September jarflies rasping shrillness in the trees and night hawks swinging down curiously, pirouetting off so near the rustle of their flight-feathers was audible, the breeze of their upward swooping felt on the cheek.

Somewhere McKee had got two good horses, and Duncan was glad to be well mounted again. From somewhere too Mc-Kee had money—"friend of our enterprise," he said, and Duncan asked no further questions. They bought food in towns where McKee had no friends to offer hospitality. They slept on

pallets in houses broken by artillery fire and on feather beds in
high-ceiled rooms where there were faded velvet curtains at the
windows but only grits and fried fatback for breakfast. They
met encouragement and antagonism.

"Think they'll ratify that Fourteenth Amendment?" some
people worried. "If they don't, we can't build railroads. Can't
build nothing. We'll get somebody running Alabama like
Brownlow runs Tennessee."

"We've had enough of you Democrats," others snorted.
"Damn near ruined the South one time. Why don't you stay
away and let us alone?"

Far to the north, blue and secret the mountains; and beyond
them, looping a coil into Alabama like a turbulent silver ser-
pent, the roiling Tennessee River, roaring and churning over
its shoaling bed. That was what they had to sell—entry into
the river ports. To iron-gray, weary men in dusty offices and
warehouses, in courthouses smelling of the spittoons; to young
men back from the war with disillusion dry as gray paint on
their set faces but a flaming heat of hate making embers of
their quick, hot eyes.

To widows, fearfully unadjusted, full of tremors of uncertainty, widows a little drugged by the newness of independence,
widows who owned land with little idea where its boundaries
lay, who owned timbered hillsides still cut into patterns by en-
trenchment, abatis, shellfire or campfire. Widows who wept or
widows who were too canny, or too cute, or too eagerly effu-
sive.

"All over the country, like a kind of illicit smoke, this neglected femaleness," McKee mused as they rode the main road
back toward Tuscaloosa. "They're a herd—a nice, rapacious,
calculating and avid herd, as dangerous as she-bears, some of
them. They've been robbed of life and fulfillment. They're terrified and tormented by fevers they've been taught not to under-

stand because to understand would be unladylike. What they need most is something male to cling to and cry on, or nag and cajole and exploit. And they know there's no hope of getting what they need in this denuded land, even when they're hardly aware that they need it."

"Fifty thousand of them in Alabama," Duncan remarked.

"And I brought you along! A handsome, single young man with a devilish eye and an arrogant charm, even though your coat doesn't fit around the neck! Like turning a he-colt loose in a desert with a lot of rutting mares! But if they persuade Papa to come to our railroad meeting, or Uncle Henry, who has a little money put away—but don't you tell now!" McKee mimicked in an airy falsetto "—that's what we have to have."

"We get our shirts washed and our horses fed. We get blackberry cobbler and peach pie."

"And languishing looks and sighs—along with the dirty glares and muttered cussing we meet up with in other places, where the Radicals are riding high. Nobody seems to think Demopolis is a good place for the meeting. Tuscaloosa, Elmore says. If we can get fifty men of consequence, with the people who'll trail along out of curiosity or to figure if there's something going on that they can be opposed to, I'll be satisfied."

It was a long road. All around was Alabama, full of loneliness, embittered too often, worried to death, and all of it, so far as Duncan was concerned, empty as a drum. In the lower lands the cotton was whitening. He must get back, he would be needed at home. Liveright, with his military supporters, might be looking for him right now with a summons. Cassius might have returned, champing for revenge. They had done well. They had rights of way tentatively promised. They had the word of substantial men that they would subscribe to the promotion of a north-and-south railroad. They had sunburned necks and blistered insteps from stirrups without boots, and now they were headed south again to Marengo County, which to Duncan would be the most desolate place of all because she was no longer there.

Emma Villerand had been kind and sympathetic when, after too much of McKee's enthusiasm before they started, he had slipped away to the Villerand place. "They left this morning, Duncan," she had told him. "Mr. Villerand drove them to Montgomery. Then they are taking the train to Mobile and go from there by boat. We want Marian to spend the winter in New Orleans. She's restless and I think unhappy too—they're so lost and pitiful now, all the young things! I'm sorry you missed seeing the girls. And, Duncan, Juliet left a message for you. Wait here. . . . I declare," she exclaimed, laughing, "I'll never get used to living now! I catch myself saying, ' 'Phrony, fetch me this,' or 'Lissa, go get my shawl,' knowing very well I'll have to go myself. You wait now."

He had carried Juliet's perfumed note a day and night before he opened it. Then, deciding that the burning awareness of it in his pocket was worse than knowing what was written on the thin blue paper, he tore the envelope raggedly.

Dear Duncan, ran the hasty script, *I am going away. Papa wants me to take Marian to New Orleans. I am not happy to go, but I think it is best for Marian. She has got so silly about you, and I know that you do not care for her at all. I know I hurt you long ago, it seems ages and yet sometimes only yesterday. Do try to forget me, as I've been trying to forget. But, oh, it is so hard! And now, good-bye.* JULIET.

In sudden irritation he had crumpled the sheet and thrown it away. Then he had gone back and picked it up again, smoothed and folded it and put it in his pocket. Because he was male and had a male's innate conceit, the note gave him a small, smug glow. But when this had cooled slow anger came in its place. So he had been deluded by his own vanity. He might have put Juliet out of his mind, but he had not severed every fiber of the

old delusion, and now with the cleverness of a woman unsatis-
fied by love, she was exploring delicately, watching to see if
some frail, unslain rootlet might push up and bloom again. She
had kept him dangling of old, smiling sweetly at his young
misery. Now, however futile the effort might be, she had to
give a little tug at the old chains to learn if a heart still hung on
the hook.

Was she lying prettily to please herself, or had he been so
brutal to eager little Marian that it had been obvious to other
people? In heavy moments of self-reproach he castigated himself for being a hound and a cad. That was the insolence of his
breed, the wild, fox-hunting, dueling, gaming, strutting young
blades who had made up the gallant, dangerous, arrogant cavalry regiments, who were born to pride and place and, now that
that place was no more, were lost, baffled and enraged at being
brought low.

Had he taken out on Marian his resentment against life as it
presented itself to him, because she was a handy victim, offering herself naïvely to a spirit that war had not tamed, only
made numb and incredulous? Had she been so much wiser than
he that she had known there could be no more splendid givers,
no more conquerors? That the givers had nothing left to give
but love and that the conquerors were all meekly conquered?

New Orleans was probably full of gay, brash young men,
Latins, Creoles like Felix Destrade, and Juliet would do her
best to uproot Duncan Wade from her sister's heart like a poi-
sonous weed. He let that thought torment him as he rode
homeward through the short, hot September days.

Then he was back in town again, surrendering the horse,
saying good-by to McKee, who was hurrying on to Selma.

"Have to begin a stiff campaign of agitation for this meeting," McKee said. "Tuscaloosa in January. Cotton will be sold
by then, maybe the legislature will have passed some kind of
assistance bill and men will have more time for public affairs."

In town Duncan walked unmolested. Lieutenant Wilkins gave him a remote nod. Horace Horning advised him to go his way but to bring his father in shortly to sign some papers.

"I'll try," Duncan agreed, "but he thinks signing a mortgage is dishonoring his forefathers."

"Getting sold out for taxes could be worse. Villerand's Yankees have gone back to Boston, they say. But Villerand's in Montgomery—no telling what he's cooking up down there. He's thick as thieves with General Swayne, maybe plotting to get himself appointed governor of Alabama. Patton's too much of a placater to suit me, but maybe he's right. Maybe we have got to pull in our proud horns and submit, but it's like yoking a stallion with an ox—never saw that done successfully."

"Say a stallion and a jackal, Mr. Horning."

"Still unreconstructed, ain't you? They went and sent your little gal off to Louisiana. Reckon you heard? Figure to go after her, do you?"

"On foot?" His tone was sharply bitter.

Horning sighed. "Hard world! No way to make it easier very soon that I can see."

Hugh Wade sat under the magnolia tree at home, mending a cotton sack. "Have to make these last. Raveled out that one that was plumb worn out to patch three others. It's you and me and Parmy to pick, I reckon. Josuff's gone and Louisa's back is stiffening on her again."

"Josuff's gone? Gone where?"

"God knows! Cabin's been empty since night before last. Found the door open yesterday morning, nobody inside. Never thought about him taking off in the night, he's been so scared lately. Couldn't even get him to unbar the door after the sun went down, poor old fellow. Parmy's acting queer too. Just rolls his eyes when I ask him questions. He may be gone tomorrow."

"Have you looked for Josuff? He's old. He may have just

wandered out, mixed up in his mind as he was. He might be lying sick somewhere on the place."

Hugh Wade shook his head. "No, son. I just haven't felt up to walking in the sun these last few days. Nothing to worry about—nothing at all," he said hastily. "I've had a touch of flux and my knees are weak and my head swims. Haven't slept much either."

That mortgage—it was preying on the old man's mind, Duncan knew, fear of it obscuring the consequences which might ensue if they refused Horning's offer of assistance. It was a hard world for the old, too.

"You need some blackberry cordial, Pa, and some decent food too. Looks as though you get thinner every day."

"Louisa couldn't make any cordial this year. Applegate didn't leave us any whisky to put in it. Bard Leonard came by Saturday—said he heard Applegate was riding high down in Montgomery—fixing to get himself elected something or other."

"Applegate? Good Lord! Old Jack Appletoddy! Villerand's in Montgomery too. Horning thinks he's trying to get appointed governor if they put us under military government."

"When he came this way Applegate couldn't even read. Took a swig out of Louisa's liniment bottle, couldn't read the label. Almost choked him to death. Soon as the sun goes down I'll go with you to hunt Josuff. Better rest a little first. That's a long walk out from town—got a blister too, didn't you? See where it bled through your sock. Was McKee satisfied? Did the boys rally round?"

"We got encouragement from some important men. Also some discouragement. Too many people are certain that anything Alabama might attempt on her own would be frustrated and futile. You'd better stay here, Pa. I'll go look for the old man."

"No, I'll go. I feel better now. Louisa stewed me up some

kind of tea—settled my stomach. Catnip, maybe. Don't know what it was."

Slowly in the fading light they took the wagon road. Days were growing short. The cotton was bursting white from the bolls. The meadow lay pinkly glowing from the drying sedge grass, wild grape vines drooped, dry and dusty, grasshoppers flung up from the rattling grass, and a quail whirled hysterically into flight as they skirted the cornfield. Parmy had left a pile of corn there between two rows.

"We may have to pull the corn too," Hugh said. "Don't know what's got into Parmy."

"It's that damn Union League business! Look here, sir." Duncan stopped short. "You've had thieves. All the corn is gone from these six rows. Or has Parmy carried it in to the crib?"

"Not an ear in yet, except what Louisa brings in to boil. That pile may be gone by morning."

"I'll carry it in myself. I'll gather and you can ride to mill, and if Parmy won't work, he won't eat—that's gospel."

The lane was empty and still. Duncan had searched every fence row, kicking aside the dusty bushes, sending birds dashing with outraged chitterings, tramped every path and the wagon road when they came to the head of the lane.

"One place he'd never go—the graveyard," Hugh said. He set off deliberately toward the house, but Duncan halted.

"I'll look there anyway."

"No use," his father argued with an odd touch of impatience. "Lately he's been scared to death of that place."

"You go along. I'll have a look." Duncan skirted the brick wall.

"You're wasting your time, I tell you!" Hugh snapped.

Duncan frowned. Parmy, he was thinking, was not the only one on the place who was behaving oddly.

"I'm searching this burying ground, Pa," he said deliberately. "You go along. Supper will be ready."

He went in through the gate, aware that his father had turned back, taken a few steps and stood waiting. Then Duncan gave a sharp yell. "Pa! Look here!"

The stone urn that topped the first Hugh Wade's tombstone had been thrown down. It lay upturned between two graves, and a few feet away old Josuff's body was flung like a sack. His face had been beaten, one eye almost knocked out, blood had run down his temple, blackening the cleared ground. Close by a heavy bottle lay shattered, its edges smeared with blood.

Hugh had come up. He stood gazing down, his face blank, drained, set. He did not speak.

"Could it have been Parmy—is that why he's acting queer?" Duncan straightened old Josuff's stiffening arms, found one gray hand tightly curled about a broken razor. "Tried to defend himself," he said. "I thought at first this marble might have fallen on him, but the bottle here—there was a fight."

Still his father did not speak. He was trembling all over, holding to the monument for support.

"Must have been a tall man to knock the top off that tombstone." Duncan studied it. "The mortar's dried out, been dry a long time by the looks of it." He glanced into the opening in the shaft, frowned, dipped his hand down and brought up a greasy sack. "What the devil? Look here, Pa! Money—money, hidden here in Grandfather's tombstone."

Hugh dragged words out hoarsely. "Josuff's money. He used to keep it hidden in the wall of his cabin. I've seen him counting it out of that sack, time and again."

"He must have hidden it up here. Likely he came to get it and they jumped him—Preacher or some of that gang. After they'd killed him they got scared and ran and didn't find the money. Pa, there's more than sixty dollars here."

"Yes, Josuff got a share of last year's crop. They took care that the Negroes got theirs, even when the white planter lost everything."

"Who does it belong to now? Josuff never had any family."

"I reckon it belongs to you. You found it . . . on our place."

"If we use it to feed the others, Parmy and Louisa—that would be honest, wouldn't it? Here, you take care of it. I'll have to do something about the poor old fellow. We'll have to bury him right away, this hot weather. I'll nail up some kind of a box. You go down and send Parmy up to help me."

"Son, I doubt if you could drag Parmy up here with a team of oxen. Maybe he knows what happened here. Maybe that's what ails him. But I don't believe he had anything to do with it."

"I'll go down and put him to sawing boards. He can do that, anyway. I'll fetch a pick and spade and start digging. I can bury him over in that corner. Have to move that brush first."

He strode across the enclosure, kicked at the piled trash, turned to find his father at his shoulder.

"No, not here!" Hugh said. "We'll bury him outside the wall."

Duncan was staring down. "Pa," he said sternly, "there's a grave here. Who's buried here?"

Hugh cleared his throat harshly. "I told you we should bury Josuff outside the wall," he repeated.

"Pa, I want the truth. There's somebody buried here—lately. You know it. You know whose grave this is. You tell me."

Hugh's face was greenish white and set, but his eyes held a high, fine anger. "A scoundrel who called himself Cassius Grant is buried here," he said.

Duncan felt sick. This was the inner, unnamed fear that had lurked in his mind all this time. Now it thrust up, raw and terrible. "You killed him, Pa! My God, they would hang you if they knew!"

Hugh seemed to relax, a kind of relief bringing color back into his face, as though the horror of concealment was removed.

"I did not kill him, Duncan. I meant to do it. I went to do it, but Josuff was there before me. Josuff killed him."

"For me," Duncan said solemnly. He went to the body and tenderly touched the dry, dead hands of the faithful old servant, laying them in repose across the still breast. "I would have killed them to save you too, Josuff, if I could," he whispered softly. "I reckon you know that now."

He could guess the torment of superstition that had made the old slave's last days terrifying. Afraid of that grave, knowing all his possessions were hidden here, the only money he had ever owned in a long lifetime. Venturing out at last, alone, shaking with fear, to be struck down by some vengeful, drunken prowler.

"We'll bury him in my old black wedding coat, Pa," Duncan said. "He always wanted that coat. I wish I'd given it to him now. Years ago."

Carefully he piled the brush again over the burial place of Cassius Grant.

Josuff's grim, frightful secret should be forever safe.

XXIV

IT WAS a long winter, long and bitter with frustration.

All through the fall, in early chill and fog or the heat of Indian summer, Duncan and Hugh dragged heavy cotton sacks up and down the rows. Sometimes Parmy helped desultorily, sometimes for days at a time he disappeared. There were meetings, Louisa reported, there were picnics, there were baptizings.

Once Parmy returned at night, terrified and retching, with the marks of a lash livid upon his shoulders.

"Dem Leaguers, dey flog 'em, make 'em come to meetin'," Louisa sputtered, stewing up a mess for Parmy's back. "Dey tell um, got to get a new name, get a new wife, get another church. That ole fool Parmy, he been baptized four times already."

"And yet if we're lucky enough to sell this cotton, we've got to share with that black idiot!" Duncan stormed to his father.

Borrowing Bard Leonard's mule to make a team, Duncan hauled their own and Bard's cotton to the gin. "Less than thirty bales. That last one is short weight," he worried as the bales were heaved into the shed. "And we'll pay three hundred dollars' tax on it if we can sell it at all."

A cotton "agent" who said his name was Carver drove into the yard with a proposition. He would ship the cotton downriver, pay the tax and shipping costs and divide the profits evenly.

"Mr. Villerand has already engaged me to market his crop,

as he did last year," he stated. "I handled it very profitably for
him. Mr. Villerand will vouch for me."

"A damn poor recommendation," Hugh Wade muttered.

"What else can we do?" Duncan countered.

The agent shed his veneer of affability. "If you leave that
cotton standing there it may be confiscated. They'll remember
that you never took the oath, Mr. Wade."

"He's right, Pa. Better a dubious bargain than a certain
loss."

December had come before Carver returned and handed
Hugh two hundred and forty dollars. "Every bale was short
weight, and much of the cotton of an inferior grade," he declared.

"How about Villerand? I suppose he raises a very superior
kind of cotton," Hugh flared out angrily.

"Mr. Villerand" was the retort "has sworn allegiance to the
government of the United States. And don't forget that your
hands get a share of the crop. The Freedmen's Bureau will
check on that."

"The wage, I believe, is a dollar a day and found. Our one
hand has worked maybe twenty hours all this summer. We've
clothed and fed him for a year. We'll likely have to feed him
all winter."

"Settle that with the Bureau, no business of mine," Carver
clucked to his sleek horse, gathering up the reins.

"Two hundred dollars after we pay the Negroes," Duncan
said, "and we owe all that to Horning and Hale—for taxes,
maybe more."

"At least we can sell what corn we don't need," Hugh said.

When Parmy had been paid he left in the night and did not
return.

"He down in that shanty town by the bridge," Louisa
snorted. "Took up with a black woman—fat, hooey!" She

opened her arms in a wide, disgusted gesture. "Us ain't got to feed um—dat's sump'in."

Andrew Johnson was battling the Radicals in Congress to save the South from further reprisals and exploitation, they heard in town. Duncan was reluctant to believe this. General Swayne and Governor Patton were both urging the ratification of the Fourteenth Amendment, prophesying dire happenings if it was rejected.

"Old Andy may be our friend as he claims," said Emanuel Hale, "but Congress is fixing to cook his goose if they can muster the votes to humiliate him. They may find an excuse to impeach him one of these days."

"Your taxes, Hugh," Horning stated casually, "were three hundred and twelve dollars. I paid 'em right quick. Hiked 'em on you about thirty per cent."

"We've got exactly two hundred dollars—plus a bit of cash Duncan has, which we need to feed ourselves. We may have a little more when we sell the corn."

"Give me half the tax bill now; we'll carry the rest. Trust we'll live to see the day you'll be selling five hundred bales again. Disappointed Villerand, I reckon, when your taxes got paid. Heard he was hanging around, drooling."

"Reckon you've heard the last of your assault case, young Wade," Hale remarked. "They threw Judge Kane out of office —sheriff too. Put in a Radical hill fellow from up Winston County way as judge. Made Judge Kane so mad he burned up every record of the court. Now they've got him in jail."

"Fellow they put in his place don't own a shilling's worth of property in this county—only been hanging around here a month or two messing with that Union League," Horning put in. "I petitioned to be discharged from your bond. Told 'em to release the bond or call the case to trial. They can't call it to trial with no record against you and no docket."

"What can they do to Judge Kane?"

"Fine him, I reckon. Anyway, if I get my bond discharged you'll be free to leave the state, young Wade, so be you've got an errand anywheres." Horning grinned.

"I'll have to trade somebody out of another pair of shoes before I can walk far."

He had begun a dozen letters to her, but none had ever been finished. They were too loverly, or they sounded too primly formal, and each, he suspected dubiously, was definitely futile. Only a scoundrel could ask a woman to share nothing at all. Debt and uncertainty, even if he was never brought to answer for the attack on Cassius Grant. Debt and an old house where an old man lived out his days with what gallant courage he could fan to life from the embers of a valiant spirit.

"Christmas is coming," whispered Horning as they left the store. "We got in a lot of pretties from St. Louis. Nice little trinkets the ladies fancy—pink soap and handkerchiefs with lace on 'em. If you take a notion to buy something, your credit's good."

"A lady—" Duncan remembered the old traditions—"may only accept flowers, music or a book from a gentleman. My mother drilled that into me, years ago."

"Only book we've got is an almanac. Says there'll be snow in January. Reckon she wouldn't care for that."

Christmas was only another day, till Bard Leonard arrived late lugging a ten-pound shoat under his arm.

"Trade her to you for some of that lumber. Picked you a she-critter so you can raise your own hams another year. That ain't all," he continued when the animal was penned and joyfully fed by Louisa, both squealing in unison. "Looky here." He rummaged the wagon and brought out the denuded carcass of a wild goose. "Shot it down in the bottoms. Reckon your old Nigra woman would cook it for us? I fetched along a little sage and an onion. My old lady always fixed 'em up with sage and onion."

"Bard, I love you!" Duncan exclaimed. "Hey, Louisa, come back here and quit making love to that pig. Christmas gift, Louisa! Christmas dinner."

They ate, after dark, on the stiff linen tablecloth. Louisa had candied yams in sorghum and baked fresh corn bread. She had even opened a jar of her famous pickle. They gnawed the bones and gnawed too the eternal problems of survival in a land tragically beset with enemies, within and without.

"Well, they voted not to ratify. But they passed the railroad bill. Sixteen thousand dollars a mile for finished construction to be endorsed by the state. There'll be a meeting in two weeks, Bard, to set up some kind of organization to build a road north to Decatur. Tap the river ports, give us transportation to the north."

"Judge Clayton be there—and Alex White and Elmore?"

"Clayton promised. I'm not sure about White and Elmore. Elmore is more concerned about the Democratic convention."

"Republicans will run Grant for President, I reckon. Be hard to beat. Who us Democrats going to put out against him?" Bard asked.

"Man named Blair is being talked about. Election's nearly two years off. A lot of things can happen in that time."

Too much happened, and little that was good for Alabama. Horning's almanac had truthfully predicted the weather. Snow fell in January, winds blew out of the hills, frigid, searching. Duncan rode the mule to Tuscaloosa, and both he and the animal were weary from plowing before they started. He was two days on the road, putting up at a planter's house where there was little fire, a cold straw tick for a bed and fried squirrel for breakfast, which he ate sparingly, seeing how little food there was for six people.

The meeting was delayed, confused, full of acrimonious argument between North Alabama men and the Black Belt representatives. The unfriendly feeling that had existed between the two sections since the second year of the war had increased, become hostile and suspicious. McKee did not come. He was sick with a lung fever, it was reported.

Duncan rode home cold, sick, discouraged. No wonder scalawags and carpetbaggers found it so easy to exploit Alabama when her own people could not unite to promote the common good. It was this miasma of fear and uncertainty that overspread everything, of course. Nobody had any enthusiasm for making plans, knowing that likely enough they would all be shattered and brought to nothing by men in Washington.

"We might as well have sold that piece of ground to Villerand," he told his father wearily. "We could have used the money and we'd have saved those extra taxes."

"I'll sell it to him at my price," Hugh declared stoutly, his jaw set. "I shan't mourn if no railroad goes hooting and smoking through this property. The river was transportation enough for my grandfather and it's enough for me."

Old men, old, Duncan thought, too tired to cavil. Alabama needed young men, the oldsters argued, yet on every side the young men beat their heads against the stone walls of what had always been, what was not done in honor, what no gentlemen could in pride and decency consider. And meanwhile the tricksters, the opportunists, the odiously vulgar and dishonest took over the courts and the ballot boxes, set men of dignity against one another, Negro against white, county against county. God, but war walked on dirty feet, and where it's legions had marched blight lay like a yellow fog, eating into men's souls. Into his own, Duncan Wade realized—a gentleman's son, who for a little had even been annoyed by his own father!

The knock on the door stirred him from bitter brooding.

"I thought I heard a wagon." Hugh got up, took up the lamp, put down the book he had been reading. *A History of the Roman Empire,* it was, Duncan saw. Applegate's ruffians had disdained the books. Applegate, he remembered, could not read.

"I'll go," Duncan said. "Probably Bard Leonard wanting some news of the meeting."

The wind caught the lamp flame and made it flare and gutter as the door opened. Hugh shaded the chimney with his hands. The wood fire fluttered too, and ashes blew out into the room. The man who waited outside the door, his blue pinched face sunk into his collar, had a familiar look. He cleared his throat and Duncan recognized him. It was Liveright, the deputy sheriff. So they had come for him. He braced himself and said curtly, "Come inside. The wind's blowing out the lamp."

Liveright shivered but stood still. "Bad night." He scrubbed his nose with his sleeve. "I've got a boy out here—hurt bad. Got mixed up in a fracas down by the river. Said he wanted to be brought here, Mr. Wade."

"Parmy—I expected this," Hugh said. "Can he walk?"

"Bled a lot—then fainted on me. They'd have taken him, I reckon, but I ain't working with that bunch of bastards no more since they locked up Judge Kane. Don't believe he can walk. Pretty weak. May have to carry him. You help me, Mr. Wade?"

"We'll bring him in here. His cabin will be cold," Duncan said.

Liveright's eyes widened. "This-here is a *white* boy, Mr. Wade. Says he knows you."

"Wait here, Pa. Try to keep that light from blowing out."

The hurt boy lay in the back of the light wagon, covered with a blanket.

"Take his feet . . . easy," Liveright directed, his arms under the boy's shoulders. "He ain't tall but he's heavy."

"Why did you bring him here?" Duncan panted as they stumbled up the steps into the house.

"Asked him did he have any friends could take care of him. He said, 'Uncle Hugh—Uncle Hugh Wade. Knows me,' he said. 'Don't take me home,' he said. Yelled it out, kinda sharp. Didn't seem to know nothing much after that."

They laid him on the floor close to the fire. He was well-dressed, but dirty, his coat soaked with blood, his red hair matted with sweat above a face mottled with coppery freckles. Duncan bent down, wiped the moisture from the twitching face, straightened, aghast. "My God, Pa! It's young Jule Villerand!"

"Villerand?" The deputy's tone was awe-struck. "But his boy got killed!"

"This is Villerand's son. We grew up together, though he was a few years younger. Where did you find him?"

"I told you. They had a ruckus down by the bridge. Some of these young hotheads in masks shot up that squatter camp of white and black trash down there. Captain Gilbert showed up with a squad of troops, afoot. There was a lot of shooting. Why the devil they don't send mounted men—Swayne's asked for cavalry times enough."

"He's been shot. Here—it looks bad. Get a towel, will you, Pa? And ask Louisa to fetch some hot water. Jule . . . Jule, can you hear me? It's Duncan, Jule."

"Going fast by the looks of him." Liveright hunkered down to struggle over buttons with numbed fingers. "I live down there, got a little place. Don't go out much since they locked Judge Kane up. This boy crawled up to my door, had a kind of robe on. I told the old lady to burn it quick. He said, fetch him here, so I hitched up quick as I could and took the back roads. But you'll have to hide him, I reckon."

"Hide him? Press that towel down here, Pa. Maybe we can stop this bleeding. Tell Louisa to bring another blanket. Or, better still, you help me, Liveright, and we'll bring down a mattress."

"I've got a little whisky here, Mr. Wade."

"Makes a hemorrhage worse. We learned that in the army."

They lifted young Jule carefully to the improvised bed. The blanket Liveright had brought was already drenched, and they used another one, thin, but clean. Hugh Wade staggered up presently, clutching at a chair. Louisa was dribbling water from the iron kettle.

"It's no use," Hugh cried. "Fetch his mother, Duncan. Ride the mule."

"Take my rig," Liveright said. "How far is it?"

"A mile by the road."

"Hurry then. I'll stay here. They might come, but they're probably still hunting for him down in the bottoms. They'll search all the houses, and my old lady was plenty scared—she might give it away if they talk rough to her."

Duncan was twisting into his coat. "Why are they hunting him?"

"He shot Captain Gilbert. Bragged about it, laughed, before he pitched over unconscious in my wagon."

Duncan drove the patient horse over the muddy road as fast as he could urge it to go. Jule Villerand! Missing from General Maury's forces at Mobile. Where had he been these three years, while his mother mourned him and his sisters wore black dresses with crepe bands? Even his father, tough, doughty Julian, had choked up when he said, "Run up a flag and shout hallelujah, if my boy came walking in." And young Jule had begged Liveright not to take him home. Why? The wagon careened in the ruts, while Duncan pondered this mystery.

The Villerand house was dimly lighted, only one window showing a pale glimmer. Duncan ran around the veranda and rapped on the glass. He could see Emma Villerand sitting there alone, some sewing in her lap. She looked up, startled, stiffening when he rapped again. He pressed close to the glass and called, "Mrs. Villerand? It's Duncan Wade. Let me in."

She got up then, came to the window. "Who's there? What is it?"

"It's Duncan Wade, Mrs. Villerand. Let me in, please."

Cold wind tore at him as he hurried back to the front door. The light had moved through the house. He heard locks being undone and the door opened a cautious crack. Emma stood there, holding the door, holding too a ready pistol in her hand.

"Oh, it is you, Duncan? I had to be sure. Is something wrong?"

"Very wrong. You have to come with me, Mrs. Villerand. Get a cloak—it's bitter cold—and hurry."

"Is it your father? I'm all alone. Mr. Villerand went to New Orleans to bring the girls home. What is wrong, Duncan?"

"There is trouble at our house. We need you. Please hurry."

"Your poor father! Wait here. No, you run to Tuby's cabin and tell him to get up and come to stay in the house."

"There isn't time. Can't you lock this door from the outside?"

"There may be a key, but Mr. Villerand would have it, I'm sure. There is a key to the back door. It hangs in the pantry. I can bolt this door and let myself out the back, with the key. Will I be home by breakfast time, Duncan? I'd hate to lock Lelia out."

"You get a cloak, Mrs. Villerand, and I'll lock the doors." He hurried her into the wagon as quickly as he could, tucked a blanket around her. He had locked the house impatiently, thinking that while she was fretting about her possessions her most precious possession of all might be slipping away. He had to tell her—but he waited till they were at the Wade door. "Mrs. Villerand, there's a wounded man here . . . probably dying."

"Is it Cassius?" she asked.

"I'm sorry, it's not Cassius. It's your son, Mrs. Villerand. It's young Jule."

"So . . . he came back." There was no surprise in her

voice, which was a breath, almost a sigh. "You might have told me, Duncan."

"You might have fainted. I had to bring you to him."

"Yes, I had to come to him. His father has been hunting him for some time. We didn't know he had come back." Composed, white-faced, erect, she walked into the room. She nodded to the others, knelt beside the unconscious boy, put a hand on his head, wiped away the icy sweat with her palm. "Jule!" she called, softly. "Jule, Mother's here."

The boy did not stir. Only the gulping, difficult breathing went on, contorting his body with every effort for air. Liveright moved to the window, cleared his throat roughly. Hugh Wade said with grave courtesy, "My deepest sympathy, ma'am."

"Thank you," she murmured. "Can nothing be done for him, Mr. Wade?"

"I fear not, Mrs. Villerand. We cannot stop this hemorrhage. He has been shot in the lung."

Duncan piled wood on the fire. The wind screeched in the chimney, shook the windows. Louisa, crouched in a corner, sobbed low. The room seemed to fill with a pressing, hostile silence, broken only by that bubbling breath, which came slower and slower so that they waited tensely for the next strangling gasp.

Emma's lips were moving. "I will go unto the altar of God," they heard her whisper. "He will sustain my soul in my trouble."

Then sharply there was only stillness. The breathing had ceased. Emma gave a little choking sound. Then her voice went on in a kind of chant, "To God's gracious mercy I commit you, my darling. The Lord make His face to shine upon you, the Lord be merciful to you and give you peace."

Hugh Wade stooped and drew the blanket up over the still face. With courtly gentleness he helped Emma to her feet, steadied her with his arm. Her face was upturned, drained, tragic.

Abruptly feet pounded on the porch, the door crashed open and the room seemed to fill with soldiers. Lieutenant Eric Wilkins came striding in, his face like thunder.

Duncan stepped forward. "Too late, Lieutenant," he said quietly.

"Shut that door!" Wilkins barked at the squad who had backed away a trifle awkwardly. One after another they removed their hats. "Who brought him here?" he demanded.

Duncan looked at Liveright, whose face had turned pale. "No one brought him here, Lieutenant," Duncan lied. "He stole this man's wagon, held him hostage with a gun. Then when he arrived here he collapsed and died."

"They're hunting for him in Louisiana," the lieutenant said. "We had orders to take him."

"This boy, Lieutenant," Duncan said, "is Mrs. Villerand's son. I hope you will allow her to mourn her dead in peace."

Wilkins looked uncomfortable. "I'm sorry, ma'am," he said. "In the army we must do what we are ordered to do. You have my sympathy, ma'am."

"I know," she said, low.

"Outside!" Wilkins barked at the squad.

They tramped out, but Duncan heard one trooper grumble, "Damn Reb would die before we had a chance to hang him!"

XXV

ONE OF McKEE'S friends up Jefferson way had insisted on giving him a bottle of brandy, and for that now Duncan was grateful. With hot water from Louisa's kettle he made hot toddies and pressed one into Emma Villerand's cold, inert hand. "I know ladies are supposed not to drink strong spirits, Mrs. Villerand, but right now you need this," he argued.

She sat, looking small and pitiful, in the chair Hugh had drawn near to the fire. She had made no sound when young Jule was covered with the blanket and carried into the cold parlor by Duncan and the deputy. When Liveright came tiptoeing back solemnly for the boy's shoes, her breath had caught in an audible gasp, but her body was still, her lips caught together tightly. Now she looked dazedly at the glass, then turned her eyes up to Duncan's face and, at his repeated command, sipped a little obediently, strangling briefly on the strong hot brew.

Liveright downed his glass at one gulp, reached for his coat, ran his hand abstractedly down the front where a bloodstain darkened. "Reckon I'd better jog along—unless you want me to take the lady home."

"We'll take her home when she feels well enough to go. We'll stay with her till her family arrives," Duncan said. "Thank you, Liveright. You risked your own freedom to help him. Mrs. Villerand thanks you too."

"Yes," she said quickly. "Oh, yes!"

"You got me out of it mighty slick." Liveright grinned. "Could have got us all in bad trouble."

"That lieutenant knows the Villerands. There won't be any more trouble."

"Hope not. Better get on now. My old lady will be in a tizzy, scared to death for fear they got me too. Good night all—and sorry, ma'am."

When the wagon had rattled away, Emma stirred. "He had killed someone. You can tell me, Mr. Wade. They came for him because he had killed someone."

"He shot a Union captain, ma'am," Hugh answered. "Very commendable in war, but in this shabby peace . . . most reprehensible."

"You knew that Jule was still alive, Mrs. Villerand?" Duncan asked.

She breathed deeply, wearily. "Yes . . . we have known . . . for weeks! He wasn't killed at Fort Morgan. The girls saw him . . . in New Orleans. They have had dreadful times there, men killed, buildings burned. Mrs. Destrade, the elder, was afraid to stir out her door. But the girls went to church one Sunday . . . and on the way they saw their brother. It was a shock, of course . . . and worse because he was in a mob of young men who were chasing some poor Negroes down the street. Juliet wrote to her father immediately, and Mr. Villerand left at once. That's all I know, Duncan: that apparently Jule has been in New Orleans since the surrender . . . and that now . . . he has come home."

A harsh sob shook her from head to foot, the drink slopped on her dress, and she brushed at the stain absently.

"I'll get a wagon and help at daylight and take him home. You'll stay here? You'd better lie down and rest."

"I'd rather sit here, if I may. I'd like to be near him while I can. Duncan—" a shrillness made her voice break—"why did he do it? We loved him! Even if he did not want to come home because he disagreed with his father, he might have written me a letter. His own mother!"

Duncan patted her shoulder. "War does strange things to men, Mrs. Villerand," he said. "We become what we would not wish to be. And when we know that we have changed, some reckless pride in us will not let us admit that we can be wrong. Jule was very young."

"Twenty-two last October," she said.

"He got caught up in some of the rash madness that hatred spawns," Hugh Wade said. "I've been thankful that Duncan was sober enough to see the folly of this night-riding business. Alabama can never be saved by more violence."

Duncan looked shrewdly at his father, turned his eyes away. No use to remind the tired old man that violence was in the blood of all the Wades, that there was a hidden grave on the hill which testified to his own belief in its final expediency.

"Do you expect your family home soon, Mrs. Villerand?" he inquired.

"They landed in Mobile last Monday. The girls are coming with their father. Mr. Destrade's mother and sisters refused to stay in New Orleans any longer, since there is so much terror there, so he is taking them to Martinique. His mother was born there. But Juliet declined to go with them, so she and Marian are coming home. They should be here any day now."

Day came at last, thinly, with more sullen spits of snow. Duncan rode the mule to Bard Leonard's place, enlisted Bard's help, and together they removed Jule Villerand to his own home.

"You'll stay with me—both of you?" Emma begged the two Wades when she had been taken home by Hugh in the creaking old buggy drawn by their shaggy mule.

"I'll stay with you, ma'am," Hugh Wade agreed. Never be-

fore had he entered Julian Villerand's house. He had thought
never to enter it, but this was trouble. He let himself remember
that Julian had helped to carry Florence to her grave.

Duncan and Bard went into town and returned with the best
coffin to be had there. Together they made young Jule ready.

"I would have liked to bury him in his uniform." Emma
sighed. "He was so handsome when he rode away." But she
did bring out from hiding a silk Confederate flag. They folded
it on a pillow under the boy's head.

"Good thing it's cold weather," Bard worried. "Hope Villerand don't take too long comin'."

In town Duncan had sought out Eric Wilkins, learned what
the lieutenant knew about young Villerand.

"He was an officer in one of those masked organizations,"
Wilkins reported. "We heard he was being sent up here to enlist men for their organization in this county. We were watching for him. Before that, from what we've learned, he'd been
in New Orleans, hanging around in gambling houses, living on
his winnings, I suppose. He shot down the captain in cold
blood, Wade. His family are lucky. He'd have been hanged
without mercy if he had survived."

"Who shot him? Does anybody know?"

"I shot him," the lieutenant returned calmly. "It was my
duty to shoot him after he'd killed an officer. But he was
mounted then and he got away fast. If they bring that 'White
Camellia' order into Alabama, we'll have to have cavalry. We
can't put it down on foot. Can't they see that it will only make
things worse for everybody?"

"They see only that decent white people are being intimidated and that their women are not safe, Lieutenant; and that
your troops are doing little to end the terror and violence."

"I do what I can," worried the young man from Delaware.
"You don't know what it's like, Wade!" he cried with a kind

of desperation. "Walled in by hate . . . knowing that the hand of almost every man is against you, and yet you're sworn to obey orders. Now the Villerands will hate me too."

"They needn't know. I shan't tell them who killed their son."

"That's white of you, Wade. I appreciate it."

"I shall not tell them because it would give them pain," Duncan said, brusquely, walking away.

There was hot coffee at the Villerand house. There were pink slices of ham and biscuits dripping melted butter. Duncan was glad to see his father eat, even knowing that he ate reluctantly at Julian's table. Emma trailed her black skirts quietly through the rooms, gave orders in a low tone to her servants, went to sit in the chilly parlor by the side of her son. The wind fell and on the second day the sun came out, wan and hesitant, but birds fought for the berries on the bushes beside the door and a lopsided moon shone at night and touched the world with silver.

Villerand had provided his family with no burial plot. There had been no need. So, after discussing it with Emma, Duncan went with Tuby to a low slope above the orchard and paced off a space where a wall could be built later. Bard Leonard volunteered to find men to dig a grave. When Duncan walked up there late on the third day, he found Parmy flinging up muddy clods with a lusty shovel.

"Your Nigra woman made him come," Bard explained. "He showed up hungry and she ain't feedin' him till this grave is dug."

"Tole me I git two dollars, Mist' Duncan," stated Parmy. "Dat white lady, she goin' pay me two dollars?"

"She'll pay you, Parmy. And Louisa will feed you too—if you stay away from that shanty town and those Leaguers," Duncan qualified the promise.

"Dat woman I git, she done lef' me," Parmy mourned. "She

gone took up wid a yeller man got him a mule. When they goin' gib me a mule, Mist' Duncan?"

"Save your money and buy yourself a mule, Parmy."

"Hope Villerand gits back tomorrow," Bard fretted. "Don't reckon we can wait no longer."

"Reckon I kin buy a mule wid two dollars, Mist' Duncan?" Parmy wanted to know. "Dat woman, she got all my cotton money."

Duncan had an inspiration. "Remember our old Derry mule, Parmy? He's still limping around the pasture. You stay home and work and I'll give you that Derry mule."

"That mule he got lame foots. Reckon I kin cure up them lame foots? Hi yah, Kingdom Come—I got me a mule!" Parmy leaped back into the grave and set the dirt flying.

"You'll have to tell her, Duncan," Bard said. "Tomorrow we got to bury him for sure, Villerand or no Villerand."

"If it stays cool it might be safe to wait," Duncan said.

"They've got friends round over the county, but she don't seem to want nobody to know they're in trouble. Mortified, the way he died, poor woman!"

At ten o'clock the next morning Bard appeared at the Villerand door, with a lean, narrow-faced man in a long-tailed coat. "This-here is Preacher Botts from up north, got the Higgs place next to me," he told Duncan. "Never did know Villerand's religion, but Mr. Botts knows his Bible pretty good, if so be she'll let him preach the funeral today."

"If I may speak to the good sister I may be able to persuade her that the funeral should be held," Botts stated. "Not many ordained men of the cloth would choose to say the Sacred Words over the body of a murderer, but I will put my scruples aside in this sad instance."

Duncan's fists tightened and his eyes blazed. "You're the man who cheated poor old Mr. Higgs out of his farm, I understand, Mr. Botts?"

"Definitely there was no dishonesty. The man was a traitor to the nation. His land was confiscated, and I was able to buy it with the help of some friends who have a missionary spirit and are eager to see this benighted land restored to sanity and salvation."

"This benighted land can save itself if you and your kind will take yourselves off and let us alone, and cease to rob and exploit us, Mr. Botts," snapped Duncan. "You'll preach no funeral in this house over the body of any friend of mine. Take your delicate scruples back to town and go now, before I teach you the meaning of decency and godliness."

Botts rolled his eyes sanctimoniously. "Another one!" he mourned. "God, how long shall the heathen rage and the people imagine a vain thing? How long shall this proud race of blasphemers, adulterers and traitors be permitted to prevail? Smite them, Lord. Smite them hip and thigh!"

Duncan took a menacing step forward. "Get him away from here, Bard!" he ordered. "Get him out of my sight before I forget that there's a dead boy lying in yonder. You meant well, but get the hypocrite off this place."

"Jest as you say, Duncan," Bard said patiently. "Come 'long, Brother Botts."

"You will repent this insult, young man," Botts threatened. "Repent now on your knees, before it is forever too late."

"The Lord may have some reservations about me," Duncan retorted, "but He would sicken at the sight of you!"

"Who was that, Duncan?" Emma asked as Bard's wagon rolled out of the yard.

"A carpetbagger preacher—the one who put the Higgses off their place. Bard was trying to help; he thought you might want that man to conduct a funeral today."

"Oh, but we will have the rector from Selma! Mr. Villerand will attend to that when he arrives. I can't think why they are so delayed. It must be the snow and the cold weather. But at least I can keep my boy with me a little longer."

It was dusk when Tuby raised a shout. Hurrying outside, they saw the carriage entering the lane.

Emma began to sob. "How can I tell them? How can I bear to tell them?"

"I'll tell them, Mrs. Villerand." Duncan strode off toward the gate.

Villerand was driving, bundled in a great coat and wool scarf, perched on the driver's seat and looking more than ever like a squat Buddha. In the carriage Juliet and Marian were huddled in shawls, their faces pale and weary. Marian gave a little cry as Duncan came up to the carriage, but Villerand reined in the horses, looking impatient and annoyed. "What now, Wade?" he demanded. "These women are cold."

"Your son is here, Mr. Villerand," Duncan said quietly. "He is dead."

Villerand seemed to deflate abruptly, all the angry color draining out of his skin, his body shrinking within its wrappings. "They got him!" he gasped. The reins slipped from his hand.

Tuby got the horses' heads quickly. "You come along, Mist' Julian," he urged. "You and the young Misses, you come git warm." He led the team to the veranda steps.

Before Duncan could help her Marian sprang out of the carriage. "Duncan! Duncan!" She ran into his arms. "I prayed you'd be here—I prayed and prayed!"

"I'm here, Maggie." He held her close.

"Marian," reproved Juliet, trailing her long skirts up the steps, "your brother is dead!"

"You were here, Duncan? You were with him when he died?" Marian clung to him, her cold hands on his shoulders.

"He died in our house. I was with him when he died."

"And you brought him home?"

"I brought him home. But I took your mother to him before he died."

Villerand rushed up the steps to where Emma waited at the door.

Marian turned her head and looked at them in rapt surprise. Never before had she seen her mother cry. Never before had she seen her father take her mother into his arms. She began to cry herself, stormily, burying her face in Duncan's sleeve.

"We begged him!" she wailed. "We cried and pleaded. We begged Jule to come home. And finally—to get rid of us—he promised. Then when Papa came we could not find him anywhere."

"He came home, Maggie." In violence, in arrogant defiance, he had come home—to meet violence armed with the strength of the conqueror's law.

Hugh Wade emerged from a shadow where he had waited. "We did what we could, Villerand," he said. "It was little, but if more could have saved him we would have done it. We'll go now—and thank you, ma'am, for your hospitality."

"Oh, no!" Emma cried quickly. "Don't let them go, Mr. Villerand! I could not have borne this without the Wades to help me. You must stay, Mr. Wade—you must not desert us now."

Julian Villerand held out his hand. "Hugh," he said, "we need our friends and our neighbors. Will you stay with us in our trouble?"

Hugh Wade straightened. He was shabby, he was weary, but the old courtliness lay upon him like a proud garment. "We'll stay, Julian," he said, taking Villerand's hand.

Marian gulped down a sob. "Isn't it beautiful, Duncan?" she

whispered. "Isn't it wonderful—to be friends again. Oh, Duncan, say you do love me—say it now!"

"I love you, Maggie."

"Forever and ever?"

"Forever and ever!"

POSTLUDE

HUGH WADE was dying.

He was an old man, broken and thin and spent, and the years had trampled with iron feet on his spirit, never taming it completely, never daunting his courageous soul, so that now he could look at death and know it for a Comforter, for a Deliverer.

He had seen his grandchildren born in his house: little Hugh, the fourth of that name, and small Juliana, now three years old, with Julian Villerand's lion-hued hair and the quick dark eyes of the Wades. Juliana stayed close beside his bed, now and then reaching a plump hand to pat the cold yellow fingers that picked and picked at the cover, bringing sloppy glasses of water that her mother took from her hand and held to the old man's gray lips.

"Who is Florrie, Mama?" Juliana whispered. "Granddaddy is talking to Florrie."

"Florrie was your grandmother, baby. She went to heaven a long time ago."

"I reckon she wishes Granddaddy would hurry up and come to heaven too," mused small Hugh from the stool against the wall where he had sat quietly all through the summer afternoon.

"Grandmother will wait. She has waited a long time—ten years," Duncan said.

The ten tragic, dreadful years! The years of Military Government, with General Pope in command, determined to crush these willful Southerners and bring them to supine humility; with Meade succeeding him, and Ulysses S. Grant in the White House, white men disenfranchised, state government a pitiful puppet affair, corrupt, degraded, subservient to the rapacious, the spoilers, the tricksters and the scalawags.

Ten years that had turned Duncan's hair gray and put a little stoop in his shoulders, that had seen Maggie Villerand Wade grow into a grave, sweet, practical woman. Juliet's hair was gray too. She had never returned to New Orleans. Felix Destrade had been killed there in the winter of 1868, when the steeds of vengeful riders made the streets of the old town ring.

Juliet came quietly into the room now. "Louisa is making coffee," she said in a low voice. "You'd better have some. I'll stay here."

"We'll stay," Marian said. "It won't be long now. But take the children and feed them, will you, Sister?"

"I'll bring your coffee here then. Come along, Hugh—you too, Baby."

"I want to stay with Granddaddy. He'd want me to stay till he went to heaven," Hugh argued.

"Let him stay." Marian reached an arm and gathered her son close. "Has Papa Villerand come back, Juliet?"

"He's outside—under the magnolia tree. He looks dreadful. Things are frightful in Montgomery, he says. Two legislatures in session in two different buildings, one Democrat, one Radical. And Papa says it appears now that the Stantons and their Wall Street conspirators have stolen more than seven million dollars from Alabama, and that the railroad will probably be thrown into bankruptcy and taken over by the state. Thank goodness, Duncan, you persuaded Papa to stay out of that venture!"

"What hope was there for an honest man, when a fellow like Applegate could be elected Lieutenant Governor of the State of Alabama?" Duncan let his old anger rise. It had been quies-

cent for a long time now. He had spent his fury on the sprouts
in the old Wade fields. He had wearied his body and his mind
under crushing sunshine in the cotton rows. Political storms
had seethed over their heads. The Ku Klux Klan had galloped,
spreading secret terrors, and then had died under the pressure
of sane men's thinking.

"Wait," said the wise ones.

All this would pass. The scalawag and the carpetbagger
would all go; already they were drifting away. The looters and
the pillagers would go when there were no more spoils. But the
land would remain, the rich, black, patient land of Alabama.

Hugh Wade stirred a little. Marian hurried to the bed and
wiped his twitching mouth with cool water. On the opposite
side Duncan slid his arms under the thin old shoulders and
lifted his father, steadying him till his gasping breath evened a
little.

"All right, sir," he said. "You'll be all right. Just hold onto
me, Pa, and you'll be all right."

Hugh's eyes opened wide. He looked about at them all
brightly, looked across the room at the open door. Marian,
turning quickly, saw that her father had come in and stood
there quietly.

Then Hugh's voice rang out, sharp and clear. "Miss Florrie!" he cried. "Miss Florrie!"

Sudden and harsh, from the door where Julian Villerand
watched, came a rasping sob. Marian looked at her father
sharply.

Now she knew! All those years—and the old hostility had
died, but now she knew why it had ever been at all.

"He's gone," Duncan said softly. He laid the still body
down, gently drew up the sheet.

"Is that all?" whispered the last Hugh Wade. "Is that the
way Granddaddy went to heaven?"

"That's all, son. I think there is happiness in heaven just now, don't you?" his mother said.

He let out his breath with a gusty sigh. "I have to be Hugh Wade now," he said. "I'll be very strong and never hate anybody. I promised Granddaddy."

ACKNOWLEDGMENTS

The authors wish to acknowledge indebtedness for assistance in research and supplying authenticity for this book to *The Story of Reconstruction,* by Robert S. Henry; *Alabama's Tragic Decade,* by John W. DuBose; *History of Alabama,* by A. B. Moore. Also to Mr. David Laurance Chambers of The Bobbs-Merrill Company, Inc., for valuable editorial aid; to Mr. and Mrs. J. Webster Garner of Birmingham, Alabama, and Miss Susie May Smith of Tuscaloosa, Alabama.